THIRTY-THREE

Going On...

GIRLFRIEND

BECKY MONSON

Thirty-Three Going on Girlfriend
Copyright © 2014 V2 Becky Monson
Cover Art by Mark Hamer

To Rob, Audrey, Max, and Violet.
Our days may be full of chaos and our nights exhausted, but I
wouldn't have it any other way.

To my most trusted confidants, Lori and Robin.
Thank you for dealing with my neurotic tendencies, so no
one else has to.

Chapter 1

I can't believe I am here.

I can't believe I'm standing here, gazing lovingly at Jared, surrounded by our friends and family, on this amazing beach with this marvelous sunset, as we make these vows—these incredible, sure-to-make-you-cry vows—to each other.

The colors are all muted, antique tones of pink, yellow, gold. My bouquet is practically bursting with soft pink roses.

My makeup is not whorish, as my sister, Anna, would have preferred, and my hair is done in perfect, long curls, half pulled up with a small, antique jeweled clip. Simple. Understated. Exactly what I wanted.

And then there's my dress. My dress is spectacular. It's timeless, really, just slightly off-white, an off-the-shoulder bodice with details of stunning Chantilly lace and a sweeping train. I heart it. I heart it all, especially Jared in his classic suit—none of that penguin stuff for him—he looks like something out of a style magazine. His pants and jacket are perfectly tailored, and he wears the antique pink tie just because I want him to.

I glance over at my bridesmaids — my baby sister Anna and my dearest friend, Betsy Brown — gazing at us with bright smiles. Anna's has an ever-so-slight look of jealousy, but I beam at them. This is the perfect day. My perfect day with Jared.

"Do you, Jared Nathan Moody, take Julia Warner Dorning to be your lawfully wedded wife? To have and to hold from this day forward, until death do you part?" the officiant, dressed in white, asks Jared.

"I do," he says simply.

"And do you, Julia Warner Dorning, take Jared Nathan Moody to be your lawfully wedded husband? To have and to hold from this day forward, until death do you part?" the priest asks.

"I do," I say as I stare into Jared's eyes. His are filling up with tears, and mine begin to well up, too.

"Then by the power that is vested in me, I now pronounce you man and wi—"

"JULIA! What the hell? What are you doing in my dress?" Anna's screeching pulls me out of my fantasy. "Geez, I leave you alone in here for ten minutes, and you think it's okay to put my wedding dress on? Mom! Tell her to take my dress off!" Anna stomps her foot in a ridiculous, childlike manner.

My mom comes in the room just after Anna and puts her hand to her mouth. "Oh, Julia dear, what are you doing?"

"Nothing! Geez, I was just seeing how it felt, that's all. Stop pouting like you're ten," I say to Anna, who is practically throwing an adult version of a temper tantrum.

What's the big deal? Anna and my mom left the room to go check out veils, and I was left in the room with her wedding dress, just sitting there, all alone. What woman wouldn't want to try it on? Especially a woman who's in her thirties, with no promises of marriage on the horizon.

I can't believe Anna is getting married. My baby sister. My sister, who's ten years my junior, is getting married. It was a whirlwind kind of thing, too. She met Jonathon at my dad's law firm where she's currently working. Jonathon is a junior partner at the firm. I once made the mistake of calling him "Jon," and that is apparently not acceptable to *Jonathon*. To say he's stuffy and pretentious is an understatement.

My brother, Lennon, and I both have our suspicions about Jonathon. Well, they are not actually suspicions, just a mutual dislike for the guy. We haven't tried to like him, to be honest, but there's only so much blather about Ivy League Schools (he went to Stanford), and amazing accomplishments (made junior partner in his first year), that we can take. Plus, the guy does nothing to help with the wedding, not one thing. That's weird, right?

They've been together for just under six months, and now they are getting married. My boyfriend, Jared, (I still have a hard time calling him that) and I have been together for a little over nine months and not a peep about marriage. We don't even say "I love you" yet. I've wanted to say it. I feel like I could have said it from the beginning, actually. Call me old-fashioned, but I feel like he should say it first. Okay, I mostly want him to say it first because if I said it first, I'm afraid his reply might be the dreaded "thank you."

That's the insecure voice in my mind that creeps in every now and then. Okay, I mean practically all of the time. I don't want to be *that* girl, but I can't help myself.

This is my first real relationship in, well, ever.

Anyway, this is not about Jared and me, this is about Anna and Jonathon. I should not compare. In with the good thoughts, out with the I-hate-my-sister thoughts.

"Well, hopefully you didn't stretch my dress out with your butt. It's bigger than mine, you know." And there are the I-hate-my-sister thoughts again. They come and go these days. To say that Anna has been acting like a diva is an understatement.

"Yes, you've said that more than once. Thank you for the reminder that my butt is bigger than yours." She helps me get out of the dress and then holds it in her arms like it's a darling baby, stroking the lace with her fingers. I expect her to start cooing at it. *Don't worry my little sweetie-pie, I won't let that mean, big-butted lady touch you again. Never, never again.* She tenderly hangs it up. I roll my eyes at her as I find my clothes on the floor in the corner and quickly start putting them back on.

I'm surprised I could get the dress on, to be honest. I've packed on about ten pounds in the last nine months. I work at a bakery. The fact that I haven't put on more is really a bit of a miracle. My friend Betsy Brown (or just Brown, as her friends call her) says it's my "I'm in a relationship weight." Apparently when you're happy in a relationship, you tend to get comfortable and start putting on a few. She claims to have done the same thing when she first started dating her now fiancé, Matt. I didn't know Brown then, and all I see is the perfectly put together pageant queen that she is now. I'm inclined not to believe her at all.

I did buy one of those ten-minute workout videos. I figured I should be able to fit at least that into my day. If only I could muster up enough energy to put the darn thing in my DVD player.

4

"Did you at least check out the options I picked out for your maid of honor dress?" Anna points over to the corner where a bunch of boring different-colored dresses hang.

Since I'm the maid of honor, I get to pick out my dress. Everyone else is wearing the same black dress, and I get to wear the same dress style, but in a color, and she's letting me pick out the color. I know she has one in mind that she wants me to wear, but for some reason she wants me to pick it out. That way, it looks as if she gave me the option, while keeping control.

"I did look at them, I like the purple one," I say, knowing full well that purple is not the color she wants. Why did she even give it to me as an option in the first place?

She scrunches her face at me. "Well, but don't you think purple will sort of clash?"

"Anna, why don't you just pick the color you want for me? I really don't mind." *I really freaking don't mind*, is what I want to say.

"No! You have to pick. Just not the purple. Anything but the purple."

"Fine." I point over to the rack of dresses. "I'll wear the olive one."

"Yes! Perfect. The olive green one will work." She goes over to the rack, picks it out, and holds it up, contemplating. "Yes, yes . . ." she trails off, probably picturing the lineup in her mind.

I should just start counting down in my head, *five, four, three, two . . .*

"Well, maybe not the olive one." Yes, I saw that coming. She hangs the dress back on the rack. "Why not the dusty rose one?" She pulls it out and shows it to me. Aha! That's the one she wanted all along. I should have known.

"Sure, whatever," I say and sit down on the couch in the all-white dressing room that looks as if it were made for a queen. And for the money we are spending in this place, it might as well be.

"If you don't want to be in my wedding, you don't have to," Anna says, as she hangs the pink dress back on the rack, an air of frustration in her voice

"What did I say?" I regard her with confusion.

"It's just your attitude, that's all." She folds her arms.

"My attitude?" I stand up and confront her, ready to spar.

"Now girls," my mother chides. "Stop arguing. Julia, you'll wear the pink. It will look lovely with your skin."

"Fine," I say and sit back down on the couch.

My mother and Anna go over to her dress and start talking about something weddingy, and I tune them out. All these wedding plans are so boring. Okay, they wouldn't be boring if they were my wedding plans. But they are not, and I am totally okay with that, totally okay.

Only I'm not. I want to be okay. Anna and I have bonded over this past year or so, and I love her to death, but I can't help but feel jealous. Who wouldn't? I'm the first born in the Dorning family, and I'm already not the first to have children. Lennon and his wife Jenny now have baby Liam (whom I adore, and I'm pretty sure I'm his favorite aunt), and now I will be the last to get married, if I ever *do* get married. I shouldn't dwell on it. I should just get over it.

And I try. I really do.

I remember when Anna came to my condo to tell me she was getting married. She used her own key and waltzed right in without knocking. I'd told her she could do that, but somehow it still got on my nerves.

"I have news!" she said, giddily.

Anna had been wearing this big, ridiculously puffy white coat because it had been snowing that day in March. While other parts of the world were starting their spring break celebrations, we still had open ski resorts and sub-zero temperatures.

I was sitting on the couch, exhausted from my day at the bakery and trying to unwind. I was glad to see her, though. Since she had started dating Jonathon, we hadn't spent as much time together, and I missed my Anna and me time.

"What news?" I looked over to see a silly smile on her face. "What's with the goofy grin?"

"I'm getting married!" she blurted out and held up her left hand. On her ring finger was a giant — and I mean giant — diamond ring.

"What?" was all I could say, while my eyes bugged out of my head.

"I'm getting married!" She started jumping up and down like a child on her birthday.

"But . . . but . . . you don't know Jonathon that well. I mean, you've only been dating for, what, like three months?"

"Three and a half months," she snapped back quickly, the giddy jumping ended. "Not you, too. Mom and Dad said the same thing. Why does everyone want to crap on my parade?" She sulked over to the couch where I was sitting and slouched down at the other end. Her puffy coat made exhaling sounds as she leaned back on it.

"Well, how did you expect us to react? I mean what about your credit card debt?" Anna had racked up a very large amount of debt and had been working at our dad's law firm to pay it off. I knew she had made a dent in it, but it was still pretty hefty.

"Jonathon isn't worried about all that. Anyway, I'm not counting on him to just pay it off. I plan to keep working at the firm until it's gone," she said, and looked down at her hands. I saw a tear escape down her cheek. Anna doesn't cry often, so I immediately felt bad.

"Look, I'm sorry, Anna. Don't cry," I said, and I scooted closer to her.

"It's just supposed to be happy news, and everyone should be excited, but it feels like all I've been doing is convincing everyone that this is what I want. It really is, Julia . . . what I want." As even more tears poured from her eyes, I knew I had to get excited, even if it was my best acting job ever.

"You're engaged!" I said brightly, bouncing up and down on the couch. (I was too tired to stand up and do it.)

"Oh, shut up," she said, pushing me away from her.

"No, really. I'm thrilled. Well, okay, I will be thrilled. Now tell me, how did he do it?"

"Well, we were at that fancy steakhouse–the new one I was a telling you about the other day." Her eyes brightened as she told me. "And when they brought the dessert out, it was cheesecake — which is not my favorite — but Jonathon didn't know that." She glanced over at me to get my reaction. I'm sure she was hoping that I was not giving her an I-told-you-so smirk, since he didn't even know her favorite dessert. But I played along.

"Anyway, so there, on the top of the cheesecake was my ring. And he got down on one knee and proposed!" Her smile broadened at the memory.

"Oh, my gosh! That is so romantic!" I grabbed her and hugged her. Anna and I are not huggers, but I wanted her to think that I was extra-excited, and that I thought it was so incredibly romantic, but the truth was I was still in shock. Plus, the old ring-in-the-dessert wedding proposal is so overdone. I didn't want her to get *that* out of my expression. So hugging it out was my best option.

"Julia," she said as she pulled away from my overbearing hug, "I want you to be my maid of honor." She smiled slightly at me, almost in a bashful way, like she was embarrassed to even say it.

"Really?" I beamed brightly at her, because I was truly flattered that she'd asked me.

"Yes. I must have you there by my side on what will probably be the most important day of my life." She bit her bottom lip and stared down at her ring.

"Of course I will be." I reached for her hand and held it briefly, letting her know how much that meant to me.

For the past two months, I've put on a brave face during this torture. But today, here in this stuffy dressing room—well, it's not actually stuffy because it's ridiculously huge, but it has a stuffy feel to it—I'm just not feeling it.

"Julia?" my mom says, a little louder than her normal tone. I look over at her and she and Anna are both staring at me.

"Yeah?" I say, realizing I've not been paying attention to them at all.

"You ready to go?" She comes over to me and stands next to the place where I'm sitting.

Oh, yes, I am definitely ready to go.

Chapter 2

Cupcake Battles. It's only my favorite show on TV right now. It's a competition show where contestants make cupcakes, and they are judged on flavor and décor and, well, it's just the best show. I've never missed an episode.

So this is what happened. Two weeks and one day ago, I was carrying one of those industrial-sized cartons of eggs into the walk-in cooler, when I literally tripped over my own feet and twisted my ankle. It was super graceful. Immediately my ankle turned into a cankle — calf plus ankle, where there is no definition from calf to foot. Jared took one look at it and took me to one of those walk-in clinics. I wasn't quite able to walk in to the walk-in clinic. Jared had to help. After an x-ray to determine that I hadn't broken anything, the doctor deemed my ankle twisted and gave me a prescription for pain relievers to make me comfortable and something else to help with the swelling.

One day after the whole ankle-twisting debacle, and hopped up on some Percocet (they make me feel lightheaded), I decided to audition to be on *Cupcake*

Battles. So in my very giddy mood, I made my audition tape. I'm about two hundred percent sure that it was total crap. First off, there was the whole Percocet thing, but also I'm not that good on camera. I've seen myself before. It's bad. In fact, I mostly avoid all cameras, even of the still variety—I alternate between one half-closed eye like a lazy-eyed-pirate, and a double chin—which is why I didn't even bother watching what I'd taped. I'd made it late night when I was alone in the bakery, did one take, and zipped it off before I came to my senses.

So I can easily say that I was more shocked than I've ever been (ever), when I got a call from one of the show's producers. They wanted me on the show. I, Julia Dorning, recently recovered spinster, am going to be on *Cupcake Battles.*

I can't believe it.

"Believe it, honey! It's happenin'!" my employee at the bakery, Patti, says with her thick Southern accent as she hugs me tightly. We're standing in the middle of the industrial kitchen in the back of the bakery. Mixing bowls and a slew of ingredients are strewn around haphazardly on the counters. It's been a crazy morning, to say the least.

"And you deserve it, darlin'. You really do," Patti says.

"Oh, stop buttering me up," I say as I pull out of the hug. "Of course you know I'm taking you with me."

She clasps her hands together and does a little cheer. "Well, I'm about as happy as a dead pig in the sunshine!"

I'm not even going to ask what that means. I'll just assume it means happy, although it didn't give me a very happy visual. But, that's Patti Farnsworth, with her big, blonde, back-combed hair and her crazy Southern sayings. I honestly don't know what I'd do without her, even if I don't understand half of the phrases that come out of her mouth.

11

I still can't wrap my brain around it. I'm going to be on *Cupcake Battles*. *Cupcake freaking Battles*! It's only been my dream since, well, since they started filming the show on The Dessert Channel.

Holy crap! I'm going to be on The Dessert Channel! I can't even begin to grasp how much exposure it will give the bakery. I'll be on national television! Millions of people will be watching!

Oh, gosh.

Cupcake Battles. National television. Millions of people. Oh, gosh.

My stomach sinks as reality sets in. This is not me. This is not something I do. What have I gotten myself into?

If only Jared had answered his stupid phone. I mean, what's the point of having a phone if it's never on? And he's far away too. I can't just drive over and have him talk me down from this sudden ledge I've found myself on. He's in Chattanooga. Or Chicago. Something that starts with a *C*. I don't know. I can't keep track.

To be perfectly honest, I hate his job. I mean, it's his consulting company that he started and blah, blah, blah. But he's always gone, it seems. And to be even more honest, it still has the teeniest, tiniest bit of sting when I think about it. That's how we met, after all. He was secretly working as a consultant at the tech company I used to work for. Oh, and the fact that he's the reason that I "used to" work for said company. He got me fired. Yes, I met my current boyfriend under very strange circumstances. My parents thought it was weird. They both love Jared now, but in the beginning it was a little bizarre. "Mom, Dad, meet Jared Moody, my boyfriend. We met at work. He got me fired."

Anyway, none of that matters. It's water under the bridge and all that. Jared was right to get me fired. I'm

12

much happier now at the bakery. The bakery that I own. Julia's Bakery. The bakery that will be featured on a national television show that I somehow have to work up enough confidence to pull off in fewer than two weeks. Twelve days. That's all I have.

Oh, gosh.

"How's the future winner of *Cupcake Battles* holding up?" my only other employee, Debbie, says as she walks into the kitchen. Her red hair is pulled up in a bun and she's wearing glasses. She looks more like a schoolmarm than a baker.

"Feeling a little queasy, actually," I say as I grab my stomach. I'm not exaggerating. I think I might barf.

"Debbie, fetch her a chair, please. Quick like," Patti instructs as she comes over to me and pats me on the back. I must look pale. The way I'm feeling, I'm probably white as a ghost.

Debbie rolls my office chair into the kitchen, and they guide me into it.

"You'll be fine," Debbie coos softly as I sit down in the chair. She starts lightly rubbing my shoulders.

Will I be fine? What if I do something stupid like, oh, I don't know, burn the cupcakes or the entire building? I wouldn't put it past me.

I didn't think this through very well, did I? I mean, I didn't even bother to think about it at all, to be honest. Which is not like me. I think things through. I'm an over-thinker. But I didn't think I'd even have a shot, so I didn't consider how I might react if they actually called.

Now that they have called, and the excitement and shock have worn off, and I'm now realizing everything, thoughts of canceling start to float around in my mind. I want to say "I'm not a quitter," but in all honesty, I sort of am. Events rarely happen to me of my own accord. I tend to have to be thrust by situations, or even people, into the direction I should go.

Take the bakery, for example. I would never have bought a bakery, nor would I have ever even entertained the idea, unless it just fell into my lap, which is exactly what happened. Okay, there was more to the story, but that is the gist of it.

Clearly, I'm not made to do this sort of thing. I think I should call the producer back and tell him I can't do it. I've never been in front of cameras or done any type of performance in front of a crowd. This is something Brown could do, or even Anna. But not me. I might be passing up the opportunity of a lifetime, not to mention an incredible amount of exposure for the bakery, but maybe that's the right thing to do.

No. I know this would be one of those things that I'd look back on in life and regret not doing. I have to do it. I have to. How could I even consider passing it up? This is exactly what Jared would say to me if he would just answer his stupid, stupid phone.

I need to pull myself together.

"You all right, darlin'?" Patti looks at me with concern as I slowly start to stand up from the chair.

"Yes, just my nerves getting the best of me," I say. Not yet willing to give up my chair, I sit back down.

Debbie snorts out a giggle. "If your nerves are already hitting you, imagine how you will be with all those cameras around you." Patti whacks her on the arm and gives her a look telling her to shut it.

"I mean, you're gonna be great," Debbie says quickly, trying to backtrack.

"Darlin', you need to pull it together. We got ourselves a lunch rush coming up, real quick," Patti motions her head toward the clock that hangs above the door. I do appreciate Patti and her non-sugarcoating approach. Even though I do love the sugarcoating, it's probably better for me not to have it. I sugarcoat enough things in my own mind.

"You're right," I agree. Maybe focusing on the bakery will help me get my mind off of things.

We get to work, preparing for the lunch rush. And it works - I'm feeling much more at ease. Granted, I've totally pushed any thoughts of *Cupcake Battles* out of my head. That is until right now, at least.

Oh, gosh.

No, I must focus on lunch. I head out to the front to help Debbie as people start to trickle in.

"What's wrong, Julia?" a sappy-sweet voice says to me as I concentrate on getting the sandwich toppings situated in their correct places. I look up quickly and find myself face to face with Lia, one of our regulars at the bakery. She comes in two or three times a week.

"Your aura is off. I can see it. It's all a dark and muddy blue color. You're fearing something." Her large blue eyes are filled with concern behind black, thick-rimmed glasses. She has short, reddish hair and a plump, round face.

Oh, no. This is so not what I need right now. Lia . . . is a *witch*. A good witch, so I've been told. I wouldn't know. It's not like I've known a lot of witches in my life. Actually, she's the first. Anyway, she's always reading our auras and telling us how we are feeling. Okay, she's right on most of the time, but it doesn't mean I subscribe to any of her hokey stuff.

"I'm fine, Lia. Really." I keep my tone kind, but my sentences short, so she knows that I don't feel like talking right now.

"You want to talk about it?" Clearly Lia may not be as

intuitive as she thinks she is.

"No, really, I'm fine." I slap on a big, forced grin.

"Well, I'll be over at my regular table if you do." She tilts her head toward the corner where she usually sits when she comes into the bakery.

"What can I get for you today?" I keep with the forced smile.

Luckily, she places her order and leaves me and my muddy blue aura to ourselves. Thank goodness.

The lunch rush goes fairly smoothly after that, and I keep sneaking peeks at my phone, hoping that Jared has heard one of my ten voicemails. That's right, ten. Don't even ask how many texts I've sent. But nothing. Nada.

I also can't help but be *that* girl and feel a little insecure that he isn't answering my calls or calling me back. I know he's busy, I do. And I do trust him. However, my mind does tend to go off on crazy-tangent thoughts about Jared and some hot secretary he's met and suddenly run away with. It's totally unfounded. First of all, I have no idea if there is even a hot secretary in the vicinity. Secondly, Jared is not the type to run off with someone. He's much more methodical about things.

"Well, now that the lunch rush is done, why don't we get started on practicin'?" Patti asks me as I come back into the kitchen after things have calmed down in the front.

"Practicing for what?" I rack my brain, trying to figure out what she's talking about.

"*Cupcake Battles*?" She gives me a strange expression, perhaps wondering if I've taken something. I probably would have, had I had something to take. A swig of some of the rum we have in the pantry did sound tempting at one point, but I needed to keep my wits about me to help with lunch.

"Yes, of course. Sorry." I shake my head. "I was trying to push it out of my mind during lunch. I guess it worked." The butterflies start creeping in again as I think about all we are going to have to do to get ready for this. And of course, the whole national television thing is looming over me.

Oh, gosh.

Anyway, my muddy blue aura and I don't have time for the nerves right now. We have some practicin' to do.

The deal with *Cupcake Battles* is that it's separated into three parts. It starts with four teams, and for the first part of the competition, you're given strange ingredients with which to make original-flavored cupcakes. The judges taste the cupcakes and eliminate the person with the lowest score, which will most likely be me, but I'm not going to think about that right now or the pukey feelings will creep back in. Let's be honest, they never left, but they might get worse, so it's best to just not think about that.

If you make it to round two, you have to make three different kinds of cupcakes. This round is judged on taste, but it's also judged on décor, which, to be perfectly honest, I suck at. But that's why I'm bringing Patti. She has a knack for that stuff. The décor usually has to do with some sort of theme that they tell you about in the beginning.

For the third round—which I obviously won't make it to so I don't even know why I'm explaining it—you get a team of assistants, and you have to make one thousand cupcakes in a two-hour period, and you get a carpenter to make a stand that you design, which also has to go with the theme. Oh, I hope I get the carpenter named Ryan. He's seriously dreamy.

Patti starts our practicing by giving me strange ingredients and asking me what I'd do with them. At first,

17

I'm totally at a loss and can't think of anything. I start to think that I can't go through with this, but then I begin getting into it, and suddenly my mind is working (surprisingly) and I'm now starting to feel creative rather than nauseated.

I might be able to do this after all. Yes, I will delude myself into believing that, pukey feelings be damned.

~*~

My phone rings, waking me up. I must have dozed off while watching reruns of *Cupcake Battles*. I was studying to help give me ideas.

It's Jared. It's about time. I guess he didn't run off with a secretary after all.

"Where have you been?" I say, instead of the obligatory "hello" most humans use.

"Sorry. It's been a rough day," he says. He sounds tired. "What's going on? I got all of your messages. Everything okay?"

"Well, I hope it is. I mean, I think it will be." The butterflies creep in as I think about what I'm about to tell him.

"So what's going on?" he says through a yawn. Nice. Glad I could keep him so interested.

"Well, you know that show *Cupcake Battles* that I make you watch sometimes?"

"Uh-huh."

"Well, in twelve days they are flying me out to compete on the show."

"Are you serious?" Now he's starting to sound like he's awake.

"Yes, I'm totally serious." I smile. The butterflies dissipate, slightly.

"But I didn't even know you auditioned," he says, sounding confused.

"I didn't tell anyone. I didn't think it would actually happen." I still can't truly believe it's happening.

"Jules, that is . . . just . . . really great news." I can envision him smiling happily. Even through the phone I know his exact expression right now.

"Is it? Because I kind of feel like running for the hills." I throw out a nervous laugh, since I'm honestly only half joking. Okay, I'm like one-eighth joking. I could totally run for the hills. What does "running for the hills" even mean? What hills? I'm picturing myself running for the hills of Austria and spinning around like Maria from *The Sound of Music*, singing "the hiiiiiiills are aliiiiiiiiive" only not with Nazis chasing me. So maybe those aren't the best hills to run for.

"Jules, listen to me. You will be great. This is an opportunity that you can't pass up. Think of the publicity you will get for the bakery."

"I knew you would say that." I smile to myself.

"Well, it's true. You would regret not doing it."

"I knew you would say that, too."

Even knowing exactly what he would say, hearing it from his voice is so much better. He's right, of course. If only we had talked when it all first happened. He could have saved me a lot of internal turmoil.

He chuckles. "This is great news, Jules. I needed it after today."

"Why? What's going on?" I ask, feeling strangely relieved to be putting my attention on him and not having to think about the upcoming competition, even with my inner voice calming a bit.

He lets out a long breath, as if he'd been holding it in for a while. "It's a long story. I'll tell you when I get home.

I don't feel like talking about it right now."

"Okay," I say, wanting to push him to explain, but also knowing Jared well enough to know that I should just wait and he will eventually tell me. Insecure thoughts creep in though, and my heart sinks a little at the possibility that it has to do with more than work.

"Miss me?" he asks, his playful tone squelching my stupid, girly inner-dialog.

"So much," I say, goofily grinning. I really do miss him. I hate this long-distance junk. I think the only saving grace is that he gets to come home, sometimes for weeks, between jobs. If we had to do this on a permanent basis, I'm not sure we could, especially with my crazy dramatic thoughts.

"Are you coming home this weekend?" I'm afraid of the answer. I have a sinking suspicion of what it will be.

"I can't. I wish I could." His voice sounds apologetic even through the phone. It lessens my desire to slap him, but only slightly. "And I don't know if I'll be home next weekend either."

"Well, that sucks," I say bluntly. I want to be supportive, but it's hard.

"Sorry, Jules. I wish I could be home with you to celebrate." His voice sounds so tired but with a hint of something else. Maybe sadness? He's trying to cover up something. I wish he would just tell me what's wrong so my mind doesn't take off running with the possibilities.

"How did the girls take the news about *Cupcake Battles*?" he asks, trying to change the subject.

I oblige. "Patti and Debbie? Thrilled, of course. I'm taking Patti with me as my assistant."

"I'd have picked her just for the comedy of it all. Who knows what she will say on camera."

Oh, wow, I never thought of that. What crazy Southern

expressions will Patti say on national television? I have no choice though. No one does gum paste décor like Patti. Even Debbie agreed, although I suspect she didn't want to go. National television wouldn't appeal to someone like Debbie. She and I are a lot alike, apparently.

We say quick goodnight and I go back to snuggling with my cat, Charlie, and watching more *Cupcake Battles*.

After a few minutes, my phone beeps signaling that I have a text.

I miss you too.

I text back an emoticon with a kissy face. I totally hate emoticons, but sometimes they just convey what I'm thinking so much better than actually saying it.

I guess one bright side to Jared not coming home the next two weekends is it will give me more time to prepare. Oh, and I also won't have to shave my legs either. Neither of those sides are very bright - more like dim, at best.

Chapter 3

I have tried for weeks to get the word "amazeballs" out of my mind. I'd never even said it or thought it until Brown forwarded me an article entitled "Things You Should Never Say After 40." Granted, I'm not forty, but for some reason she felt the need to forward it to me. Maybe because I went through a phase of saying "whatevs" and she really hated it. Well, the joke's on her because "whatevs" has now been replaced by "amazeballs." I don't even know what it means. Like super-duper amazing? Or maybe something dirty. I have no clue.

I mention this because that is the first word that entered my mind when I walked into the bakery this morning. The smell of baking bread is, well, amazeballs. Honestly, I still can't believe that I'm the owner of a bakery. After six months of being a business owner, I still feel like I should pinch myself. This is my sanctuary, for sure. Although, lately my sanctuary has been bombarded with wedding stuff (I'm making cakes for both Brown and

Anna), and now it will be attacked with *Cupcake Battles* practices.

It's Friday, the end of the week for us. Since our clientele is mainly businesspeople, and they tend to stay clear of downtown on the weekends, it's not worth it to stay open. It's nice to have my weekends, especially when Jared is around. But this weekend I will be practicing with Patti for the competition, so I guess it doesn't matter that Jared isn't coming home, although I could use his moral support right now. His job sucks. He really needs a new one.

How do you tell your boyfriend, who's pretty much the love of your life (although not admitted aloud), that you don't like the company that *he* started, and you want him to find a new one? You don't, that's how.

Patti and Debbie are in the back, already getting everything started for the morning rush. I love it that I have people that work for me that I can count on to be here before I can drag my lazy butt out of bed. They are the best employees. I didn't find them. They came with the bakery when I bought it, but I wouldn't have it any other way. We have a great thing going, the three of us.

Patti doesn't actually need to work. She's an empty nester—all three kids are off starting their own families and her husband is retired. I suspect she works here to get away from home and have some time for herself, though she has never admitted that. Patti is a doer. She gets things done, doesn't need direction, and she keeps me in line. She also lets me run the bakery how I want to and doesn't step on my toes. Like I said, we have a good thing going.

Debbie, on the other hand, is more of a sugar-coater. Don't get me wrong, she does her thing and does it well (her scones are a must-try), but she's not quite as direct as Patti. Like Patti, Debbie is an empty nester, except for one son that seems to keep coming back home. She's also a widow — which is where I think the sugarcoating comes from. She's been through a lot and therefore empathy and sympathy come easily to her. She's perfect for running the front of the bakery.

"Well, hello there, missy," Patti says when she sees me walk into the back.

"Good morning, ladies." I smile as brightly as I can at five in the morning. My brown hair is twisted in a damp bun on top of my head. I need to put my alarm clock across the room from me so I have to get out of bed to shut it off, although I'd probably still find a way to get back in bed. I'm not a morning person, and I still can't figure out how to be one, even after six months of owning the bakery.

"How are you feeling about everything this morning?" Debbie asks as she mixes the dough for the scones. I can smell orange. My favorite kind of scone — orange cream.

"Better, I think. Jared was excited." They both grin at me when they hear Jared's name. Both Patti and Debbie are Team Jared and have been since even before we started dating, back when I tried to hate him for getting me fired from my job. They always wanted us to end up together. Their hopeless romanticism was super annoying during that time.

"Well, I'm glad to hear it. Speaking of Jared, settle a bet for us," Debbie says.

"What bet?" I ask as I put my apron on.

"If you had to choose between an outdoor wedding and an indoor one, which would you pick?" Debbie raises her eyebrows in interest.

"Oh, geez, you two. Stop planning my freaking wedding, this is getting ridiculous." Okay, so the hopeless romanticism never stopped, even after we started dating.

24

Now they have moved on to our upcoming wedding, the one that has never even been discussed between Jared and me. They clearly have way too much time on their hands and I need to give them more work to do.

"Just answer the darn question!" Patti points the whisk at me that she's using to mix icing for the cinnamon rolls.

"No way. I refuse to add more kindling to that fire." I roll my eyes and start pulling out the tools to make croissants.

"Come on, just indulge us," Debbie says, giving me sad little begging-puppy-eyes.

"Oh, fine." I let out a sigh. "I guess if I had to choose, I'd say outside, depending on the weather of course."

It really isn't something "I had to choose" as much as something that I've planned out and thought about in ridiculous amounts of detail. I can't help but think about it. Until *Cupcake Battles* came along yesterday, weddings had been in the forefront of my mind, especially with Brown and Anna getting married. I'll never admit it, though.

"Told you," Debbie bobbles her head at her, and Patti sighs loudly. She hates to be wrong.

"Anyway, would you two cut it out?" I say as I start measuring out pastry flour. "It's not like it's even been discussed. Plus there are no guarantees. I mean if it all works out."

"Oh, please stop with yer 'if it all works out' trash," Patti cuts me off, raising her voice as she tries to imitate me. "Honestly, if I had a dime for every time ya said that, I'd be richer than three feet up a bull's rear end."

Debbie and I look at each other. What the heck is rich about a bull's butt? Is there a Rosetta Stone for Southern talk? If so, I need it.

"Well, there are no guarantees." I shrug my shoulders

at her. Sometimes my internal thoughts come out of my mouth as well.

"I've seen the way he looks at ya, and he ain't going anywhere." She shakes her head at my insecurities.

I do realize I should be more secure in my relationship with Jared after nine months of dating. But up until nine months ago, I thought I'd die a lonely spinster. Sometimes I get caught up in my doubts and still wonder if that's where I'll end up, just me and my cat, Charlie, with no one to be there when I die from choking on a double chocolate fudge cookie (if I'm going to die from food, it better be worth it).

The morning goes by quickly as we bake and get everything ready. At seven, I go unlock the doors. There are already people outside in the cool May morning air, waiting to come in for their morning coffee and pastry.

"Morning, George," I say as a middle-aged, portly man with graying hair comes in. He's one of our regular customers. Thank goodness for regulars. They are the bread and butter of this place.

George mumbles a "good morning" as he walks (more like clomps) in and makes a beeline for the counter. Debbie is there waiting for him.

"Well, good morning, George!" she says brightly and warmly.

"I'll take my regular," George grunts out. We've learned that George is not a morning person and pretty much a total grump in the afternoon, too. Debbie seems to make her greetings louder and brighter every time he comes in (which is most days), just because she knows he hates it.

I peer out the window as I switch on the open sign, and more and more people begin to file in through the doors. The sky is ominous with clouds; looks like more rain today. Unfortunately for Denver, that means there is a fifty-fifty chance it could turn into snow. After the crazy winter we had, spring has not been very springy.

I go back behind the counter and start helping Debbie. The morning rush is a busy one today, which is good and bad. Good because we are making money, and bad because we run out of scones rather quickly. It's one of those things that just happens: make too many scones, it's a slow day. Make too few, it's a busy day. Murphy's Law can stuff it.

After a couple of hours, things finally start to slow down. I leave Debbie to work in the front and go back to help Patti with the cookies for the lunch rush. Today we'll also be plotting out what kinds of things we'll be doing to prepare for *Cupcake Battles* while we get ready for lunch. We are going to have to do a lot of multi-tasking for the next eleven days.

"Someone's here to see you, Julia," Debbie says as she comes into the back. I'm mixing snickerdoodle dough while Patti is writing down our plan of attack.

"Who is it?" I say as I wipe flour-covered hands on my apron.

"You'll see," she says, raising her eyebrows high on her face.

Could it be? No. Jared is in . . . someplace that starts with a *C* and wasn't coming home this weekend. He just told me on the phone last night.

But as I come out to the front, there he is, looking tired and ragged in jeans and a T-shirt, and also looking totally hot.

After all this time, I'm still taken by the sight of him. His sandy blond hair, his striking blue eyes, his manly, strong body. I should be over all of the butterflies at this point, shouldn't I? But I'm not.

27

In a totally out-of-character move, I run and jump into his arms, throwing caution to the wind and not caring about me and my extra ten pounds. I wrap my legs around his waist and I kiss him hard on the lips. He wraps his arms around me, holding me up and against him. Gosh, I love to kiss this man. I can't get enough of him.

"What are you doing here? You just told me last night you weren't coming home this weekend," I say between kisses.

"I took an early morning flight from Charlotte. Thought I'd surprise you." He kisses me again lightly on the lips.

Charlotte, right. I knew it started with a *C*. My legs are still wrapped around him, and I'm hugging him tightly, closing my eyes as I take in his scent, that amazing, manly scent.

"Ahem." I hear a clear voice and I open my eyes, face-to-face with none other than Bobby, Jared's mom, who I'm quite sure doesn't appreciate watching the love fest that is going on with her son right now.

"Bobby!" I say, a little over-enthusiastically and jump off of Jared, stumbling just slightly as I try to catch my balance. Honestly, I cannot stop myself from doing the stupidest things around this woman. She has got to think I'm a complete moron at this point. I can now add this to the list of embarrassing things I've done in front of her, right under tripped and fell flat on my face. Yes, that happened.

"Jared, you didn't tell me your mom was here." I shoot him a look that says "thanks a lot."

"Well, how could I when you attacked me like you did?" He smirks slightly at me.

"Oh, geez." I laugh nervously. "I didn't 'attack' you. Ha ha ha . . ." I trail off, shaking my head.

I'm such an idiot.

"Wonderful to see you, dear," Bobby says in flighty yet matronly tones, smiling in a faintly patronizing way, as she often does around me. Her tailored raincoat is slightly splattered on the shoulders with drops of rain. She starts to shrug off her jacket, and Jared is quick to come to the rescue and help her take it off.

He's amazing with his mom. I've heard that you're supposed to watch how a man treats his mom to know how he will treat you, and if that is true, I will be doted on and treated like a queen forever . . . I mean, if it all works out.

"Great to see you, Bobby!" And there comes over-the-top-butt-kissy Julia. Why can't I just be normal? "Can I get you anything?"

"Oh, I'd love a scone."

Crap. Of course she would. "We're all out of scones, I'm afraid. What about a lemon poppy seed muffin?" I point over to the display case, which is lacking at this point, to say the least. The morning rush wiped us out.

"Oh," she says, disappointed. "A lemon poppy seed muffin it is, then." She takes a seat at one the tables nearest her. Jared follows suit, sitting down across from her.

"Anything for you?" I ask Jared. I'm so excited to have him back.

"I'll have the same." He beams at me with a smoldering gaze. I so heart him, even with the off-putting unexpected appearance of his mom and the slightly compromising position we were in when I saw her. A smile from him and I feel instantly relaxed.

Too bad it doesn't last long. Just one glance over at Bobby and I'm back to being flustered.

Bobby isn't that scary of a person, honestly. In fact, she has a very kind look to her. She glides into rooms with her

29

long, skinny limbs that always use fluid movements. She always seems light on her feet, like a dancer. Her clothing is unpretentious. She mostly wears a simple pair of jeans and a white-collared button up. In fact, I don't know if I've ever seen her in anything else. She seems very conservative in the way she dresses. I've yet to see her in the summertime and have often wondered if she will continue with the jeans and white button up, even in the heat. Something tells me she probably will.

She doesn't wear a ton of jewelry, just a few rings. And she always wears a diamond solitaire necklace. All gifts from her late husband, I'm sure. She seems very loyal and sentimental like that. I don't think she has been on a date since his passing, nor does she care to. Her hair is the same color as Jared's — sandy blonde — and is cut short and well kept. She wears minimal makeup because she doesn't really need it. At sixty-two, she's actually quite striking.

I'm not sure what I was expecting when I first met Bobby. I guess someone a little stuffier, with fur coats, diamond-saturated fingers, and the like. I just figured Jared would refer to her as "Mummy" in her presence, and they would spend their time drinking tea with their pinkies extended, talking only of politics and other highbrow discussions. But they are nothing like that. The conversation is mostly lighthearted and fun, and Jared refers to her as Mom, or even just Bobby most of the time. My mom would have us imprisoned and possibly hung for referring to her as Katherine. She's "Mom" to us, and that's how she likes it. Bobby doesn't mind when Jared calls her by her given name, and even seems to enjoy it.

"How was the morning rush?" Jared asks, weariness in his eyes. I still want to know what he didn't feel like talking about on the phone last night. I doubt he would want me to bring it up in front of Bobby, so I'll have to wait. He's very protective of her and doesn't want her to worry.

"I think the rush went pretty well." I glance around at the bakery and see perused newspapers messily laying around on some of the tables, crumbs on the floor, and a display counter that is practically empty. I'd say this morning was a success.

"So Jared tells me you're going to be on some sort of competition on television," Bobby says, holding a cup of coffee between her palms.

"Yeah, yes. *Cupcake Battles*," I say.

Bobby has clearly never heard of *Cupcake Battles*. The silence confirms that.

"It's on The Dessert Channel," I tell her.

Bobby has clearly never heard of The Dessert Channel.

"It's five channels away from Fox News, Bobby," Jared pipes in.

"Oh!" She sets her cup down and clasps her hands together, giving me a little cheer. "Well, isn't that wonderful. What exactly will you be doing?"

"Well, I'll be competing with three other bakeries to see who can make the most creative and flavorful cupcakes," I sum it up, not wanting to go into detail. I doubt she wants to hear it anyway, since it's not up her alley of television programs. Perhaps next time I'll have to try to get on Fox News to get the attention of Bobby Moody.

I hear the jingle of the bells on the door and in walks Lia. We must be getting close to lunchtime. As if on cue, Debbie comes into the room and starts bustling around, straightening up before the rush.

"Hello, Julia," Lia says in her sickly sweet voice as she approaches the table where we are sitting. She's wearing a strange ensemble of clothing, a long chevron skirt with a mismatched striped shirt. She wears a strange headband that wraps around her forehead rather than up on top like the rest of the world wears it. I wonder if it's some sort of witch thing.

"Hi, Lia," I say and then give her a closed-mouth smile. She stands there as if waiting to be introduced to Jared and Bobby. Really?

"Uh, Jared and Bobby, this is Lia. She's one of our favorite regulars." Favorite is a slight exaggeration, but it felt weird to just say "regular." "Lia, Jared and Bobby." I motion over to Bobby and Jared.

"You and Jared must be dating," Lia says matter-of-factly.

I blush. "Uh, yes, we are." I glance over at Jared and he winks at me. "Lia is quite clairvoyant, actually." I leave out the whole witch thing and pray she doesn't bring that up.

"I figured that out because I see that you both have red auras," she says, gesturing between me and Jared. "And red can mean a lot of things, but between two people it tends to have a sexual context."

Bobby coughs uncomfortably.

Oh, my dear heaven. Please let me die right here. I'm totally ready to go, just take me now.

"Okay," I say in a high-pitched crazy manner, "thank you so much for that, Lia. Can I get you a muffin? On the house!" I jump up from my chair and escort her over to the counter. I now wish she would have brought up the witch thing. Then maybe Bobby would be focusing on that rather than on my sexually-charged red aura. Oh, dear heavens . . .

After I get Lia sorted out, I grudgingly come back to the table. Finding a rock to climb under sounds more appealing.

"Sorry about that." I take a seat at the table. Bobby

looks composed, but I can tell Jared's been laughing.

I do not see the humor in this. At all.

"Well, on that note, I should get Bobby home." Jared stands. "But wait, Jules, didn't you have some sort of marketing thing you wanted to show me?"

I'm pretty sure I go fifty shades of red. I can feel the fire in my face. And honestly, right after the whole Lia debacle?

Marketing is *code*.

"Uh, sure. I mean, yes," I stammer, obviously not as good as he's at acting calm and cool. Can you blame me? Lia the Witch just told my boyfriend's mother that her son and I have red auras. Lusty red auras.

"It's in my, er, office." I get up from my chair, not making eye contact with Bobby.

"Be back in a second, Mom," Jared says.

"It was great to see you, Julia," Bobby says, a pleasant smile on her face.

"You too, Bobby." I flash her what I'm sure is a ridiculous grin.

Jared takes my hand and guides me toward the back office.

"Marketing stuff," I spew out quickly to Patti as we walk by.

"Sure, sure." She gives me a knowing glance, which I ignore completely.

Once inside the office, with the door shut, Jared grabs me and pushes me up against the door and kisses me with so much passion, my legs go wobbly.

"So, I guess Lia was right?" I say between kisses.

"Totally right," he says as I tighten my hold around him, kissing him with slight force.

"Dinner tonight?" he asks as the kissing slows down to soft pecks intermixed with him tenderly moving my hair out of my face. My hair twist had come undone.

"Of course." I grasp the hand that is playing with my hair and kiss the inside of his palm.

"Okay," he says, gathering himself. "I'll call you later, then." He kisses me softly one more time, and then he opens the door and goes back out to the front.

I sink down into my office chair, heart racing with what I'm sure is an ultra-red aura burning brightly.

"That was pretty fast marketin'," Patti says loudly so I can hear her.

"Shut it, Patti," I yell out the door, and then close my eyes and spin in my chair like a giddy little girl.

Chapter 4

"Hmm, I don't know. I was thinking something more like red velvet or chocolate," Anna says, underhandedly questioning my wedding cake ideas. Mind you, cake ideas I haven't even *told* her about. She's already in full Bridezilla mode, and it's only ten in the morning.

It's Sunday and we are at brunch with Mom at one of our favorite breakfast spots. It's called Snooze, and they make this pineapple upside-down pancake that I'd like to marry.

"Well, I was thinking we could do different flavors for each layer," I say, hoping to get her off of the red velvet idea.

"Like what?" She eyes me, dubiously.

"Like I was thinking the base could be a chocolate hazelnut with a white chocolate mousse filling."

"That sounds lovely," my mother pipes in, and Anna agrees.

"And for the middle layer, I was thinking a coconut cake with an almond cream filling," I tick off the layers with my fingers as I tell her my ideas.

"Let me stop you right there," Anna cuts me off as I start to move on to my idea for the third layer. "Coconut and almond? Together?"

"Oh, yes." I dip my chin once. "It's all the rage right now." It's not really, but Anna will be all over it if I say it is. It truly is an amazing combination, though. I happened upon it by accident, and it was quite the tasty accident, if I do say so myself.

"Hmm." She purses her lips, considering it.

"And for the top layer, I was thinking a lemon cake with English lemon curd filling."

"Well, that actually sounds good," Anna says snidely. "I can't believe you came up with that on your own." Then she gives me a playful look. She's teasing, of course. I do like it when old Anna makes an appearance. Crazy Wedding Anna has taken over and has been driving me nuts. I've been missing old Anna.

"Yes, I do have my talents." I give her my best smirk. "Anyway, you might want to run over that with Jonathon to make sure that works for him."

"Oh, Jonathon doesn't care about the details. He's leaving it all up to me." She smiles smugly.

"So that's why he hasn't been helping much," my mouth says without asking my brain first. It does that more than I'd prefer.

"What do you mean?" she snaps. Oh yes, excellent, Julia. Great can of worms to open up right now. It's been bothering me though, so I might as well go with it.

"I mean, he just doesn't seem to want to do much." I search my mom for help, but she's just staring at me. Part of me wonders if she has had the same thought as well. How could she not? Jonathon hasn't done one thing for this wedding. He hasn't even helped with any of the decisions, not one. Except for the proposal part, that was it. "Maybe he's just too busy," I add, seeing the appalled look on Anna's face.

"Yes, of course he's busy!" Anna practically spits it out at me. "He's a junior partner after all." She looks to the side, exasperated.

I want to say, *you're kidding! He's **a** junior partner? I had no idea! Neither of you have ever, ever mentioned it before. Ever.* But being sarcastic right now would probably not be helpful.

"Anyway," Anna takes a deep breath, "I don't need his help. He's fine with just showing up at the wedding."

"But what about the parts he's supposed to do? Isn't the groom's family supposed to do the rehearsal dinner or flowers or something?" I only know this because Brown and I had this conversation recently when she nearly had a nervous breakdown because her fiancé Matt's family wanted to do the rehearsal dinner at the Golden Corral. I don't think Brown has ever stepped inside a Golden Corral in her life. She was not going to do it the night before her wedding, that was for sure.

"I've spoken with his mom, and we are working out all of that. She's very busy as well and doesn't have time to help out, so she has left it up to me to pick the venue. She just gave me a check to pay for it all."

"Anna, you can't do all of this on your own," I say. I truly am concerned. Taking on a whole wedding, and doing it with only a little time to get everything done — isn't this the stuff that breakdowns are made of?

"I can handle it. I like it. Besides I have you and Mom." She regards my mother strangely. Mom still hasn't piped in, and Anna is obviously confused by her silence. So am I. By now our mother would have said something to bring peace to the conversation (she's the peacemaker of the family), but instead she has just sat there and listened. I think my suspicions are correct. She's been wondering all of this herself but has not had the nerve to ask it.

The truth is she hasn't asked my mom and me to help with much anyway. She's dragged us to dress fittings and food tastings, but she never truly wants our opinion. It's like we are there because that's what you're supposed to do — drag your mom and your maid of honor around with you when planning a wedding (and your fiancé as well, but that is obviously not going to happen), but she has no actual need for us to be there.

Silence awkwardly lands upon the discussion. My mom stares intently at her food, avoiding eye contact.

Anna clears her throat. "Anyway, the wedding is still over a month away, and there isn't that much left to do."

I want to scoff at her, but I just keep it to myself. There's so much left to do, I don't think she even realizes.

"Julia, didn't you have something you wanted to tell us?" My mother finally pipes in, not just trying to bring peace to the conversation, but to bury the topic completely.

"Yes, I do." I smooth down the napkin in my lap. "I just found out that I'm going to be on *Cupcake Battles!*" I do a little dance in my chair. It still seems so surreal. The dancing also covers up the pukey feeling that rears its ugly head whenever I say the words "*Cupcake Battles.*"

"*Cupcake Battles?*" my mom says, confused.

"Yes, you know the competition show I love to watch?"

She's clearly still confused.

"It's on The Dessert Channel?"

Still. Not. Registering.

"It's five channels away from Fox News."

"Oh, well, isn't that fun," she says. Yet another person

impressed that I'll be five channels away from Fox News.

Clearly my mom and Bobby could bond over their love of Fox News since that seems to be *all* they watch. Honestly, there is other programming out there.

"When is it?" Anna asks. I'm surprised she didn't pipe in earlier since I make her watch it with me sometimes. Or I used to, before she went all wedding nut-jobby.

"I leave in ten days." My stomach sinks as I say that. I shouldn't be here. I should be practicing. But Patti and I practiced for hours yesterday, and we decided we needed a break. I'm suddenly wondering if that was the best idea. Ten days is not that far away.

"But what about my wedding?" Anna looks incensed.

"Are you serious?" She's seriously going to make this about her? "I'll be back two days later. An entire month before your wedding." I scrunch my face at her. Does she honestly think my entire life revolves around her wedding? Can I not have a life of my own outside of her stupid wedding?

She shakes her head as if to bring herself out of a trance. "Right, okay. Of course. I didn't . . . mean to say that." She tucks some hair behind her ear, mumbling something that sounds sort of like "sorry." I'm not exactly sure, but I think that's what she said.

And that right there, ladies and gentlemen, is an Anna apology. A pretty good one, actually. It's very difficult for Anna to apologize in any way. I'm pretty sure she's allergic.

One time after a heated argument at dinner with the family, she came down to the basement apartment at my parents' house (when I used to live in their basement), and said, "Mom told me I was rude to you at dinner. I don't think I was, but sorry if I was." And then she ran back upstairs. I yelled, "Apology accepted!" up the stairs, but

I'm pretty sure she had run lightning fast to her bathroom and immediately jumped into the shower to scrub any apologetic feelings she had off of her body before the hives set in.

"Well, I'm excited to hear how it turns out. How much money do you win?" my mom asks, trying to bring the conversation back from the turn it was about to take, a turn where I wring my sister's neck.

"Ten grand, and then you also get to have your cupcakes at a huge party — usually with famous people in Hollywood — and get tons of exposure."

"Oh, well that sounds like fun," my mom says, still trying to lighten the mood.

Anna doesn't say anything. I think she might still be reeling from her pseudo-apology, or she feels ashamed for going where she did in the first place.

"So, Anna, are you all set with the wedding favors?" My mother eases back into wedding stuff, seamlessly.

Anna settles back into bride mode immediately - did she ever even leave? I try to be involved, but I mostly just sit there and only offer my opinion if asked, which is pretty much never.

I go back to paying attention to my pineapple upside-down pancake and bask in its nothing-to-do-with-weddings-or-cupcakes qualities.

~*~

"You're late," Betsy Brown says as I rush into the restaurant in lower downtown, or Lodo, as we locals like to call it. This has been quite the busy day today, not to mention caloric. And I still have dinner with Jared tonight before he leaves to go back to Charlotte tomorrow.

I wish I'd worn my fat pants. These skinny jeans are

cutting off my circulation.

"Yes, I'm late. You're surprised?" I shrug my shoulders.

"No, I'm not. Sit down. We have much to discuss." She motions to the chair next to her.

"Thanks," I say and take a seat.

She has no idea how much we have to discuss. I'm about to tell her that I'm going to be rushing out of town to compete in a cupcake baking competition during the week of her wedding and will return only two days before the actual wedding. I wish I didn't have to do it face to face. A text would be so much easier.

"How are you holding up?" I ask, hoping that she's not going to be full of the wedding drama. I have enough of that from Anna.

"Oh, I'm pretty much a disaster," she smiles feebly.

No such luck. Aaaaaand, now would not be the best time to tell her about *Cupcake Battles*. I think I'll just wait. Maybe I can send her a wimpy, cop-out text later.

And then the craziest thing that has ever happened in all of the time I've known Brown happens. She starts to cry.

"Brown?" I ask, almost as if I'm not sure it's her, like she has been taken over by an alien. "Are you okay?"

"Yes," she says through sniffles and desperate attempts to stop the tears now rapidly coming out. "I mean, no. Not really."

"What's wrong? Is everything okay with Matt? With the wedding?"

"No," she shakes her head, dabbing her eyes with her napkin. "Everything is fine with Matt. I mean, I guess it's fine."

"What do you mean you guess it's fine?"

"I don't know." She stares at her hands, her fingers

41

nervously playing with a small piece of string that is hanging from one of the corners of the cloth napkin in her lap. "It's just . . . it's just . . . Oh, never mind." She shakes her head again. "You wouldn't under — I mean, you don't want to hear about it."

Nice cover, Brown. She's right, though. I wouldn't understand. I've never been engaged. I can tell by her expression she feels bad that she went there. I'm not even going to give it any acknowledgment, although the devil on my shoulder kind of wants me to. But then the angel on the other shoulder is reminding me that I'm going to be ditching her right before her wedding. So I think I'll let it lie.

"Try me." I give her a supportive grin.

She sits in silence for a moment, still playing with her napkin. The waitress comes by and I shoo her with my hand, tilting my head toward breaking-down-Brown. The waitress nods, catching on, and turns and walks away.

"It's just that . . ." she trails off, as if to find her wording. "It's just that, I'm not sure I can go through with this."

"Go through with the wedding?" I try to keep my eyes from bugging out of my head, but they don't listen and do it anyway.

"Yes, this whole institution of marriage. It's kind of archaic, isn't it? I mean, I'm a modern woman. I should be doing more modern things." She slams her fist down on the table. A balding, portly man at the table behind her swivels his head around to see what's going on.

"What kind of modern things should you be doing?"

"I don't know. Focusing on my career, making more money . . ."

I take a deep breath. "Brown, where is this all coming from? I just saw you last week and you were fine, excited even. Why are you just coming up with this now? Only two weeks away from your wedding?"

Oh, wait. Cold feet. I should have known as soon as she cried. I'm not sure why it took so long for that to occur to me. It might possibly be due to the fact that my feet have never had the chance to get cold.

"Matt wants to have kids, like right away," she spurts out, before I have a chance to bring up the whole cold feet thing.

"Okay?"

"Well, I'm not ready to have kids yet," she says a little louder than is appropriate for a nice restaurant. The man behind her turns around again. He appears to be slightly annoyed.

"Did you tell him that?" I ask, ignoring annoyed guy.

"Yes, I did."

"And what did he say?"

"He said that he thought we were on the same page with children, that we both wanted them."

"Do you want them?"

"Yes, I do." She shakes her head slightly. "Just not yet. I'm not ready."

"Did you tell him that?"

"Yes."

"And what did he say?"

"He said he would wait, but not too long." She gazes out into the restaurant, contemplating.

"Well that sounds like a fair compromise to me." I try to make eye contact, but she's still staring off.

"I guess. We also got in a huge fight over me taking his last name. Another archaic tradition." She rolls her eyes.

"Why is that such a big deal?" I would totally take Jared's name, if everything works out, that is. I'd be Julia Moody. Julia Warner Moody. JWM. This is obviously the first time I've ever thought of that. I haven't practiced writing it a zillion times on printer paper at work. Or shredded said printer paper in case someone were to see it.

"Because!" Brown says, bringing me back to her. She looks at me like I've lost my mind. "Why would I want to go by Betsy Whitehead?"

"Whitehead?" I furrow my brow.

"Yes, his last name is Whitehead. She stares at me, probably wondering how I could possibly not know this.

I'm wondering the same thing. How did we make it this long as friends and her never telling me Matt's last name? Probably for the same reason she doesn't want to go by it. She hates it.

"I don't know how he expects me to be named after a zit, for hell's sake." She closes her eyes, disgust in her expression.

I stifle a giggle. I mean, obviously that was my first thought—whitehead equals zit—but hearing her say it out loud is a little hilarious. Or really, a lot.

I try hard to push back the giggle that is trying to escape and to squelch the smile that is trying desperately to appear on my lips. It's a difficult plight, and it isn't long before I can't control myself and I start laughing.

"Yes, ha ha. It's *so* funny. Laugh at the future Mrs. Whitehead," Brown says, and then I see her trying to keep herself from joining in, but she's unable to hold herself back as well, and she starts laughing.

"Okay, so I might understand that one," I say through giggles as I try to calm them.

She wipes her wet eyes. "I wish Matt did."

"Well, I'm sure you can come to a compromise on that. Can't you just take his name, but keep Brown for work?" I ask, feeling a little proud of that idea. That seems like a fair concession to me.

"Maybe," she offers, a slight frown appearing. "It's just all hitting me really hard right now. All of that, plus the job thing in Atlanta."

That catches me off guard. "What job in Atlanta?"

"Didn't I tell you?"

I shake my head. "No, you didn't."

She bats a hand through the air as if to minimize it. "Oh, I got a job offer from a software company in Atlanta with, like, incredible pay. But Matt doesn't want to move to Atlanta. He thinks we have good roots here and should stay in Denver." She rolls her eyes.

"Oh, well then I'm glad you didn't take the job," I say giving her a closed-mouth smile. She echoes the expression, knowing that I wouldn't want her to leave. I love that we can communicate without actually having to communicate, since I'm the queen of not being able to say how I'm truly feeling, especially when it takes on a cheesy quality.

"Anyway, I thought about just going and coming back on weekends until we figured things out. Maybe the money would make Matt change his mind. There's a lot of financial potential at this job."

"And?" That doesn't seem like that horrible of an idea. And at least I'd have Brown on the weekends.

"Oh, Julia." She pats me on the arm. "Long-distance relationships are a dumb idea."

"Why? I mean, I can see how it would be hard, but why?"

"They just don't work." She sits back in her seat folding her arms.

"They don't?" I hate to sound naive here, but I guess I am.

"No. At least not in my experience, they don't. And in my friend's experience, and pretty much anyone that I know that's tried it. It's just too much time apart from each other. Time apart to grow apart."

"Huh." I tilt my head to the side, taking in what she just said. I guess that makes sense. She does have first-hand experience. When she moved here from California, she left a boyfriend there that she tried to make things work with. And since she's marrying Matt in two weeks, that obviously didn't work out.

"Anyway, I turned down the job, and I'm sure it was the right thing to do. I love Matt too much to risk it." She glares at the ceiling and exhales loudly. "Gosh, I seriously could use a cigarette." Annoyed Man does a little glance over his shoulder at the word "cigarette." Now he's just eavesdropping. Rude.

"Yeah, why did you pick three months before your wedding to quit anyway?"

"Because I promised Matt I would. I should have done it afterward. I see that now." She reaches across her body and rubs the nicotine patch on her other arm, her frown deepening.

"Well, you're too far into it. No turning back now." I pat her nicotine-patched arm.

"Anyway," she sighs, "I need your help."

"Sure, what with?" I'm already doing the cake I'm not sure what else I can do.

She pulls out a piece of paper and gives it to me. "My maid of honor lives in a different state, and so I really need your help with this stuff."

I gape at the list. There must be thirty items on there. "Are you serious?"

"Yes, I'm serious! I can't do this all on my own, Jules. I need your help." She pleads to me with her hands as she starts to tear up again.

Oh, gosh. How am I going to get ready for *Cupcake*

Battles and do all of the things on this list for Brown? There's also the issue that I haven't even told Brown about the competition. I'll just add that to the list right under "call flower shop three days before wedding to confirm." That's right in the middle of taping. Perfect. How will I even do that? Ask them to hold off taping for two minutes while I make an important call? That's going to go over well.

Crap.

She needs me. My friend needs me. Of course I have to help. I'm just going to have to make it work. I'm not sure how, but I'll figure this out.

"I've got this." I wave the piece of paper back and forth.

"Oh, Jules, thank you so much. What would I ever do without you?" I can see the relief in her face.

"I have no idea, Mrs. Whitehead." I wink at her.

"Oh, shut up." She slaps me lightly on the arm.

~*~

"You seem tired," I say to Jared as we are seated at the Paramount Café. We are in the back corner booth, yes the same one where I freaked out and ran away from him so many months ago. That seems like a lifetime ago, honestly. We come here often. I'm not sure why. It's like a super weird sentiment.

"I *am* tired," he says, sitting back in the rounded booth. I like this booth. We can sit next to each other and we don't seem as creepy as those couples that sit on the same side of the table together. I mean, essentially we are doing that, but it just feels different.

"Everything okay?" I tilt my head to the side, searching his face for answers.

"Not really." He puts his hands in his lap and gives me a sad half-smile.

"What's going on?"

"I don't want to worry you about it. We can talk about it after *Cupcake Battles*." He takes my hand in his, rubbing my thumb with his.

Insecure Julia rears her ugly head, which is stupid. At least, I hope it's stupid. I hate the unknown. And frankly, by now he should know that I hate the unknown and would rather just get it out in the open, whatever it is. I suppose I know that I shouldn't push him. He will tell me when he's ready. He always does.

But still, I don't like waiting.

"So how goes all of the practicing for the competition?" he asks in a feeble attempt to change the subject.

"Good, I guess. We wore ourselves out yesterday, and decided we needed a break today." I let go of his hand and pick up my menu.

"I'm sorry I can't be there to cheer you on," he says, sounding disappointed.

I set the menu down and grab his hand again. "I know you are. Honestly, it might be more of a distraction to have you there."

"Why's that?" He gives me a little smirk.

"Because I'd probably be wishing I was spending time with you instead of focusing. This way I can be across the country from you and that won't even be an option." I scoot closer to him, even though there wasn't much space between us, but sometimes even two inches can seem far away.

Jared looks down at our hands, intertwined, and then up at me. There's more in his eyes than tired. It's almost a touch of sadness. A chill goes down my spine. The bad kind. Why won't he tell me what's going on?

"Everything's okay with us, right?" my mouth says before my brain is able to stop it. I honestly don't even know why my brain bothers. My mouth tends to say a lot of things without clearing it with my brain first.

"Of course it is. Why would you even think that?" he says without pausing.

Because I'm an insecure idiot, is what I want to say.

"Sorry, it's just that . . . never mind." I angle my face away from him, but still hold on to his hand.

"Hey." He puts his hand on my cheek, gently moving my head so I'm looking at him again. He rubs my cheek lightly with his thumb. "It doesn't have to do with us, okay?"

Okay, Jared, right now would be the perfect time to tell me you love me. Just say it. You know you want to. I swear if I have to hold it in for much longer, I might just spew it out. Seriously though, shouldn't I be taking a card from Brown's school of thinking? I'm a modern girl. I can do modern things. It's not the 1950s, for heaven's sake.

I open my mouth to say it. I'm just going to tell him. *I love you, Jared.* How hard can it be to say four little words? Four words that mean a whole lot. Oh gosh, I think I'm sweating.

Before I can will myself to say anything, Jared has moved in even closer, and in the blink of an eye, his lips are on mine, kissing me tenderly. His hand that was on my cheek moves to my back, and he pulls me into him. Suddenly the tender kissing has taken on a whole new, intense tone.

Wait, wasn't I just going to tell Jared something? My mind goes blank, and it's a good thing we are sitting because I'm pretty sure my legs have gone all wobbly. Talk is overrated. This is much better.

It should be duly noted that I'm completely against

public displays of affection. However, right in this moment, and since it's me doing the PDA, I don't care.

Chapter 5

I think this might have been the quickest week of my life. I'm so tired and busy. I'm about ninety-nine percent sure I didn't brush my teeth this morning, and I'm hopeful I did it last night because I'm not confident of that, either. Gross.

Patti and I have been mind-numbingly practicing for *Cupcake Battles*, so much so that I contemplated using my bra to measure out flour. That's right, my bra. I was in the middle of a drill, trying to bake a batch of cupcakes within forty-five minutes from start to finish, and I couldn't find a measuring cup to save my life. Patti is screaming "Make it work, darlin'! Whaddya think they're gonna do if ya can't find a measurin' cup? Ya gotta be quick on yer toes! Like a dead pig in the sun after it's been up a bull's rear end!"

Okay, that wasn't the Southern saying she actually used, and honestly, I'm not even sure what the one she used meant, so what's the point of remembering?

Anyway, I kept trying to think of things I had on me

that would be useful for measuring, and all of a sudden, my bra popped into my mind. I'm a C-cup, that's probably at least a cup or around it. So, yeah. I can't even explain where my brain was. I'm fried. Needless to say, in a small moment of clarity, I dropped the bra idea and just eyeballed it.

Guess what happened? The cupcakes were . . . disgusting. So bakers cannot "just eyeball it," as my arch-nemesis Rachael Ray would say. (Yes, we are arch-nemesis status now since she just keeps getting more famous.) Anyway, she's a cook, not a baker.

It's Friday. I leave for *Cupcake Battles* on Tuesday. Every time I think about it, my heart races and I start to get the cold sweats.

It's also a little worrisome that I'm leaving the bakery to function without me. I'm sure it will be fine. In fact, I know it will be. Beth, the previous owner, has agreed to come and help Debbie run everything. Even knowing that it's in good hands and will be totally fine, I still find it hard to leave, even when I know it's a must. It feels like I'm leaving my child or something, although I wouldn't know since I don't have any children. I once compared taking care of my nephew Liam to taking care of a kitten (that went over about as well as expected), so I probably should just refrain from using any baby metaphors at this point.

And then there is Jared. Jared, the man I love, whom I have still not yet told, the man that is supposed to be supporting me with everything, the man that will be in Charlotte this weekend instead of here with me. I knew he wasn't coming home, but I still hate it. I know he won't be surprising me this weekend, either.

The truth is I don't really need him here. He can't bake, he doesn't even know how to sift flour, or even what that means. (He asked me once after he heard me say it to

Debbie and I was like "really?") But it's the moral support that I need. And I just want him here. I sincerely don't want to hate what he does for a living, but I do. I can't help it.

"Would you just bug off?" Debbie says to Patti as I walk out of my office where I've been sulking.

"I'm just sayin' he seems mighty into you," Patti says, raising her eyebrows.

"Oh, please, George doesn't even seem into the scone he eats for breakfast every morning." I can only see her from behind, but she's in full defense mode with her hands on her hips and her feet pointing to the swinging door that goes to the front of the bakery, as if she expects to walk off at any moment. I can't see her aura, but if Lia were here, I'm pretty sure she'd say it's the one that means angry.

"Ooh, maybe he has a thing for redheads." She does a double eyebrow raise.

"Hmph," is all Debbie says and then she pivots and walks out to the front.

"What was that all about?" I ask, as I take in the disastrous kitchen. We need to clean up and lock up so Patti and I can get some more practicing in. We are down to the wire. But honestly? I seriously don't want to do any of it. I'm so fried.

"Oh, nothin'. I was just tellin' Debbie that she should ask George out."

"George?" I say louder than I intended. "That total grump? I don't even know if he can say more than a grunt. What would they even talk about?"

"Well, she ain't getting any younger, and she needs to put herself out there. You know she hasn't been on a single date since Roger passed? That's like ten years ago."

"Maybe she doesn't want to date? Maybe she's fine

53

being alone?" Even as I say it, I know it's not true. Debbie doesn't complain out loud, but you can tell that she's lonely.

"Are you ready to practice?" she asks, clearly not wanting to discuss it further. She's cleaning up from the lemon bars that she made for the lunch rush, the lemon bars that sold out in about ten minutes. They are a top favorite here.

I sigh. "I guess. I'm just so drained." I lean against one of the stainless steel counters. This one is covered with flour and pieces of dough left over from the spring flower sugar cookies that we frosted with my newest frosting creation. It's my normal buttercream, but with a touch of almond and a touch of coconut. It's amazeballs. I mean, it's amazing. I have to stop thinking that word. It will inevitably come out of my mouth if I keep thinking it.

"Yeah, but we only have until Tuesday." She stops cleaning and looks at me.

"You're right, let's get to work."

We clean up enough space to get started. There's no use in cleaning up the kitchen before we make a mess of it again, as Patti so Southernly pointed out (at least that's what I think she was saying).

Today we create three different cupcakes and then decorate them. We'll sell them at the bakery tomorrow, so it's even useful.

I attempt making little flowers out of fondant, and they basically look like little balls of colored garbage. So in essence, they suck. Patti's look fantastic, thank goodness. I'm too tired to do another round so we call it a day and go home.

~*~

It's dark and foggy and I don't know how I was convinced to do this. I thought a nice night in would be more fun, but I was out-voted.

"Come on!" Anna screams at me as she and Brown each grab a hand and drag me out to the dance floor.

Have I mentioned before that I hate clubs? Well, I do. I totally don't fit in, and my dancing is about as graceful as a giraffe on skates. I saw a video of myself dancing when I was a kid and it was basically like I had long, ill-proportioned, gangly arms moving haphazardly around while my body stood completely still. The picture of grace, I am not. My brother, Lennon, made fun of me (he still does to this day) and that was the end of my dancing career.

But here I am, in the middle of a dance floor. Brown and Anna are both slightly tipsy and dancing around without a care. I'm doing a little snapping thing that I hope suffices. I make eye contact with a guy across the room, and he gives me a little head-bob.

I hate clubs.

I'm not sure how I let Brown and Anna convince me to do this. They've totally bonded over wedding stuff, even though initially Brown seemed a little ticked that Anna was getting married so quickly and taking away some of her thunder. She got over it, though. They are totally not the same person, and I have no idea how they've even become friends, but they have. Maybe it's that whole opposites attract thing.

So it's just the three of us tonight. A little pre-wedding girls' night out, not to replace the bachelorette parties both are having, which will probably involve more clubs and dancing. Oh gosh, how can I endure any more of this? I'll have to think of a way out of it.

Brown's is tomorrow night, actually. I'm a little

nervous about what might be going on. She won't tell me, probably because she knows I won't come if I know.

I finally fessed up about doing *Cupcake Battles*. She was totally excited and supportive until I told her when I'd be going. She was noticeably upset, but covered it up well. Then she proceeded to take away most of my assignments and slapped them on some other bridesmaid. Crisis averted. At least she was helpful and supportive and didn't make it all about her like Anna did. See? Total opposites.

"Come on, Jules! Loosen up a bit!" Brown yells over the music, grabbing my hand and dancing around with a drink sloshing everywhere in her other hand.

The song ends, thank goodness, and I pull out of her grasp quickly and make a beeline back to the bar so as not to get stuck on the dance floor for another song that I've never heard. Brown and Anna follow.

"What's wrong, Julia?" Anna asks as she joins me by the bar. She waves down the bartender. He glances over at her and she points to her drink, signaling that she needs a new one.

"Nothing, just tired." I smile, half-heartedly. I wish Jared was here, although he wouldn't be invited if he were. But maybe I could have texted him and he would have met me here when Brown and Anna were drunk enough not to care.

I pull out my phone to send him a text to tell him that I miss him.

"Hey, this is a no boy night," Brown says as she sees me texting. It's not hard to deduce who I'd be texting since my texting audience has pretty much three people and two of them are standing right here.

"I know. I just wanted to send Jared a quick text to let him know I'm thinking of him. He's not having a great time right now," I say, abandoning the text and putting the phone back in my purse. I can't concentrate enough anyway.

"What's wrong with Jared?" Anna pipes in, overhearing what I just said to Brown.

"I don't know. He won't tell me." I slump my shoulders, wishing I knew what was going on with him.

"I know how you could cheer him up." Anna nods her head conspiratorially. "You should send him a little sexy text." She gives me a clever look.

"Are you crazy? I'm not sexting my boyfriend," I say loudly, thinking that I'm talking over the music that has actually just stopped. Everyone within hearing distance turns and stares at me. I'm probably as red as a beet. I can feel the heat in my face. The music starts back up and everyone goes back to their own conversations, thank goodness.

"No, that's a good idea," Brown interjects, agreeing with Anna.

"You guys, I'm not doing that. No way." I shake my head. Maybe they are more than tipsy.

"Oh, Julia, stop being such a prude." Anna bats a hand at me. "You don't have to send him a body part or anything. You can just do a little sexy picture. Like of your bra strap or just the top of your thong." She looks to Brown who's silently agreeing with everything she's saying.

"Guys like that?" I ask, looking back and forth between the two of them. "A thong?"

"Oh, yeah," Brown says, raising her eyebrows, her head bobbing in affirmation.

"I send texts like that to Jonathon all the time," Anna says, and I internally gag, for many reasons. I believe that is the thousandth time she's mentioned Jonathon, and also

I'd rather not know my baby sister is sexting her fiancé. So many levels of *ew*.

"I don't know." I stare down at the floor. "I'm not even wearing any, and I haven't even had a pedicure."

"What are you talking about?" Anna regards me strangely.

"A picture of my thong?" I point down at my feet. They both bust out laughing. I don't follow.

"Jules, she's talking about thong underwear," Brown says through her amusement.

"Oh, my gosh, Julia, no one even refers to flip-flops as thongs anymore." She wipes the pooling tears away with her fingers.

"Well, Mom does!" I say, trying to defend myself.

"Julia, Mom still refers to her pants as 'slacks.'" They both start laughing again.

Okay, so that was a flimsy defense.

"I'm just saying you could pull the side of your thong out and we could snap a picture," Anna says once she's able to compose herself. "Like this," she pulls out the side of her underwear for a split-second and from behind us a bunch of guys whistle. How did they even see that? It's like they all have a sixth sense of knowing when underwear is exposed.

"Well that's not possible," I say and shrug.

"Oh, come on, Jules, we'll go into the bathroom." Brown prods me.

"No, it's not possible because I'm not wearing a thong." I purse my lips together, feeling uncomfortable that we are discussing my underwear.

"You're not wearing a thong? Then what are you wearing?" Anna asks, confusion in her voice.

"Um, just my normal underwear. I don't like thongs." Why would I want something purposely going up my butt? Isn't the point to *avoid* a wedgie?

"You're wearing granny panties?" Anna snorts out, and I shush her as more glances come our way.

She and Brown start laughing again, and I scowl at them.

"Okay, fine. Jules, just take a picture of your bra strap," Brown says, grabbing my arm. "You *are* wearing a bra, right? Or do you have a sports bra on?" She and Anna start up again.

I'm so thrilled to be the comic entertainment for the evening.

With lightning speed, Brown snatches my phone out of my purse and Anna tries to pull my shirt down so my bra-strapped shoulder is visible.

"You guys! No way," I say, pulling away from them and adjusting my shirt. "I'm not doing this in the middle of a club."

"Oh, you spoilsport," Anna says. "Fine, we'll just do it in the bathroom."

"Yeah, come on," Brown agrees. "Do it while you have liquid courage."

Little do they know I've been drinking soda. Someone has to drive us home, after all.

They start dragging me, and I mean, literally dragging me, to the bathroom, giggling the whole time. I hear Anna say something about granny panties and then her and Brown bust out in hysterics again.

We get to the dimly lit bathroom and Anna pushes me into one of the leather lounge chairs. I have no idea why it's even in the bathroom. Do people actually hang out here? She pulls down my shirt so just my shoulder is revealed, and Brown starts snapping pictures of my shoulder with my exposed bra strap.

When she feels like she's taken enough, she and Anna

go through the pictures and finally settle on what they think is the perfect one. Brown gives me my phone.

"There. Send him that one." She looks over at Anna and they both nod their heads like they've found the perfect picture.

It's my shoulder. With my bra strap showing. That's it. I start thumbing through the other pictures and they are all the same. Why is this particular one the best?

"Come, on, just send the text already," Anna says.

"Okay fine," I say while rolling my eyes.

I type a quick "thinking of you," attach the picture to the text, and send it off without overthinking it like I want to.

We stand around waiting for a beep, some kind of response from Jared. I won't lie, I'm kind of feeling a small bit of excitement. This is daring of me. I don't do daring things like this.

My phone beeps.

Everything okay?

I read the text out loud and give the girls a strange look. They gaze back at me, confused as well. That seems like a weird response for Jared to send back.

I scroll up to reread my text, just to make sure what I sent him was clear and that's when I see it. The word "Dad" at the top of my screen.

"Ahhhhhhhhhh!" I scream and practically drop my phone. How did this happen? How could this happen?

I've just sexted my dad.

"What's wrong?" Anna asks, grabbing my phone away from me. It takes a minute for her to figure it out, but when she does, her eyes widen and she immediately collapses on the bathroom floor, unable to control the laughter. I take my phone away from her.

I need to do damage control. Must do damage control.

"What's going on? What's so funny?" Brown looks from Anna to me.

"I sent the text to my dad," I say, horrified.

"But . . . but . . . how?" Brown gawks at me and then glances down at my phone.

"I don't know. My dad is listed right under Jared's name in my favorites. I guess I pressed the wrong person." I want to throw up. Is there a bridge nearby for me to fling myself off of?

Brown has now joined Anna on the floor, laughing so hard she's unable to speak or get up.

"Oh, my gosh, I can't wait to tell Jonathon this story!" Anna says through fits of giggles.

"No!" I yell loudly. "No one is telling anyone anything. Understand? We will never speak of this again. Never!" I point my finger back and forth at each of them, trying to emphasize the importance of never talking about this with anyone.

They both start laughing again. I have a feeling this will be spoken of, and quite often.

What do I do? What do I say to my dad? "Gee, Dad, sorry. I was trying to send a sexy text to my boyfriend?" No, I can't even admit to it. The horror of it all.

I text back.

No, everything's fine. Don't worry about it. Anna was playing with my phone.

Yes, that's right. I blamed Anna. She's the darling of the family, they won't even question it.

And this is why, boys and girls, you should not sext. Sexting is bad. Very, very bad.

Chapter 6

I'm clearly a girl who can't say no. It's becoming very obvious that this is a fatal flaw of mine, and just might, in fact, be the death of me if I keep going like I am.

After spending all day Saturday and all day Sunday practicing and practicing and practicing until the smell of cupcakes literally became gag-worthy, plus staying up until the crack of dawn for Brown's bachelorette party Saturday night (it was more clubs and no strippers, thank goodness), somehow, I unknowingly agreed to dinner with my family on Sunday night.

Unknowingly, because my mom caught me in a moment of complete exhaustion when she asked me to come, and I agreed to whatever she was asking just to get her off of the phone. It wasn't until I got a text Sunday morning asking if I'd bring dessert that it finally registered. I doubt anyone will be surprised with what I bring for dessert — cupcakes, of course.

We have had so many cupcakes to sell at the bakery, I'm starting to wonder if my patrons are getting sick of them, too. I doubt it, though. The flavors have been exciting and different from anything we've ever served. It's been great to have so many taste-testers. The most popular cupcake flavor so far? Oddly enough, it was jalapeño. Granted, the jalapeño was very subtle and gave just a little kick at the end.

Right now I'm sitting in the sitting room (how fitting), trying to have a moment to myself before I go into the kitchen where the chaos that is my family is currently gathering.

It once again really stinks that Jared didn't come home this weekend because it would have been nice to have him here with me. As it stands, I'm the only person without a significant other with me. Lennon and Jenny are here with baby Liam, and Anna is here with Jonathon, of course. I'm so excited to hear about how smart and amazing Jonathon thinks he is. *So* very excited.

"There she is," my dad says loudly as I enter the kitchen. And here I was trying to just blend in. So much for that.

There has been no word about the text to my dad, so hopefully he just let it go. I did find his phone and deleted the picture and the text that went with it. That way if he ever looks back at his texts, it won't be there to remind him that his oldest daughter sent him an inappropriate text that was actually supposed to be inappropriately sent to her boyfriend. Just the thought of it all makes me want to die all over again.

It would have been so much better had it gone to my mom instead of my dad. Well, I mostly wish it had just gone to Jared, its intended recipient. But my mom would have been the better other (unfortunate) option. She's not text savvy. For example, about five months ago my grandma was sick and in the hospital, and my mom sent out a group text that said, "Grandma is in the hospital, please keep her in your prayers. LOL." She thought it meant "lots of love." I doubt she has any idea what sexting even is. She probably would have texted back "oh Julia, isn't that bra strap darling!"

I spy Jenny and Lennon over by the large kitchen island, playing with Liam. I walk over to them and hold out my arms and Jenny hands him over without any protest. She knows better. I tend to be a baby-hog when it comes to Liam (or so Anna has referred to me). To say that I'm head-over-heels in love with little Liam would be an understatement.

"You can be my date tonight, okay wittle Wiam Wiam Wiam?" I say in my best baby voice as Jenny gently gives him to me. I glance over at Lennon who's staring at me with much disdain. Lennon does not like baby talk, and we've all been strictly forbidden to talk that way to Liam, which is why I do it even more when Lennon's around. It's my job as his older sister to be as annoying as possible. Plus, it's hard *not* to talk that way around Liam. He is, after all, a baby.

"Nice to see you again, Julia," a pompous sounding voice says from behind me. I turn around to find Jonathon staring at me. Or rather, *Jooonathon*. You must accentuate the "Jon."

He's in a suit, which is no surprise. I don't know if I've ever seen him out of one. He's not bad looking, but he's not my type at all. There's no way else to describe him, except that he looks smart. Perfectly coiffed, light brown hair, glasses over unspectacular blue eyes, and a smug little expression that sometimes makes me feel like punching something. To be fair, I haven't really given Jonathon a chance to try to like him. And tonight it won't be happening either. I'm just too dang tired.

I say a quick hello and then start dancing around and smooching on Liam, giving Jonathon the hint that I'm not up for small talk. He's actually rather astute. He gets the hint and walks away. I feel a pang of guilt but shake it off. There will be plenty of time to get to know Jonathon, since he's about to become a permanent fixture in my life.

The dinner table is set, and we finally make our way to the table to start eating. Thank goodness since I'm starving and for something more than cupcakes. I feel like that's all I've eaten for the last ten days. I may never eat cupcakes again at this point. That's a lie. I'll still eat them.

The conversation is light and fun and it feels refreshing. I'm feeling glad that I came to dinner tonight, even after my initial reluctance. I do have a wonderful family, and now that I'm not such a disappointment (they never made me feel that way, but come on, I lived in the basement for ten years—not something your parents would brag about), I can appreciate them for what they are: my family, and really, my friends.

Geez, what the heck was that? I'm getting all sentimental and sappy. This whole *Cupcake Battles* thing must be frying my brain.

"Jonathon has some news," Anna says, interrupting everyone else's conversations, and my out-of-character cheesy thoughts. Everyone's attention moves to Anna and Jonathon.

"He won the Marxton case!" Anna says, beaming proudly. Everyone starts clapping. I'm just joining in to be nice, because I have no idea what the case was about or even who this Marxton person is, if it even *is* a person.

So that must be why he's too busy to help with the wedding plans. I guess he will have the time now. I go to say something about just that, but then stop myself. No need to open that can of worms.

I peek over at Lennon and raise my eyebrows. He just shakes his head at me and sits back in his chair. It's been nice to bond with Lennon over our mutual dislike for Jonathon. That sounded harsh. It's more like our mutual not-really-loving Jonathon as much as we should. He's going to be family soon, after all. We'll just have to learn to deal.

"Well done, Son," my dad says after everyone has quieted down. Jonathon smiles pompously. Okay, it wasn't pompous at all, but I'm sure there was underlying pompousness to it that was just undetectable.

My dad, on the other hand looks proud. Lennon works at the firm, too. I wonder if it bothers him that my dad is so enamored with Jonathon. One glance at Lennon and I can tell he couldn't care less. Lennon has never been one to feel inferior, a trait I wish I had picked up.

I suppose there's no threat. Lennon is a senior partner, and when my dad retires, which will be soon, if my mother has anything to do with it, Lennon will take over the firm. A win for the firm is a win for Lennon, too.

We settle back into smaller group conversations. My mom and Anna talk about the wedding (of course). My dad and Jonathon talk about the Marshton/Martin/Moab case (whatever the name was), and Jenny and Lennon make googly eyes at Liam while Lennon bounces him around on his knee. I just sit there in silence, pushing the food around on my plate.

I hear a clinking sound and look up to see my dad tapping a knife against a glass. "I'd like to say something before we all finish dinner and go our separate ways."

We all look at him. My dad is not a man of many words and tapping his glass to get our attention is not something he would normally do. In fact, I don't know that he has ever done anything like that in my entire life. If he wants to get our attention, he usually makes my mom do it.

"I think we all need to drink a toast to someone who has made some amazing strides recently." Oh great, more *Jooonathon* accolades. Gag. "And that person is Julia."

Huh? What? I glance around the room as everyone looks at me with big grins, agreeing with what my dad is saying.

"Julia, we are so proud of you and how far you have come with the bakery. And we wish you the best of luck in the cupcake competition." He beams proudly at me. He struggled with the words "cupcake competition" as if he couldn't find the words to say. Obviously he's never seen *Cupcake Battles*. I wonder if anyone told him it's five channels away from Fox News.

I'm speechless, which is not something that happens often. I look at everyone and at my dad and suddenly tears sting my eyes. Oh gosh, public crying. I hate it. Honestly though, I'm not sure my dad has ever given me a look of pride. I have not given him a lot to be proud of, even though he's never said anything. The proud looks were always for Lennon, or Anna (albeit undeservedly). I know I've gotten it before, but it's been a long while.

"Thanks everyone," I choke out, my tight throat constricting my voice.

"We brought everyone here tonight to wish you well and also to give you this." He reaches under the table and pulls out a gift bag.

And here comes the waterworks. This dinner was for me?

"Sorry, you guys. I'm super tired." I apologize for my tears. I'm so great at ruining a moment. Can't I just let my crying show them my appreciation without downplaying it? I'm terrible at emotional, sentimental moments. It's probably good Jared hasn't told me he loves me. I'd probably make some weird joke and laugh it off, totally ruining any romance. It's what I do.

My dad hands me the bag across the table. I take it and start pulling out gobs of decorative tissue. Obviously the wrapping was done by my mother; I'm not sure my father would know what to do with decorative tissue. At the bottom of the bag is a package wrapped in more tissue paper. I pull it out and gently and carefully pull the tape off.

Just kidding. I hate it when people do that. I rip right into that sucker. Inside there is a chef's hat that has my name embroidered on it, and a fancy, black and white polka-dot apron with "Julia's Bakery" embroidered in light blue on the front. It's adorable. I'll totally wear it. I tell them that and thank them so many times it gets awkward. I'm not very good at thank you's and especially sentimental ones.

My dad raises his glass. "To Julia," he says, and everyone else raises their glass and echoes him.

I don't think I'll forget this moment for as long as I live.

Chapter 7

Well, this is it.

I don't even have time right now to indulge in the pukey feeling that is lying dormant, probably waiting for the worst timing ever to rear its ugly head.

I'm on a plane to California to tape *Cupcake Battles*. Me. Julia Warner Dorning. The girl who just over a year ago was living in her parents' basement, working at a dead-end job, with no thought of ever meeting anyone or dating.

Now I own my own bakery, live in my own high-rise apartment, date a total hottie, and am about to appear on a national television show.

And there's the pukey feeling. National television show. What the hell am I thinking?

Yesterday was the craziest day with all the preparations for the trip. Beth came in and helped out at the bakery (thank goodness), and Patti and I worked through breakfast and lunch, baking and intermittently getting everything ready for the competition.

I stayed mostly in the back, but I did pop out to the front once to check how everything was going and Lia was there. She gave me some sort of witch's blessing (at least I think that's what it was) and told me that if I just "focus on the light that is all around us" I'll be just fine. I have no idea what that means.

I slide up the airplane window shade to see if the light makes me feel any less nauseated. It only succeeds in making me temporarily blind and gives me an instant headache. So much for focusing on the light. What a bunch of malarkey.

"You doin' okay there darlin'? You look a little green." Patti reaches into the pocket on the back of the seat in front of her and fishes out the airsickness bag. "Here. You might need this." She gives it to me.

"Thanks," I mutter grimly as I take it from her. It might very well be useful.

"Listen, darlin', you're gonna be just fine." She reaches over and pats the top of my hand.

I let out a large breath that I didn't even know I was holding. I nod my head and then close my eyes and lay back against the hard, leather airplane seat.

I'm not sure I'll be fine, but this is happening, so I'd better find a way to fake it.

~*~

You know those drivers that hold signs for people they are picking up? Well, I've always wanted that to happen to me. But, of course, there was never a reason for it . . . until now. There is actually a guy holding a sign that says "Julia Dorning" on it as we come down the escalator to baggage claim. I feel so famous.

Would it be weird if I had Patti take a picture of me and

this guy with the sign? Probably. I'll take a mental picture. I'll probably have to take a lot of mental pictures over the next couple of days.

The schedule goes as follows: Today we go to the hotel, get settled for about two seconds and then a shuttle will take us to a store to purchase supplies. We worked out our list yesterday so that we would be ready to go. Tonight, we'll try to get some rest. I have a feeling that probably won't happen. Tomorrow we get up bright and early and the shuttle takes us to the studio. We tape all day tomorrow and then . . . that's it.

Then it's home on an early flight Thursday, just in time for me to lick my wounds from losing and start working on Brown's wedding cake. The rehearsal dinner is that night and the wedding is on Friday.

If I survive this week, I'm pretty sure I'm Superwoman.

On the shuttle ride, I make Patti go over our list for the hundredth time (only a slight exaggeration). I'm sure we'll leave something off, and I'm feeling a little panicked over it. I could tell Patti was not thrilled at having to rehash it once again, and she tried to soothe me by offering words of wisdom that I'm sure would have been very helpful had I only been able to decipher them.

We check into the hotel, and they weren't kidding about the two seconds we had to get settled before the studio sent over a van to take us to the supply store. We barely had time to put our luggage in our room before the phone rang to tell us the shuttle was on its way.

Walking through the lobby on our way to the waiting van, I keep my eye out for our competition. There will be three other bakeries represented, and I'm dying to see who they are. Of course, no one is walking around with "I make cupcakes" on their shirt, so it's a lost cause. I'll meet them tomorrow anyway.

What I do keep seeing is people from all walks of life and nationalities, carrying these little unicorn stuffed animals that I remember from when I was a kid. They aren't just carrying them. They are on their shirts, backpacks, headbands . . . everywhere. One guy has a bright blue unicorn tied to his shoulder, so it looks as if it's perched up there. It's quite odd.

"My Tiny Unicorn!" I say out loud when I remember the name.

"Huh?" Patti asks as we walk out to the front.

"Those unicorns we keep seeing everywhere? It's a toy that came out back when I was a kid. I always wanted one, but I never got one."

We walk outside to try to find the van that will take us to the store. To my left, standing in the taxi line is a guy — a grown man—with a tail, a unicorn tail, actually. It's fluffy and has rainbow coloring.

We get in the van and once the door is shut, Patti clicks her tongue, disapprovingly. "Now that's just not right." She bobs her head over at the guy with the tail. "He's about as confused as a fart in a fan factory."

Wait a second. I think I understood that one. Maybe I'm starting down the path to becoming fluent in Southern sayings. I may not need that Rosetta Stone after all.

"Uni's," the driver says, matter-of-factly. He's a skinny kid. Twenty-one at the most. He has that know-it-all look about him. It reminds me of *Jooonathon*.

"What's that?" I say, confused.

"They call themselves Uni's. It's a My Tiny Unicorn convention. They have them every year."

Patti and I look at each other with confused expressions.

"People really come to a convention for a unicorn toy?" I say as we pull away from the hotel.

"Oh, yeah. From all parts of the world, actually. It's pretty crazy," the driver says. "The men call themselves Unibros and the ladies go by Tinysisters. It's quite the cult following."

"I had no idea." I sit back in my seat. I suddenly feel like I'm sheltered in the two-mile radius of Denver that I barely ever venture out from. My knowledge of what goes on outside of it is limited at best. Maybe staying in a bubble isn't the worst thing. You don't tend to see grown men wearing tails in my little corner of the world.

"So are you excited for the competition?" young driver dude says. I ask him his name. It's Jordan.

"Well, I'm not sure about excited. More like nervous," I say and laugh slightly, rubbing my sweaty palms on my jeans.

"Aw, you'll be great," he says, glancing quickly at his rearview mirror. He smiles at me with an oversized toothy grin.

"You probably say that to everyone," I say and give him a half-smile.

"Don't sweat it. The judges aren't half as scary as they are on TV," he says, looking forward at the road. I was starting to get nervous that he was glancing in the rearview mirror too much and not focusing on the driving.

"They aren't?" I say, surprised. "How do you know?"

"I'm one of the interns at the station. I work with the production team for the battles." He bobs his head up and down, sort of like one of those bobblehead dolls.

"They make the interns shuttle us around?" I ask, slightly dumbfounded. Okay, that was a dumb question. Of course that's what the interns do, the boring work.

"Well, we do more than that," Jordan says, sounding a little defensive.

"Yes, of course you do more than, uh, that," I say, trying to recover and doing it horribly.

"Whatcha got on the judges?" Patti pipes in from next to me on the bench seat in the van.

"Oh, well, they're cool," he says, bobbing his head up and down again.

She shakes her head. "I was lookin' for more info than that."

"Oh, well . . ." he trails off.

"So I take it you don't know much 'bout them, do ya? Haven't worked with them much?" she asks, and I nudge her for being rude.

"No," he says quickly, "I've worked with the judges a bunch. That's like, a big part of my job."

"So tell us what they're like," she says, her eyes staring intently into the rearview mirror.

Jordan hesitates, slightly. "Okay, well you know Josef?"

"No, that's why we're asking ya," Patti says. I nudge her with my arm again. Where did the Southern hospitality go? Oh, right, she never had it.

"Right. So Josef, he seems super mean on the show, right?" He glances at us through his rearview mirror and we both gesture that we know. "Well, he's not. Like, at all. He's actually one of the nicest guys you'll ever meet. And with the history that guy has, he's like pastry royalty."

It's true. Josef Dehne comes from a long line of bakers and confectioners in Austria. The shop he runs is world-renowned, with only two locations, one in Austria and one in New York. I've been to the one in New York. I ordered a cream cake. I seriously started to tear up after the first bite. It was that good.

"I can't give you too much info, but I'll tell you to stay away from making any red velvet. He doesn't like it."

I knew that tip already. His disdain for red velvet is obvious on the show, yet so many competitors think they can change his mind. News flash . . . they never have. I'm not a fan either, so that won't even be a temptation for me.

"So what about the gal, uh, whatsherbucket?" Patti asks, cluing Jordan onto the fact that Patti does not watch the show all that much. In fact, I'm pretty sure she only just started watching when she found out we would be on it.

"Ah, Ginger," he says dreamily.

Ginger Preisser is quite attractive with her flowing, curly red hair and her big pouty lips. If the competitors are male, drooling and flirty comments ensue. Ginger runs a famous cupcake bakery in San Francisco. I've been there, too. What can I say, my vacations tend to revolve around food. Maybe I didn't order the right thing, but I wasn't that impressed with the cupcake I had. It was good, don't get me wrong. But it was nothing close to the level of the cream cake I had at Josef's shop.

"What do we need to stay away from for her?" Patti prods.

"Well, she's not a huge fan of coconut."

"Really?" I'm surprised by that. She never seems adverse to it on the show.

"Yeah, it's one of those things that Josef makes her fake because coconut is a dessert staple. But if you notice, she never raves about coconut."

Crap. My coconut-almond frosting is out then. I wasn't sure if I'd get a chance to use it, but I was hopeful.

"Any info on the guest judge?" Patti asks. I shoot her a look, trying to convey with my eyes that I think she's pushing it.

"Oh, I can't tell you anything about that," he says. He seems pretty set on not answering that one. Patti won't be able to rudely Southern that answer out of him.

It gets quiet for a minute or so. I notice we've gotten off the interstate and are driving through a more urban area.

"Okay, I will tell you one thing about the guest judge." He gazes at us through the rearview mirror.

We both look up in full attention. I'm feeling a little bad that we've (well, mostly Patti) coerced him into telling us things. It almost feels like cheating.

"Go ahead," Patti eggs him on.

"Think far, far away." He winks at us through the mirror.

Patti and I stare at each other, searching for answers. Far, far away. That could mean so many things. I abandon my thoughts of being rude and cheating and start to nudge Patti to see if she can get him to say anything else, but as soon as I start, we turn into a strip mall and I see the supply store. We'll have to see if we can get more on the way back.

Time for us to focus on the supplies. This is one of those things that will make or break us. If we forget something important, we are in trouble. I start sweating just thinking about it.

Jordan parks the van and Patti and I get out. He tells us he will wait in the van for us and that we have about forty-five minutes.

Upon entering the supply store, I stop and gawk for just a moment. This is a baker's dream, right here. We don't have anything like this in Denver. I could spend hours here, seriously, hours. It's like a large warehouse with rows upon rows of everything I could ever want.

I'm abandoning my fantasy of marrying Jared on the beach. I want to get married here, right between the bakeware and the cake decorating aisles. I'm in love.

Unfortunately, there is no time for wrapping myself up

in one of the vast colors of fondant on display in the front. We have shopping to do. I'll have to come back here, though. It's now on my bucket list: come back to the large, bakery supply store of my dreams and spend hours basking in its glory. I don't actually have an official bucket list, but if I did, that would be on it.

Patti and I race around trying to find everything we need. It's hard, but I keep my mind focused on the task, although I do get slightly sidetracked when I see the huge selection of pastry molds.

At just under forty-five minutes, we finish up our list and head to the front to check out. We were able to find everything on the list, although that nagging feeling in the back of my mind is telling me we forgot something. It's kind of like that feeling you get when you pack before a trip, the thought that keeps eating and eating at you during the entire drive to the airport. *You forgot something important. You forgot something important. You forgot something important.* Until you board the plane and realize that there's nothing you can do about it now. That's when you remember. You forgot underwear.

We check out and Jordan helps us load the van with our supplies, and then we head back to the hotel. The drive back is not a chatty one, and I'm not sure how to get us back into the conversation we were having before. Patti must not feel like trying to push Jordan any further because she's quiet and thoughtful in the seat next to me.

The "you forgot something important" keeps nagging at me in the back of my mind. Actually, it's more in the frontal lobe of my brain. Just digging right in. I try to push it away, but when I do that, the "what the hell are you doing here?" thoughts creep back in. I think I might need some therapy for my thoughts. They are out of control.

Glancing around as we drive down the interstate in

L.A., (at an alarmingly fast rate, I might add—what is it with California and the crazy fast driving?) I'm once again having a hard time believing I'm here. I'm going to be taping a television show tomorrow. Me. Julia Dorning. I thought moving out of my parents' basement and buying a bakery was stepping out of my comfort zone. Being on a cupcake baking competition for millions of people to see really takes the cake. Or rather, the cupcake.

Back at the hotel, we find a bellman to load our stuff and take it up to our room. We weave our way through the jumble of My Tiny Unicorn fans, or essentially cult followers. They have assembled themselves in the lobby and appear to be getting ready for some sort of group outing. Perhaps they are traveling together to find the end of the rainbow. It did just rain a few minutes ago.

I get a head nod from a Unibro, or maybe it's a Tinysister. It's hard to tell. I want to say "Oh, I'm not one of you," but I decide I'll just leave it.

We get back to our room and start checking off everything we have and putting things strategically in bags so that we'll be able to easily unload them for the taping tomorrow.

Before we know it, it's nearly ten at night, and we realize we need to wind down and try to get some sleep. I'm not sure if it will happen. I feel riled up, but I know I need to try.

Right at ten o'clock on the dot, my phone rings. It's Jared. He's in Charlotte still so it's one in the morning for him. I'm not surprised he's still awake. Jared likes staying up late, which makes it hard for me when he's home in Denver and wants to hang out late at night. I think he forgets I have to work so freaking early in the morning.

I grab my phone, go out to the deck, and shut the door behind me so I can have some privacy and so Patti doesn't have to hear me. She's reading a book, which she "made darn sure" had nothing to do with cupcakes or baking of any kind. I think it's all getting to her as well.

"Hey," I say after pushing talk. I take a seat in one of the chairs. It's a breezy night, but it feels great. The fresh air feels good on my skin.

"Hey," he says back. "How you holding up?"

"Oh, you know. Just peachy." Oh, gosh, did I really just say "peachy"?

He chuckles. "Jules, you will survive this. I promise."

I let out a sigh. "Well, I'm glad you're sure. I'm not so confident." My shoulders slump. I didn't realize how much tension I was holding in them.

"Well, I'm proud of you," he says.

"Thanks," is all I say. The warm butterflies start spinning around in my stomach. "How are things for you? Any better?"

He sighs. "Not really, but they will be," he says, not very confidently. It sounds more like he's trying to convince himself, like if he says it out loud, it might come true.

"I wish you would talk to me about it. Maybe right now would be a good time. It would get my mind off of tomorrow."

"I don't even want you to think about it right now, Jules. Just push it out of your mind. You have more important things to think about. Really, it's all fine." Again, I can hear something in his voice that makes it seem like that's not how he truly feels.

"Okay," is all I say. He's probably right. I should just focus on the task at hand. This major, crazy, out-of-character, outrageous, task at hand. And now my shoulders are tense again.

"Anyway," he says, shifting the conversation with his

tone, "you want some advice?"

"Sure," I say flatly.

"Don't let that German judge push you around. And if worse comes to worst, you could pull your shirt down a little and show some cleavage. That might get him on your good side."

"He's Austrian, and that's fabulous advice. I'll definitely be using that on national television," I say, sarcastically.

"Fine, don't take my advice. I'm just trying to help."

"Of course you are. I never doubted that. The cleavage is a good idea. Maybe I'll get a date out of this."

"Whoa, whoa. Let's not take this too far," he says, a teasing tone in his voice.

I love to tease Jared, even when he's far away. Too far away.

"I wish you were here."

"Me, too. I'll be at home waiting for you when you get back."

"Yes, be waiting with a box of tissues. I'll probably need it." I try to make my voice convey that I'm joking, but most of me is not. "Although according to my contract, I'm not allowed to talk about the show until it's broadcast. I'm not sure how I'll keep that from you. So I might cry, but I won't be able to tell you why."

He chuckles some more. I can picture him in his hotel room, lying on his bed in a T-shirt and boxers, his hair ruffled. I'd give anything to be there right now, instead of here, on the verge of a panic attack.

"Well, I'll let you get to bed. Just know that I'll be thinking of you tomorrow. You'll do great. I love you and I'm proud of you."

"Wait. What?"

"I said, I'll be thinking of you tomorrow and you'll do

great—"

"Yes, I heard that," I say, cutting him off. "What was the other thing you said?"

"I'm proud of you?"

"No, the other thing."

"I . . . love you?" He says it more quietly this time, but I heard it. I definitely heard it. "I love you, Jules," he says it again, but much more seriously this time.

"Um, you've never said that before," says my stupid mouth. Honestly, why do I even have a brain?

"I haven't?"

"No. You haven't."

"Well I've felt that way for a while."

"You have?"

"Yes, I have."

My heart is pounding in my chest, and I'm pretty sure he can hear it over the phone. And I'm smiling. I'm smiling like a lovesick schoolgirl.

"Jules?"

"I'm here," I say, still smiling. "And I . . . um . . . love you. As well."

Wow. Just wow. I have got to be the most eloquent person I know.

"I'm sorry. I couldn't hear that," he says in a mocking tone.

"I love you." I spit out quickly, so that I don't stutter this time.

"Good."

"Yes. Good."

The phone goes silent. I'm still grinning from ear to ear and wondering if he's doing the same. He chuckles lightly into the phone, confirming that he is.

"Okay, we both need to get to bed."

"Yes, I guess you're right."

"Call me during one of your breaks tomorrow, if you can."

"I'll try to."

We say goodnight and hang up. There is so much more I could have said, and wanted to say. I probably shouldn't lay all my cards out in one night, though. *I want to marry you and have all your babies!* And he's right, I probably should try to get some sleep. But I've got giddy feelings in my stomach, mixed with looming nausea. I'm not sure I can sleep.

Jared said he loves me. He loves me! It wasn't declared in the most romantic setting, but it was totally perfect in its own way.

Chapter 8

This is it. It's go time. Thank goodness I remembered my pants.

I had a dream—more like nightmare—last night in which I was not wearing pants. And I kept going to get cupcakes out of the oven, only there was nothing there. When I finally had some cupcakes to present, they were red velvet with coconut frosting. The judges hated them, and I was cut in the first round. Also, Patti was a goat that kept eating my ingredients.

I didn't share that part of the dream with Patti.

It was a stress dream and I should have seen it coming. It's just been so long since I've had one. The last time was when I was working at Spectraltech, and I had a dream that my old boss Mr. Nguyen wanted an accounting report, and when I went to print it, it just kept printing and printing and printing. I had that dream often. I'm not sure what it meant.

Maybe I should have Lia analyze my dreams. Only I haven't had any stress dreams since I started at the bakery. Huh. I just realized that. Maybe you don't have stress dreams when you love your job?

Currently we are waiting in the green room while they get a few last things situated, and then we're on. We've had someone touch up our hair and makeup. The look of death Patti gave the poor stylist who attempted to touch her bouffant was hilarious (and probably scary for the stylist). Needless to say, Patti's hair is just as it always is, big and back-combed.

We're wearing matching T-shirts that have "Julia's Bakery" on the front, and "You are what you eat, so eat something sweet" on the back. They're the same shirts we wear at the bakery. Well, I wear them. Patti wears "whatever she darn well pleases." But she had to conform today, even if the hot pink color of the shirts reflects off her big, blonde hair, giving it a slight pink hue. I wanted to go with black, but one of the other teams called it first.

Speaking of the other teams, we've finally met the competition. Two husband and wife teams and one sister team. I'm the only one here without family, although Patti has become like family so that counts. Everyone seems nice and a bucket of nerves like me. All of us except for one team that is, the Somethings (also known as the black-color-shirt-stealers). That's not their actual name, I just can't remember. Brady and Something Something . . . I'm not good with first names either. I only remember Brady because I immediately thought of *The Brady Bunch* when I met him. Not just because of his name, but he also has a strange resemblance to the oldest brother, Greg, down to the curly dark hair. I'm expecting him to say the word "groovy" at any moment.

The Somethings are those type of people that "get the party started." Bordering on obnoxious, their game-on approach to this whole thing has been quite the spectacle.

Every once in a while, completely out of the blue, mind you, they will scream the name of their bakery and high five. My heart has jumped a couple of times, it's that loud and that out of the blue. I pray the producers tell them not to do that when the cameras roll. Who knows what I might do under the pressure of the cameras and their screaming? I might throw a cupcake at their heads. It would be completely accidental, of course.

The other two teams I've named The Tallies (the other husband and wife team—they are ridiculously tall, like basketball player tall) and the Sisters (that one is pretty obvious).

My stomach aches from being so tangled up and nervous. I'm not sure if I want to pinch myself and make sure I'm not dreaming, or kick myself for being here in the first place. I curse everyone who convinced me to do this.

"We are about to go to the kitchens," Jordan says, making my stomach ball up even further.

Coincidentally, Jordan was the intern that was assigned to assist Patti and me with all of the backstage stuff. Interesting fact about Jordan, the head bobbing is not a car thing. It's an all-the-time thing. It's really starting to get on my nerves. In Jordan's defense, my nerves are easy to get on right now.

Patti reaches over and gives my hand a quick squeeze. My other hand has a death-grip on my phone. Jared and I have been texting back and forth all morning. We are not supposed to have our phones on us at this point, but I figured what's the harm if we are in the green room and the cameras aren't rolling.

I text Jared.

It's time to go. Wish me luck.

My phone buzzes back almost immediately.

You'll be great.

I wish his vote of confidence would make me feel better about everything. Like a cheesy chick-flick movie where the man's love is what makes the heroine do incredible things.

My phone buzzes again.

Love you.

Okay, that does bolster my spirits a bit. I giggle, grinning at my phone, then text him back a "love you, too" reply. This is fun. I've never loved someone before, or had them love me back. Well, I mean, not in *this* way.

"Who ya textin'?" Patti glances at my phone.

"Jared," I say simply, still smiling giddily at my phone.

"He sendin' you a sexy picture or somethin'?" She raises her eyebrows at her inference.

"No!" I say quickly, "Jared doesn't do that."

"Oh, you two. So boring." She clicks her tongue, disapproving.

"You do that with your husband? Wait. Nope," I hold up a hand, "I don't want to know the answer to that."

Patti and her husband Randall walk the pervy line, always pinching each other's butts anytime they are around one another, even in public. That's the worst kind of PDA. They think it's fun to make an innuendo out of everything. It's really not fun for the rest of us. I'm sure they sext each other, and I don't need details.

Patti shakes her head and chuckles softly to herself. "Nah, Randy would never do somethin' like that. But the guy before him, now that would have been right up his alley," she says with a reminiscent look.

"You never told me there was a guy before Randall," I say, grateful to think about something else other than cupcakes or battles. It's probably not the best idea, but I'm too nervous. I need the distraction.

"Yeah, Roger was his name. I think in another life I woulda married him."

"What happened?"

"Oh, ya know. He joined the Army. We tried to keep things goin', but the long-distance thing kinda ruined things." She shakes her head, that reminiscent expression still on her face. "But, Roger was a lot of fun," she says, giving me a wink. "*A lot.*"

Ew. I stop asking questions because frankly, I don't want any more information.

"COOL CAKES!" Team Something screams from across the room, as their intern leads them out to the studio.

"I'm gonna slap those two," Patti says, visibly shaken by the sudden outburst from Team Idiot (I may change their name to that). I jumped a little, but not as big as the first time they did it.

"Yep, we are ready to go," Jordan says, talking into his headset. He stands up and motions for us to stand, too.

My heart starts to beat rapidly, like very rapidly. I wonder if I should ask Jordan if there is a medic on staff to help when people faint, because if not, they should have one waiting in the wings for me. I've never fainted before. I'm thinking today it might happen.

Patti grabs my hand and gives it another quick squeeze. We glance at each other and I take a deep breath. There's no turning back now. Well, I could make a run for it, but I'm already in this deep, I may as well finish.

Anyway, what's the worst that could happen? I could

embarrass myself in front of millions of people. No big deal.

Jordan turns on our microphone packs, which is slightly awkward since mine is attached to the back of my pants.

"Let's go." He starts to walk out of the green room and we follow.

Here we go.

Chapter 9

"Can you say that again with a little more excitement?" the cameraman says to me.

"Um, sure," I say reluctantly. I thought I *did* say it with excitement.

I take a step back. Maybe my problem is that the camera is so close it feels like they could see the pores on my nose.

"Okay, try it again," Hal the cameraman demands. We are on a first-name basis, Hal and I, mostly because I keep tripping over myself, running into things, dropping things, and not using enough enthusiasm (allegedly). This has all happened only in the first ten minutes of taping.

It's going to be a long day.

"I'm Julia, from Julia's Bakery, in Denver, Colorado!" I shout brightly and raise my eyebrows up, so I seem more excited, but I'm pretty sure it's going to come across as deer-caught-in-headlights. I don't care. Let's just get to the baking part of this competition. The introduction and cheerleading part of this thing is not my forte.

"That should work," Hal the cameraman says with his mouth, but his body language and facial expressions say otherwise. He's probably thinking he got the short end of the stick when he was assigned to my kitchen.

He moves on to Patti, who I'm sure will give him more of what he's wanting. Or if not, a not very understandable Southern saying. Either way, she's bound to be more entertaining than me.

There are four open kitchens, one for each of us in the competition. So far, we have stayed in our own kitchen areas and done our intros there. Except for a few whoops and chanting of "Cool Cakes, Cool Cakes, Cool Cakes" by the Somethings, everyone else has been pretty quiet. Hopefully they are all as flustered as I am. I'd hate to be the only one.

I'm not sure what impression I gave them during my audition tape, but obviously I made it seem like I was good on camera. In my defense, I was by myself, I had nothing to lose, and I was hopped up on Percocet. This time I've got two cameramen practically up my butt, lights everywhere, and a swarm of production crew members all in my personal space. It's fairly disconcerting. I need something chemical, something to get me moving. I'm pretty sure Percocet would be a bad idea. Plus, the bottle is at home.

Time to bring in the big guns. I search for Jordan. I spy him over in the corner, using his headset with an air of importance. Oh, brother. He makes eye contact with me and I signal him to come over to where I'm standing.

"Any chance you can get me one of those Rock Star drinks?" I say in a whisper when he gets close enough to hear.

"Sure," he bobs his head up and down, and then speed walks out of the room.

The studio gets oddly quiet as the judges come out and take their seats, as if royalty has just entered the room. Well, they sort of are royalty in our little baking world, but I'm not sure why everyone is quiet.

"Why's everyone so quiet? Do I have something in my teeth?" Josef says, with remnants of an Austrian accent. He pulls up his lips to reveal his perfectly white teeth and shows them to Ginger, who inspects and then shakes her head no. Spots of laughter filter through the production crew.

I feel a little more at ease with his playfulness. I guess Jordan was right, he's not as scary in person as he's on camera. At least in the last five seconds he hasn't been.

Jordan runs back into my kitchen and hands me the caffeinated drink. "You have thirty seconds to chug that down," he says, slightly breathless.

"Okay," I say and I quickly pop the lid and start chugging.

"What was that?" he says, looking straight at me.

"I said . . . okay?" I say after gulping down some of the fruity flavored drink.

He holds up a finger as if to shush me and holds his other hand on the earphone signaling me that he wasn't talking to me.

"Okay, it's time to go meet the judges," Jordan says. I show him with my eyes that I registered his comment, but I continue to chug the Rock Star. I pray this works, and that I don't get heart palpitations (that's happened before).

Jordan walks Patti and me up to the front where the judges are, and we stand in a semi-circle with the rest of the competitors.

The host of the competition, Franky Jackson, comes out and the Somethings start to clap obnoxiously. Everyone else joins in. Franky, a rather handsome man with black hair, striking, deep brown eyes and a goatee, does a slight bow toward us, tucking his chin into his chest and closing his eyes in an overdramatic fashion. He seems unamused and not excited to be here. This show has been on the air for nearly a year now. It's probably hard to get continually excited about cupcakes. I still get a little giddy when I see a good one, so maybe it wouldn't be so hard for me.

"Welcome, competitors, to *Cupcake Battles*," he says in a voice that makes women want to undress. It's deep and sultry and slightly breathy. "You have been chosen from many entrants, so you should feel proud of yourselves for making it here." He looks us over as he talks, probably silently judging us.

The Somethings start clapping again. Really? This is getting a little ridiculous.

"Before we get started, Josef wants to say something to you," Franky says, motioning to Josef with his hand.

"Yes, thank you Franky," Josef says, nodding his head at Franky and then toward us. "Welcome to *Cupcake Battles*. You were picked to compete from among some of the most talented bakers in America."

"Cool Cakes!" the Somethings chant. Josef does not seem thrilled. Oh, please let them get cut first. Or let me get cut first. Either option will do.

"Yes." He shakes his head, trying to recover. "Anyway, both Ginger and I want you to know that we are looking forward to this competition and that we know you will all bring the best that you can because you're all very talented."

I brace myself for a "Cool Cakes" explosion, but nothing happens. Thank goodness.

"I say all this to you because I want you to know that when the cameras start rolling, we'll be a little tough on you, and that is just for the cameras and for the show. We are really just sweet little bunnies pretending to be bears. Well, I am. I'm not so sure about Ginger." He glances over at Ginger who appears to be appalled at that inference.

I wonder how many times this exact speech has been given. It's obvious by how unamused Franky seems, that this is not the first time.

I have to admit, I was nervous to meet the judges, especially Josef. He comes across as intimidating and not very approachable. I guess there's more acting going on during this show than I had thought. Of course, everyone knows reality TV is not entirely reality. For example, my over-the-top enthusiastic introduction of myself. That is *so* not reality.

"Good luck everyone!" Josef gives a little cheer in the air with closed fists.

I make eye contact with the Tallies and the Sisters, silently saying good luck to one another. The Somethings just stare forward at the judges, as if to butt-kiss them from afar.

We've yet to meet one judge, who is essentially the most important piece of this whole show. The third judge — the surprise judge — will be introduced as soon as the cameras roll so that our expressions of surprise when they tell us the theme of the show, will be real.

The sounds of cameramen shuffling to get into position fill the room. This is it. The action starts now . . . I think. I've actually thought that exact thought a few times already, only to have to wait for five minutes while they adjust some sort of lighting, or something to do with the sound. But now, this feels like the real start.

As if to solidify that this is it, a producer counts down from five and signals with his hand to Franky that the camera is rolling.

"Welcome to *Cupcake Battles*, where four teams will compete to be crowned king of cupcakes. Only one team can take the crown. And the rest? Well they will have to go home with their tails tucked between their legs."

Oh, gosh. I don't want to go home with my tail tucked between my legs. I think I just realized right now that I have to give this all I've got. So far I've mostly just wanted to get through it, with very low expectations; no expectations is more like it. But suddenly I realize that there are people counting on me to at least do my best. I don't want to have to explain to everyone why I didn't win, why I couldn't pull it off. And if I have to give that explanation, I need to be able to say that I tried everything.

Suddenly a boost of adrenaline rushes through me, or it could be the caffeine. Whatever it is, I'm going to go big or go home. Time to get my A-game on.

But first . . .

"Can I just . . . hold on a sec . . ." I say as I wave my hand frantically at Hal the cameraman to tell him to shut it down.

"Julia?" Patti gapes at me, her eyes wide.

"I'm sorry." I cover my mouth and run out of the room.

I make it just in time to the nearest trashcan before the contents of everything I've had to eat or drink today, come up.

Chapter 10

Caffeine was a bad idea.

"You all right, darlin'?" Patti rubs my back as I drink the water that Jordan brought over to me after I spewed everything in front of a room full of practically strangers. Practically strangers that are taping a show that will go on national television.

Apparently, Hal didn't shut it down as I had signaled for him to do. One of the producers motioned for him to follow me, and my puking has now been caught on camera. I was apparently not the first contestant to throw up on *Cupcake Battles*. I was, however, the first person to be caught on camera doing it. The others made it to the bathroom.

I. Am. So. Freaking. Lucky.

They gave everyone a small production break to let me get myself put back together, and for the makeup girl to do some touch-ups.

"You think you're ready?" Jordan asks.

"Um, I guess," I say, and then exhale deeply. I'm pretty

sure that was a one-time puking. At least I'm not feeling like throwing up at the present moment. I have no idea what could happen later, though. The producers don't seem angry in the slightest. In fact, they were delighted by the drama of it all. I'm obviously no expert, but I'm pretty sure that kind of stuff is ratings gold. Probably right up there with passing gas, which I pray is not next for me.

Jordan leads me and Patti back to the studio, where everyone is waiting for us, still in their same positions. It's the strangest feeling. Since I've puked, gotten cleaned up, drank some water, and gotten back here, I could swear it's been at least an hour. But in truth, we haven't even been gone for more than ten minutes.

It's going to be a long day.

I wish I could have called or even texted Jared, just for some moral support. It would have been nice to hear his voice, even if just for a second. I could tell him that I just threw up on a national television show, and he could tell me that it's all going to be okay. Or he might just laugh. Knowing Jared, it would be both.

Everyone gets situated, Ginger gets one last-minute touch-up on her lipstick, and then one of the producers is counting down and we are off. Again.

"Welcome back to *Cupcake Battles*. Are you feeling better, Julia?" Franky says to me, and I can feel Hal the cameraman to the side of me.

"Uh, um, sure," I stammer. Yes, perfect. Add stuttering onto the list of freaky things that Julia will do on camera. I'm doing well today. Right now, I'm wishing it were tomorrow.

"Let's introduce the judges, shall we?" Franky says, angling toward the judges' table situated to his right. "First, we have the lovely Ginger, owner of Frost in San Francisco. To her right, we have Josef Dehne, world-renowned pastry chef and owner of Dehne Sweets in New York City."

Franky appears so confident on camera. Like he could do this in his sleep. He probably could.

"And now the judge we've all been waiting for, and the reason we are all here to compete today. Cupcake bakers, allow me to introduce your guest judge," Franky pauses, I suppose for dramatic effect, "Kenneth Landers from NASA!"

Huh? Who the heck? I hope my face hasn't given away my instant feelings of disappointment. I was hoping for someone a little more famous.

Kenneth, a tall, lanky guy who appears to be a little computer nerdy, comes out and waves to all of us. I glance over at the group and the Somethings look delighted. Of course they do.

"Welcome to *Cupcake Battles*, Kenneth," Franky says as Kenneth takes his seat next to Josef. "So competitors, today you will be competing for that ten thousand dollar prize, and the winner will have their cupcakes featured at the 55th year celebration of NASA in Pasadena, California!"

I notice that the other competitors are all smiling brightly, so I follow suit. But I mean, come on. Is this only slightly disappointing to just me? I know I should be thrilled by the opportunity, but I was honestly hoping for something more like cupcakes to celebrate the birthday of Jay-Z and Beyoncé's kid. I'm sure they would need at least a thousand of them.

"Are you ready, competitors?" Franky says, bringing me back to my current reality. "For our first round, you must use the secret ingredient to make one cupcake for the judges to taste and critique. And the secret ingredient is" — pause for dramatic effect — "astronaut food!"

Our attention is directed to a medium-sized table being wheeled into the room, with a display of different packets of freeze-dried astronaut food.

Freeze-dried what-the-crap? Seriously? This was definitely not something we practiced.

"Bakers, you have forty-five minutes to come up with something that will wow the judges, and you must use something from this table. The first round of *Cupcake Battles*, beeeeeeginnnnnns, now!"

Everyone takes off running toward the table with the secret ingredients. I'm still standing there, trying to think of what I'll do with freeze-dried food. Patti takes my hand and pulls me toward the table.

We don't have much time to check out the table of ingredients because we have to get started. But a couple of things catch my eye. Freeze-dried strawberries and bananas. My first thought is a banana split type of cupcake, but then I see the Neapolitan freeze-dried ice cream and the light bulb in my head goes on.

"What's the plan?" Patti asks me, eying the packets of astronaut food I'm carrying.

"Okay, I'm thinking a Neapolitan ice-cream cupcake."

Patti stares at me, blankly.

"Trust me, it will be good. At least, I think it will be good. I've never worked with freeze-dried food before."

She signals silently that she agrees. If we've learned one thing in practice, when we went with my gut feeling on something, it would always pan out.

"Could you say the kind of cupcake you're making again, with a little more enthusiasm?" Hal the cameraman asks.

"Oh, sure," I say, shifting slightly to him. I forgot he was there, actually. Jordan is right behind him, bobbing his head, agreeing.

I say the line again and it seems to suffice because Hal gives me a signal with his hands to keep going.

We get to work. Having never worked with this type of food before, I'm not entirely sure about the consistency. All I'm looking for is the flavor. I have Patti take the blocks of Neapolitan ice cream and cut them up by flavor and then grind each flavor to fine powder.

I work on the batter, first making the chocolate, then the strawberry. I'll layer those as the cupcake base and then the frosting will be a vanilla ice-cream buttercream. I have no idea how it will turn out, but I'm just going to pray it does.

Patti and I work side by side, trying hard to make sure we are good with our time. Hal makes me re-say things a few times, but for the most part, I do okay. Or at least I get by.

I'm in my element now. Once we get baking, all my nerves with the cameras and the crew subside. Okay, not totally, but at least a little. The baking is what I know, so it comes naturally to me. Plus, now that I've barfed for a nationwide television show, what's the worst that could happen?

Oh gosh, I hope I didn't just jinx myself.

I should have brought Lia along to do some kind of un-jinxing witch thing whenever I think things like that. I'll just concentrate on the light around me, because there is a lot. Seriously, how much light do they need in these studios?

The cupcakes are in the oven so I get to work on the icing. For the icing, I use the ground up vanilla and incorporate it into my buttercream.

"Holy crap. It tastes like ice cream!" I squeal to Patti after I do a taste test. It's amazing. Like, I'd-sell-this-at-the-bakery amazing.

After trying a taste herself, Patti says something about how it made her want to smack her granny. She runs off to get the cupcakes from the ovens, so I don't have time to ask her what that has to do with anything. Honestly, I'm not sure why I even bother.

"Fifteen minutes, bakers," Franky announces from across the room.

Patti puts the cupcakes into the refrigerator to cool them down quickly, and I grab a piping bag to load the icing.

"Patti, we need something for the topping," I say in a panic. Crap. I totally forgot about some sort of décor.

"Darlin', I'm already sweatin' like I stole something," Patti says, pulling her shirt collar away from her neck, an attempt at trying to cool off.

"I know, me too," I agree. It's ridiculously hot in here, and we are only on round one. If this keeps up, I'll be a big pile of sweat by the end of this. If I make it that far, that is.

"Patti, can you just go over to the table where all the freeze-dried stuff is and see if you can find anything?" I ask as I slop icing on the floor, missing the piping bag completely. I stifle the cuss word sitting on the tip of my tongue. I know they will bleep it out when the show airs, but my mother will still know I said it.

Patti runs over to try to find something that will work, while I finish filling up the bag and then try to clean up the icing on the floor as much as I can. The last thing I need to do is slip and slide around the kitchen, although I'm sure the producers would love it.

When Franky yells that there are five minutes left, we rush to get the cupcakes out and frost them. Topping them with crushed chocolate wafers that Patti found with the freeze-dried ice-cream sandwiches. They aren't gorgeous, but I think it works. At least I hope it does. I only have one shot to make it to the next round, and it's all wrapped up in this Neapolitan ice cream cupcake.

"Time!" Franky yells, and we all hold our hands up to signify that we are no longer working.

I have sweaty pits and once again, mentally curse the Somethings for taking the black shirt color. These hot-pink shirts are sure to show off my sweaty pit rings.

"Gather around bakers," Franky calls from the judges' table. "It's time to find out who will stay, and who will be rocketing back home."

And the puns have begun. Franky is known for his puns on the show. On one of the past episodes, the winner got to feature their cupcakes at The Comedy Place in Los Angeles. The puns were in abundance. I almost had to turn it off, it got so bad.

We all line up in front of the judges' table. Well, sort of in front. Actually, we are back about ten feet so that the cameras can tape our expressions from the front, and cameras can tape the judges as well. So it's the judges' table, a crew of cameramen, and then us.

The judges are presented with cupcakes from the Tallies first. They have made a cookies and cream cupcake using the cookies and cream astronaut ice cream. A dark chocolate base for the cupcake, cookies and cream filling with a marshmallow cream top, and crushed Oreos for décor.

Not too exciting, in my opinion. And cookies and cream has been way overdone on this show.

The cameras are on the judges as they cut into the cupcake with a fork and try a bite. Well, everyone except Kenneth. He just pulls off the paper with his fingers and takes a big bite, not quite *Cupcake Battles* etiquette.

"So, let's hear what you think," Franky says, giving his

attention to Ginger.

"First, let's start with the positives." Uh, oh. That's never a good start from Ginger. If she has to start with the positives, it means there are a list of negatives. "I liked the presentation, and the cupcake itself was dense and had a rich chocolate flavor. However, I could barely taste the cookies and cream flavor in your filling, and the marshmallow cream frosting just did not do it for me."

Ouch. We are off to a scary start. I start to sweat even more, worrying about how ours will go over.

Next up is Josef. "We've had this flavor on the show a lot. This cupcake has potential, but I agree with Ginger. It's not enough of the secret ingredient. So it's a no for me."

Kenneth tells them basically the same thing.

The next cupcake on the judges table is the Sisters. "We've made a banana liquor cupcake using the freeze-dried bananas as the base flavor for the cupcake. We filled the cupcakes with a banana and rum cream filling, and topped the cupcake with buttercream frosting and chopped banana chips for a garnish," the shorter of the sisters explains to the judges.

We watch as the judges taste-test the cupcakes, looking to see if anything registers on their faces. As usual, they give nothing away.

"Tell us what you think, Ginger," Franky says, leaning up against the side of the judges' table.

"You're lucky that I love banana because if I didn't, this cupcake would not have gone over as well as it did. Overall, I really liked this cupcake. The use of the freeze-dried bananas in the cupcake gave it a nice banana flavor, but not an overwhelming one." Ginger nods her head, red curls bobbing all around.

"This cupcake makes me want to dance!" Josef says

when it's his turn to critique. He starts to do a little dance in his seat and I inwardly cringe. Josef saves that line only for cupcakes that really please him. It's rare. I also cringe because he looks like an idiot when he does his chair dance.

It's a winner for Kenneth as well. So the Sisters are almost guaranteed a spot in the next round. I've just got to be better than the Tallies and we are in.

Next up is the Somethings. I hold my breath, waiting for a "Cool Cakes!" but nothing happens. I peer over at them and detect a bit of something. Could it be nervousness? Well, I'll be darned. They aren't just overconfident buffoons after all.

"Cool Cakes Bakery, tell us what you've made today," Franky says while staring at his nail beds, proving once again that none of this is very enthralling for him.

"Today we have made you a cinnamon apple coffee cake cupcake. The base of the cupcake is a cinnamon apple coffee cake with a custard filling. Topped with a cream cheese frosting and some streusel for garnish," Mrs. Something says. She does a little fist pump after her description, which makes me internally gag.

The judges come back and it's a hit. Everyone loved it. Dang it. Chances are high that they will make it to the next round.

My cupcake is up next, and I'm starting to freak out that it's not enough. I tried it; it tastes amazing. Literally like an ice cream cupcake. But is it enough?

"Next up? Julia's Bakery. Tell us what ya got, Julia," says Franky.

"Um, so today," I clear my throat, which is a fabulous start to my explanation, sure to win over the judges. Ugh. "So today we have made you a Neapolitan Cupcake that we call the . . . um . . . Buzz Aldrin." I inwardly cringe when I say the name. Patti made me do it, she said it would be clever. I'm thinking she has no idea what clever is.

Surprisingly, it was. All of the judges give smiles of approval, and Franky actually winks at me, which is weird.

I watch tentatively as the judges taste my creation.

"Ginger? Give us your thoughts," says Franky.

"Well, let's start with the positives."

Oh, crap.

Chapter 11

It's a sullen feeling in the greenroom as we all sit and wait for our fate in *Cupcake Battles*. Even Cool Cakes is keeping their cool, which must be difficult for them.

We've been sent back here to wait while the judges assess our creations and decide who moves on and who goes home. While we wait, we are intermittently taken back to do individual interviews with a producer about what we experienced and felt during round one.

I think my interview went well, except for the one time that I snort-laughed. I hate it when I do that. Patti said I was good, though.

I'm a ball of nerves. I'm torn between wanting to see this whole thing out and being relieved if it's all over. I know I'll be disappointed if I'm the first one out. I think I've had this internal thought process that if I just make it to round two, this will have been worth it. But the first round? Not sure how I will take that.

It's iffy with my cupcake. Two to one—Josef and Kenneth liked it. Ginger, not so much. She's apparently not a huge fan of strawberry and wished I would have done a strawberry base with a thicker chocolate center. Josef did not do a dance with my cupcake, either. He did say he liked it, though.

"They're ready for us," Jordan says from off in the corner. The cameras have been on us as we sit and wait. I'm not sure why they need so much footage of us sitting and waiting, but apparently they do. I hope I didn't do one of those nose scratches that actually look like you're picking it. Oh gosh, did I?

No time for me to dwell on that as we all get up and follow the interns to the studio to await our fate from the first round.

After we are lined up in front of the judges, the cameras roll and my stomach starts doing twists and turns.

"Bakers," begins Franky, with a very serious expression. "You were asked to make an original cupcake using astronaut freeze-dried food. Some of you skyrocketed to the task, and some of you were left sitting on the launchpad."

Make. It. Stop.

The room is quiet. You could cut the tension with a knife. Literally. Okay, not literally, but it feels literal.

"Just Cupcakes," Franky says, and we all turn to the Tallies. "I'm afraid your shuttle will not be taking off. You are off of *Cupcake Battles*."

As if planned, in unison the Tallies hang their head in disappointment. Seriously, did they practice that? Was that something we should have practiced? I never practiced a losing face, or a winning face for that matter. I was just practicing my get-me-through-this face.

The Tallies are off. I've made it to the next round. Holy crap, I've made it to the next round! I realize right now would be a really bad time to dance around and celebrate that I made it, so I give my best "I'm sorry" look to the bakers that were just kicked off, while internally celebrating.

I've made it to round two. I've hit my goal. The rest is just gravy. Except now that I've made it this far . . . What if?

"Bakers, congratulations, you've made it to Round Two of *Cupcake Battles*," Franky croons coolly after the Tallies are escorted off the set.

"Are you ready for your next challenge?"

"Cool Cakes!" The Somethings say in unison. The rest of us try to hide our disdain, some of us more poorly than the other (ahem, Patti). Brady Something beams with pride at his wife, and for a split second, I can see the love between the two of them, and it makes me miss Jared. It would have been so great if he were here to cheer me on.

"Okay, let's get started on Round Two," Franky says, bringing the attention back to him. "For Round Two, you will be judged on appearance first and taste second. You will make three different flavored cupcakes where the décor will bring in the theme of today's show — the 55th Celebration of NASA. You have seventy-five minutes. And it starts" — pause for dramatic effect — "now!"

The big clock on the wall immediately starts counting down from seventy-five minutes. We have no time to lose. Patti and I go back to our kitchen and try to regroup and decide on flavors for our cupcakes.

"I think we should ditch the Neapolitan one," Patti says and I agree. Previous contestants on the show have sometimes included their original cupcake in the second round if it went over well with the judges. I think it would be too risky with Ginger, even if we had a thicker chocolate layer. Plus, if we make it past this round we have to make one thousand cupcakes, and I'm not sure we could make 333 Neapolitan cupcakes fast enough. So, like the Tallies, the Neapolitan cupcake's spaceship has left the launchpad. Oh, the puns.

It's not hard to come up with flavors for this part because we've practiced this. I already know the cupcakes we are going to do, and even though it's risky, I'm bringing in my coconut-almond frosting. The coconut is subtle. I'll just have to pray that Ginger likes it.

"Watcha wanna do for décor?" Patti asks, her vacant face telling me she has no ideas.

"I don't know." I rub my temples. How the hell do you represent NASA with cupcakes? I don't want to go with the obvious décor — shuttles, launchpads, etc.

"My Tiny Unicorn!" I yell out after we stand there contemplating for a minute or so. Patti regards me like I belong at that wacko conference back at the hotel.

"What do those fruit loops have to do with this?" she says, eying me dubiously.

"Not the people. The characters. The cupcakes we are doing are original flavors that hopefully the judges haven't had, or haven't had too much experience with, right?"

"Sure." She gestures that she understands, but I can tell she's still not following.

"Let's do an 'Out of this World' theme, and the décor can be inspired by the My Tiny Unicorns!" I say excitedly. Hal, the cameraman, better be getting this uncharacteristically enthusiastic moment I'm having. If he asks me to say it all again, so help me . . .

"I'm not sure I can make a bunch of little unicorns, and I'm not sure what the heck they have to do with NASA." She folds her arms, cocking her hip to the side.

"Not the unicorns, the décor. The My Tiny Unicorns are supposed to be from another planet. On their planet, there are rainbows with shooting stars everywhere. Think bright colors and sparkles." I do jazz hands with spirit fingers when I say sparkles because it feels right to do it, but then I remember I just did that on camera. Crap. Well, I can't take it back now.

Patti starts nodding her head faster, and I can practically see her mind moving as she starts to come up with ideas. "I like it," she finally declares.

"Good, let's get started."

We start grabbing the supplies we need, not paying attention to any of the other kitchens. There's not enough time to snoop and see what they are doing, so there's no point.

I start working on the cupcakes, while Patti works on the décor. For the first cupcake, I make one that was a favorite at the bakery, chocolate lime jalapeño. It sounds weird, but they are incredibly tasty and won't be that typical flavor the judges will expect. We decide to put a rainbow with a shooting star on this one. Patti makes the star sparkle with edible glitter. Totally adorbz. That's the next word I plan on adding to my list of words to annoy Brown with. Adorbz.

The second cupcake we make is a bananas Foster cupcake with a banana cupcake base, caramel filling, and a banana buttercream frosting with a dash of rum. We drizzle some caramel over the top to complete it. For this one, Patti makes a planet out of marzipan that even has a single ring around it, like Jupiter. Or one of those planets with a ring. (I was never good at astronomy.) They look perfect.

The third cupcake we make is a snickerdoodle cupcake with the coconut-almond buttercream. The cupcake itself is more along the lines of safe, but the frosting will be what makes this cupcake shine. Or at least I hope it does.

Patti makes large stars with the numbers 55 on them, for the 55th NASA anniversary. She does them in different colors, so it makes the color pallet very bright and almost cartoonish.

The time flies, and Franky yells that there are five minutes left before I know it. It creeps up on me so fast that I have to check the clock just to make sure he didn't make a mistake.

We plate the cupcakes quickly, all three flavors on a plate for each judge. I'm loving this out-of-this-world theme.

"Time's up!" Franky yells, and I stop fidgeting with the décor on one of the cupcakes.

On the taped version of the show, it always seems as if it's down to the wire, like all the competitors have five minutes left and the cupcakes still need to be frosted. We must have had luck on our side because we were able to get it all done with time to spare. I wonder how the other contestants did. I guess it's time to find out, since Franky just called for all of us to come over to the judges table.

Here we go.

Straight out of the gate, the Sisters did fair with their cupcakes and décor. Ginger said the décor was lacking (rockets and NASA logos abounded) and felt like they could have been a little more daring with their flavors. Josef wasn't dancing, but he didn't hate it, either. Kenneth thought the décor was perfect for the celebration, which made my stomach turn a little since we went a different direction.

Next up is us. My stomach starts to twist and turn even more. I'm regretting doing the coconut-almond frosting. Why would I think I could change Ginger's mind? So many contestants make this same mistake with Josef and the red velvet cupcake. Who do I think I am?

I give the judges quick descriptions of my cupcakes, again naming them after former astronauts. The Neil Armstrong (chocolate lime jalapeño), The John Glenn (bananas Foster), and The Sally Ride (snickerdoodle), respectively.

"Ginger, tell us what you think," Franky says, gesturing to the half-eaten cupcakes on Ginger's plate.

"Julia, I'm impressed by your décor. It's fun. It's eye-catching. It's not what you would expect to see, and I like it." Okay, we are off to a good start. "As far as your flavors go," she points to her plate, "I think the chocolate lime jalapeño might be one of the best cupcakes I've had on this show."

Shut. Up. Did she just say that? I could be done with this competition right now and be happy. Actually, I could *die* right now and be happy. Best. Compliment. Ever.

"One quick question." Ginger looks at me. "Was there a hint of coconut in the frosting for the snickerdoodle cupcake?"

"Um, yes," I say somewhat sheepishly.

"Not bad." She gives me a small dip of her chin, as if to say "hats off to me." By my side, Patti taps me with the back of her hand.

Holy crap, she liked it. She liked it all. Well, she didn't say anything about the bananas Foster one, but that means she didn't hate it. She would have said something if she did.

"Josef, what ya got for us?" Franky interrupts my internal celebration.

"This is odd for me. For once, I agree with Ginger." He gives a sly smile to Ginger, and she whacks him lightly on his arm. "I think that chocolate jalapeño thing might be one of the better cupcakes I've had on the show. In fact, it makes me want to dance."

Oh, hell yes, he can dance as much as he wants if it has to do with my baking skills.

Wait, could this mean . . . could I have made it to round three? I'm going to push that out of my mind right now. I just got a huge compliment on this show. I should just bask in that. No need to get ahead of myself.

"Kenneth? What do you think of Julia's creations?" Franky bobs his head in my direction.

"You know, when I first saw your decor, I wasn't sure I liked it. It was a little too fantasy for me. But after tasting the cupcakes, I think it all goes very well together and would be a great feature for the celebration." He gives me a closed-mouth smile of approval.

We are three for three. Now butterflies start multiplying in my stomach. I could make it to the next round. And then what? I couldn't actually win, could I? Oh, now I'm *really* getting ahead of myself.

The Something's are up next and I'm so caught up in thoughts of the possibility of making it to the next round that I don't pay much attention. Overall, I gather that the vibe from the judges was that their flavors and décor were well received.

Back in the greenroom, the tension is even worse this time. I feel fidgety and wish I could have my phone right now to text Jared. I probably could go get it, but I'm next up for my interview with the producers and I don't want to get caught, so I'll just wait. Maybe there will be time after my interview.

The interview goes by quickly and in the blink of an eye (it honestly felt that fast), we are back in front of the judges.

I'm excitedly sick, that's the only way to explain it. It's quiet in the studio, and I'm feeling this crazy need to yell out something like a "whoop" or a "yippee" or even a "Cool Cakes." This must be killing the Somethings.

Franky jumps right in. "Bakers, we asked you to come up with three original cupcakes with décor that will represent the 55th anniversary of NASA. You were judged on taste as well as décor. This was a tough decision for the judges. You moon rocketed them with your creations. The first round was also taken into account when this decision was made. Unfortunately, only two of you can continue on."

Patti and I look at each other. My stomach is a bunch of butterflies twisting and turning. I didn't know the first round would be included in this. I barely skated through with that one. That does not bode well for me.

"Cool Cakes," he says and the cameras all move toward The Somethings. Both of their faces are pasty white. All of the color has drained out.

No way, they are getting kicked off? I did not see that coming. I honestly saw myself getting kicked off. Wait, so that means . . . Holy. Crap.

"Cool Cakes, congratulations. You've made it to the final round and have a chance to win the title of *Cupcake Battles* champion!"

Well, that makes a lot more sense. Suddenly the world is righted again, in an unfortunate way.

The Somethings start jumping up and down and chanting "Cool Cakes" repeatedly. It actually gets so over the top that they have to shut down production for a second to get them to calm down. I wonder if they are regretting their decision to put them through.

So it's between us and the Sisters. I know my cupcakes were better than theirs, at least in the second round. But will it be enough to get us into the third?

Franky stares at us, looking back and forth between me

and Patti and the Sisters. Patti gives my hand a couple of reassuring squeezes.

"Two Sister's Sweets," he pauses for dramatic effect. I hold my breath because this could go either way. "I'm afraid you will not be shuttling off today. You're off *Cupcake Battles*."

The sisters hug each other and I think one of them has started to cry.

"That means, Julia's Bakery, you have made it to the final round."

Wait, what? I was so focused on the Sisters that I totally forgot what that all means. It means I've made it. I can't even believe it! I've made it to the next round of *Cupcake Battles*!

Patti gives me a hug and then we realize at the same time that our celebrating is too soon since the Sisters are still hugging each other, but in a sad way. So we go back to standing and waiting for them to be escorted off before we resume celebrating. This is crazy. I did not expect to make it to this round.

I wish I could tell Jared, but according to my contract, I'm supposed to keep everything quiet until the show airs. I doubt I'll be able to do that when I see him tomorrow night, but I should at least stay within the guidelines of my contract during the time that we are filming the show. That just seems like the logical thing to do.

"We did it!" Patti says as soon as the Sisters have walked off the set.

"We did it!" I echo back, and I give her a tight hug.

We look over at the Somethings and I give them a head nod. They both gape at me with slightly menacing expressions that seem to say "Oh, it's on."

Seriously, did they practice that? I apparently need to work on a game face. So far, I think I've only given my dumbfounded face, my excited face, and my puking face, all of which will probably not make for good television. Well, the puking one probably will.

The producers direct our attention back to Franky and the judges. They had taken a few minutes to rearrange us after the Sisters left.

"Julia's Bakery and Cool Cakes." Franky stares us down with a serious expression. "You've made it to the third and final round of *Cupcake Battles*. Congratulations. For this round, you will need to make one thousand cupcakes and an original display designed by you. We'll provide you each with a carpenter to make the design and a team of helpers to assist you in this round." He motions over to our left and there are two teams of six waiting in the wings to help us.

I see the team dressed in hot pink T-shirts, our helpers, and I notice Jordan. Wait, the interns are the assistants? Really? I had read a couple of former contestants blogs that said they were surprised at how not helpful the assistants were. Now I see why. I guess I never paid attention to the assistants when I've watched previous shows. If I had, I might have recognized Jordan from the beginning.

"You have two and a half hours on the clock. And your time, starts," — pause for dramatic effect — "now!" Franky says.

We run over to our team, now stationed in our kitchen. We don't even have time to get their names. We just start throwing out tasks. Since I'm nervous, they won't be that much help, so I have them do the very basic stuff. They will be making the cupcake batter, under my supervision of course, and the frosting. Patti will take two of them with her and focus solely on the décor.

This is what we had practiced back at home, albeit

mediocrely, since neither of us expected to get this far.

The carpenters enter the room. We get Ryan, the hot one. I try desperately not to flush when he starts asking me how I want my design, but it's a lost cause. Hopefully, I just appear red from all of the stress and work we've had to do.

"Tell me what you're thinking," Ryan says and I blush even further. Why now? Why am I such a circus freak? And Jared is going to see me blush over Ryan on television. Oh, he's going to *love* that.

I lick my lips and try to pull myself together. I tell him my design idea, drawing a rough (extremely rough, I'm no artist) picture of what I want. Since Patti and I had no time to prep for this part, I'm pretty much pulling it out of nowhere. I just hope it works out.

My quick on-the-fly design is a basic shape of a shuttle with wings and stabilizers. I ask Ryan to put shelves inside the shuttle to stack the cupcakes on. Afraid that Cool Cakes will make something similar, I add some lighting to make it stand out.

Once Ryan is squared away and off to make our stand, I get to work with the interns and Patti. Our kitchen is a hodgepodge of disarray, with everyone running around trying to get everything done in time. Patti is barking out orders and throwing out a random Southern expression every now and then. "Y'all are slower than cream risin' on buttermilk!"

I'm about a second too late to stop Jordan from putting flour in a KitchenAid running at full speed. Flour goes everywhere.

If we survive this round, it will be an act of God.

Chapter 12

We aren't going to make it. We aren't going to make it. We aren't going to make it.

I realize this is not the chant I should be doing right now, but I can't help myself. I seriously don't think we are going to make it. The countdown clock says thirty minutes left and we haven't even started frosting.

We aren't going to make it.

"Would ya stop with the face?" Patti says as she starts slopping large amounts of frosting into piping bags. This is going to have to be a full team effort, so we'll need lots of piping bags full of frosting.

"What face?" I say, grabbing a bag and following suit.

"That defeated face. It's not even over yet." She pauses to pick up a random paper towel that is balled up on the counter. She wipes her brow with it. I don't even let my mind go where it wants to go. Like, where was that paper towel *before* she used it? Ew.

"Well, I just keep seeing the clock and then looking at what we still have to do. It's kind of hard not to feel that way."

"It ain't over 'til the fat lady sings," she says. At least that's one I've heard before. Franky is neither fat, nor a lady, but when he says it's over, it's really over.

We frantically work to get the cupcakes frosted and decorated. At least the interns aren't doing a horrible job with the frosting. It's not that hard, but most of the tasks I've given them weren't that hard, and they still seemed to have questions or problems. I guess I think what I do is easier than it is.

"Fifteen minutes," Franky yells out and my stomach sinks. I really, truly, don't think we are going to make it. I've never seen a show where the competitor doesn't make it in time. At least not in this round. But I'm the first to visibly throw up on the show, why not add this to the list? It might make for more good television drama.

I glance over to see Ryan the carpenter guy rolling my display in. It looks good, I guess. Not spectacular, but the focus is the cupcakes, and with the colorful décor, it will really bring it to life. At least I hope it will.

We magically finish frosting the cupcakes with just ten minutes to spare. We immediately start loading the cupcakes onto the display, careful not to have any topple over. In hindsight, having shelves stacked this way was not my best idea. It's hard to get our hands in there without getting frosting on the shelf above. We have to stop and do a wipe down a couple of times.

Franky announces that there are five minutes left, and now I'm just telling everyone to get the cupcakes on the display. I don't really care how it looks at this point, just that they get on there.

Time is called as one of the interns literally puts the last cupcake on the stand. We all stand back from the display. We did it. We freaking did it. I don't even care at this point if I win. I'm just so happy I have a finished product.

Okay, that's a lie. I do want to win. I mean, I've made it this far.

I stand farther back to take in the entire display and my eyes bug out of my head at what I see. But not in a good way. With all the rounded cupcakes on it, my supposed-to-be awe-inspiring NASA shuttle, has now taken on a whole different shape. It's, well, **phallic**.

"Oh, my," says Patti, as she steps back to see the whole thing. "That right there is a penis, darlin'." She's pursing her lips and pointing at our cupcake stand.

My shoulders sink. I've just created a seven-foot wiener for the world to see. Well, there goes my chance to win. I mean, seriously. I've most definitely lost this battle and probably killed any extra business for the bakery.

Then to make matters worse, before I can scream "Noooooo!" Ryan the carpenter plugs it in and the flashing lights start dancing.

It's a big, flashing, cupcake-filled penis.

What's the aura color for wanting to die? Because I'm pretty sure that's the light I'm sending out to the universe right now. I know I've mentioned before when things go wrong that death would be welcomed, but I was just bluffing then, because now I know what it feels like to actually wish for death. It would be so much easier than what I have to endure right now. And there's nothing I can do about it. I can't fix it or change it. What's done is done.

We are asked to go back to the greenroom while the judges check out our displays and come to a decision. We should have just stayed in the studio. This will be a quick judgment.

Upon entering the room, Brady turns to me with a cunning smile. "Nice display, Julia." He snickers, and he and his wife high-five. I was so caught up in my display disaster that I didn't even pay attention to theirs. I'm sure they think they've got this one in the bag. They probably do.

I really hate them.

I walk over to my purse and try to subtly retrieve my phone, not wanting to get caught with it. I power it up, ignoring the many text pop-ups that start coming up. Most of them are from Brown, Anna, and Jared. But I see some from my family members and one from my grandma. Grandma? I didn't even know she knew how to text. Oh, yes, my grandma was very excited about this, being a fan of the show and all. Imagine her surprise when she sees what her granddaughter created. Awesome.

I send Anna, Brown, and Jared a quick group text.

Just made giant penis for national television. Would like to die now.

I hit send and turn it off. That was probably against my contract, but at this point, who cares? It's not like they will even understand what I'm referring to. Oh, but they will when they see the show. Everyone will. Even my poor, dear grandmother, not to mention Jared's mom, Bobby. I somehow failed to remember that lovely fact until right now. There goes my endorsement as future daughter-in-law.

And what about Jared? Will he be disappointed and say this isn't the kind of exposure that I should be getting for the bakery? Will he look at me differently? My stomach drops at the thought. I wish I would have never done this stupid show.

"It's gonna be all right," Patti says soothingly as I sit down next to her on the couch. She puts a hand on my leg in an attempt to stop it from shaking. It doesn't work.

"Is it? Because I'm thinking it's seriously bad, in so many ways."

She stifles a giggle, trying to cover it up with a sniff of her nose.

"Really? You think this is funny?" I'm not a woman of violence, but I wouldn't mind slapping Patti right now.

"Well," she sniffles and her body shakes next to me, trying to hold the laughter in, "it's kinda funny, if ya think about it."

I close my eyes and lean my head back against the bright red leather couch. This situation is so *not* funny. And I don't see it being funny in the near future. Or even the distant one for that matter.

Jordan comes in the room. "It's time for your interview with the producers, Julia."

Oh, crap. I forgot I had to do that. I grab Patti's hand. "Come on, you're coming with me."

She gives me a perturbed look, but gets up and follows me anyway.

~*~

Tears are literally streaming down my face. It might be that I'm super tired, or that it's been a really, really long day, but I've actually brought myself to tears. Tears of laughter. So okay, maybe this whole phallic display thing *is* funny right now. I know I thought it was no laughing matter before, but hearing the story out of Patti's mouth for the interview with the producers, and watching them rock with amusement, well, it became contagious, and I could no longer hold it in.

We're all trying to catch our breath at this point. It's difficult because one of us will look at the other and then

121

start laughing again. I'm pretty sure this will not be a very useful interview for the actual show.

After trying unsuccessfully to answer the follow-up questions, one of the producers calls it good and Patti and I go back to the greenroom to await our fate.

We wait for what seems like an eternity, but when I glance at the clock, it has only been thirty minutes. Still, that's a long time to wait for this part of the show. Plus, this should be a no-brainer for the judges. I made it super easy for them. It's pretty obvious who the winners will be, the stupid, annoying Cool Cakes. They think they are so great with their non-penis display. Whatevs.

"They're ready for us," Jordan says as he holds his earphone to his ear. I think he thinks it makes him seem more important than he is. It doesn't.

I look at Patti, and she nods her head, silently saying "Let's do this" with her eyes.

I was actually silently saying "Let's make a run for it," but I'm pretty sure she didn't catch that.

We walk back into the studio and take our places in front of the judges, as we have done three other times today.

The vomit butterflies are back, but I'm pretty sure I can keep it together. I'm just going to envision being done with this. In with the thoughts of being home and seeing Jared, out with the thoughts of wiener-shaped cupcake displays.

The judges all have stern expressions. That's essentially the only look they ever have when it's time to announce who wins. They probably practice so that they don't give anything away. Honestly, the winner is so obvious here, there's no point in them trying to cover it up.

"Bakers, in the first round, you were judged on

creativity using the secret ingredient, which today was astronaut food. For the second round, you were asked to make three cupcakes that were judged on flavor as well as décor. And for the third and final round, you were asked to make one thousand cupcakes and an original display. The winner of *Cupcake Battles* will get ten thousand dollars and have their cupcake display featured at the 55th anniversary of NASA." He glances first at Cool Cakes and then over at us.

I glance over at the displays, my lit-up phallic display sitting next to Cool Cake's presentation. Theirs is just a large table with varied layers, and a revolving solar system as the center focus. It seems like some sort of display for a science fair. And this is what is going to win? Nice.

"This decision was one of the hardest for the judges. But one of you stood out as the winner. And the winner is . . ."

I immediately shift to my left and hold out a hand to Cool Cakes to congratulate them. Meanwhile Patti is awkwardly hugging me from behind. Honestly, I'm not that downtrodden from it all that I need a hug right after I've lost. I'm just happy to be done. I made it to the final round. That's something to be proud of.

Mr. "Cool Cakes" Brady is not returning the handshake. Wow, what a sore winner. I've heard of these kinds of people, but I've never met one. Until now, that is.

"We won!" Patti spins me toward her, grabbing both of my hands with hers and jumping up and down, her big blonde hair bouncing around.

"Patti, I think the chemicals in your hair spray are getting to you." I move to look at the Somethings and they are hugging each other, but not in a happy way. I turn back to Patti. "Wait. We won? But, but, how?"

"Julia," Ginger says, and I shift toward the judges' table. I'm not entirely sure what just happened. I think I might be dreaming. "This was a tough decision for us, but at the end of the day, your cupcakes had the best flavors overall."

"And your décor really captured what I was hoping to have at the celebration," Stephen pipes in. "Your display may, um, need a little tweaking," he says, his cheeks reddening as he says it.

"I . . . I . . ." I have no words. I don't even know what to say. We won. We freaking won *Cupcake **Battles***, and with a phallus-shaped display, no less.

Patti grabs me and hugs me tightly. "We did it!" she says as she squeezes me.

We did it. I can't believe it.

Chapter 13

"You really aren't going to tell me?" Jared asks, as he leans against the counter in the back of the bakery.

The rest of the trip was a whirlwind. There were interviews and pictures and a celebration dinner with Patti where she got a little tipsy and told me personal stories that I'll never be able to scrub out of my brain. They are burned there forever.

I had no time to do anything when I got home from the flight this afternoon but come to the bakery and start on Brown's cake for the wedding tomorrow. I also had to see with my own eyes that my store hadn't burned down while I was gone.

"No, I'm not telling you." I grab a damp rag and try unsuccessfully to towel-whip him on the leg. He's too fast. Or I suck at towel-whipping. I used to get Lennon pretty good, back in the day. I'm probably a little rusty.

"You know I can tell just by the look on your face," he says, a knowing grin peering through his lips.

"Maybe I'm just an amazing actress," I say, giving him

my best smirk.

He laughs heartily at that, a little too loudly. Hmph. So apparently, I'm a horrible actress.

"Come on," he chides, grasping me around the waist and turning me, pushing me up against the counter. He leans in and kisses me. It's tender and loving, and for a split-second, I almost forget about having to make Brown's cake or whatever the heck we were just talking about.

"Okay, fine," I say as he kisses down my neck. That's my biggest weakness and damn him for using it against me. "I won."

The neck kissing stops abruptly (dang it), his eyes quickly move to mine. "I knew it!" he yells loudly. He wraps his arms around me in a tight hug, lifts me up, and spins me around.

"Yes, I won," I say when he ends the spinning. "But you can't tell anyone, and I can't tell you the details, but just know there was a phallic display involved, and it's going to be incredibly embarrassing when it airs." I close my eyes, picturing my display and feeling a slight pit in my stomach.

"Yes, I got your text. Although I'm now putting two and two together." He starts chuckling.

"It's not funny!" I say as I grip the damp rag again and towel-whip him.

"Ow!" He yells out and grabs his leg where the end of the towel hit him. Yes! I've still got it. He moves to take the towel to get me back, but I ball it up and throw it across the room and then I grab him and kiss him, hoping he would rather kiss me than get me back. It works.

"So now are you going to tell me what's been going on with you?" I ask, hoping that I don't ruin his mood with the question.

"Well, I could. Or I could do this." He kisses me tenderly.

I should probably pry more, but he's in the best mood I've seen in a while. Why ruin it?

After more kissing and no baking, I finally kick Jared out of the bakery so I can get this wedding cake done before the rehearsal dinner tonight.

I'm about ninety-nine percent sure that's not going to happen. Brown will not be happy.

~*~

"Where's Betsy? Has anyone seen the bride?" the wedding planner yells frantically over the laughing and talking of the bridesmaids. Time for wedding number one. Brown's wedding. We are in the bridal suite, doing last-minute hair and makeup.

I barely finished the cake in time for the rehearsal dinner, but I made it. Patti and Debbie are all set to bring it over today and add the finishing touches. Thank goodness for them.

By the end of the rehearsal dinner last night, all the lack of sleep and overused adrenaline had hit me hard. My mind was a muddled pile of goo at that point, and I'm pretty sure I made a fool of myself one or two times. Of course, I probably would have done that without the muddled brain. It's what I'm known for, after all.

I stare into the full-length mirror in the bridal suite and look myself over. I've been completely overdone. My hair is twisted up, curls everywhere. I have makeup on every millimeter of my face. My eyes are done in smoky colors that really do bring out my muddied, green-colored irises. I'd say that I might try the smoky-eyed makeup on my own, but I already know that's a lie. I'm wearing a plum-

127

colored chiffon, one-shoulder draped dress and a pair of shoes I'm pretty sure I'm going to face-plant in. Brown made me wear them last night at the rehearsal. No one else had to wear them, just me. I'm apparently the only one in the group (or the world, as Brown said) who doesn't wear obnoxiously tall shoes on a regular basis, so I needed the extra practice.

"Anyone? Has anyone seen Betsy?" The wedding planner looks absolutely frazzled. The shirt on her business suit has come un-tucked. And her chignon is less, well, chignon-y. I've never planned a wedding, but losing track of the bride would probably be pretty stressful, especially an anxious bride like Brown. I mean, she was freaking out on me, so I can't even imagine what she's put that disheveled soul through.

"I'll go find her," I say to the poor thing. I'm the only who's still not primping, anyway. I don't primp. I don't like staring at the mirror for long amounts of time. Eventually I start to see things I don't want to see, like fine lines and sun spots. It's best to avoid the mirror as much as possible.

I walk out of the room and into the hall, feeling the cool breeze of the air-conditioning. There is so much body heat crammed into that suite, it's hard to believe my makeup hasn't sweated off.

Going purely on a hunch, I walk down the hall (more like clomp, in these ridiculous shoes) and out the glass door that leads to the back of the hotel.

That's when I smell it. Cigarette smoke.

"Brown? Brown, I know you're out here," I say as I search around, peering behind tall bushes and trees that are scattered around the grounds.

"Over here," she says, and I see a hand wave at me from behind a large maple tree about twenty feet away.

The large trunk hides her completely.

"Brown, are you smoking?" I say as I walk over to her, careful not to fall in these ridiculous shoes.

"Shhh! Would you shut up?" she loud-whispers when I get closer.

I round the tree, coming face to face with Brown, and the first thing I notice is that she's stunning in her form-fitting, white lace dress. Her hair is pinned up, similar to mine, but seems so much prettier on her. Her makeup is perfect, of course. It's not much different from her normal everyday wear, just a little more striking.

And to complete the look? A cigarette hanging out of her mouth.

"Brown! What are you doing?" I reach up to snatch the cigarette from her, and she bats my hand away in a ninja-fast move. "You've made it so long! Why mess it all up today?"

"Oh, Julia," she rolls her eyes, "it's just one cigarette. You know, to take the edge off. I'm not messing it up." She blows the smoke out of the side of her mouth, away from me.

"But you'll smell like cigarette smoke," I say, pointing to her most-likely expensive gown.

"That's why you will ward off anyone from finding me until I can air out." She points the burning cigarette at me.

"Well, how long will that take?" I ask, unconvinced that's even a possibility. Smoke, especially from a cigarette, does not go away easily.

"Long enough for me to get it together so I can walk down the aisle." Her shoulders slump.

"Oh, Brown, you aren't freaking out again, are you?" I take a step closer to her and put my hand on her lace-covered arm.

"No," she says unconvincingly. "Maybe."

"What are you freaking out about now?"

"Oh, you know, just marriage and being stuck with someone for the rest of my life. No big deal."

"Brown."

"Yes?"

"Do you love Matt?"

"Yes." She stares down at the ground.

"Do you think there is someone else out there that you might be missing out on?"

"No. There's no one better." She looks at me and gives me a small, thin smile.

"Then what is the problem?" I raise my eyebrows at her. If I wore glasses, I'd peer down at her through them.

She takes a drag from her cigarette and blows it out, slowly. "I guess there isn't a problem. I think I'm just nervous."

"Betsy Brown? Nervous?" I feign shock with the back of my hand against my forehead. "I never thought I'd see the day."

"Shut up." She punches me lightly on the arm.

"Come on," I hold out my hand, "give it to me."

She reluctantly hands over the cigarette and I hold it pinched between my thumb and pointer finger, as far away from my body as possible. Smoking is seriously so gross.

"Okay, I'm going to take this and throw it away. You work on airing yourself out." She nods her head, indicating that she will. "You have five minutes to get your butt inside and get ready to walk down that aisle and marry the only man that will put up with your crap."

She rolls her eyes at me, but a small smile appears on her lips.

"I will come out here and drag you inside if I have to." I point the burning cigarette at her.

"Okay, okay! Now leave me alone for my last few minutes of being single." She gives me an I'm-only-half-kidding smile. I start to walk away. "Oh, and Julia?"

"Yeah?" I turn back to her.

"Thanks."

"You're welcome." I say and then turn around and walk back into the building, tossing the cigarette into the trashcan as I go.

Chapter 14

I will not trip and fall as I'm walking down the aisle.

I repeat this to myself as I walk down what seems like a ridiculously long aisle to the front of the large ballroom where Brown is about to get married. Matt is standing there, next to the officiant, looking handsome with his dark hair and light, olive complexion. He's like something out of a magazine, wearing a more traditional tuxedo. I'd have thought that Brown, with her fashion-forward thinking, would have had him in something more modern. Or maybe traditional is modern now. Clearly, I don't know much on the subject.

The string quartet is playing classical music. It's more fast-paced than the CD we used to practice with at the rehearsal last night, but I somehow find my groove as Matt's brother, Paul, escorts me down the aisle. Paul's got nothing on Jared, but he's a good-looking guy. Once upon a time, Brown wanted to set me up with him. But that was back when I was frump-girl. I've since "blossomed," or so I heard my mother say not too long ago. It made me feel like an adolescent tween that just grew boobs.

Making it to the front without any embarrassing tripping or falling, I breathe a sigh of relief as I take my place next to Brown's sister, Amy. Like Brown, Amy is beautiful. Actually, everyone in Brown's family is gorgeous. It seems a little unfair that so many pretty genes were given to one family.

Behind Brown's family is a group of people from Spectraltech, my former employer. This is the first time I've seen some of them since the layoffs last year. Some of them come visit me at the bakery, namely, Mr. Calhoun and Martha. Turns out Brown's and my hunch that they were having an affair was right on. They are together now, which really is . . . gross.

I wonder how they all feel about the fact that I'm now dating "the enemy," although Jared isn't the enemy to the people who are here at Brown's wedding. They still have their jobs. Most of them don't even know Jared was the one behind the layoffs, since that's how he does his consulting, mostly under-cover. As far as they know, he was one of the employees that was laid off.

I angle my head just slightly to the right and spy Jared sitting about three rows back across the way from the Spectraltech folk, probably not by mistake. He's next to Anna and Jonathon. Jonathon looks as pompous as ever. Jared flashes me a wide smile that sends butterflies floating around in my stomach. Since we said the love word, his glances at me are different. They have new meaning behind them: love.

That was ridiculously cheesy, and I don't care.

The quartet starts playing the bridal march, and the officiant asks everyone to stand. This is it. All eyes are now on the back of the room.

Now, I've been to a few weddings in my day, and

when the bridal march starts, that's when the bride is supposed to walk down the aisle, right? Because we are halfway through the song and no Brown. Whispers start rustling through the crowd and eyes start shifting toward Matt. He doesn't seem fazed at all. In fact, he just keeps his gaze on the entrance. Maybe he's willing her to come through the door. I know I am.

We make it through the entire march with no Brown. I glance at the officiant just as he signals for the quartet to start the song over. Everyone turns to stare at the back door once again. I glance quickly at Jared, who gives me a look of concern. I give him a little shrug. Then Anna does the same thing as Jared and I give her a shrug as well.

Oh, come on, Brown. Don't do this. I internally roll my eyes. This is just so cliché, isn't it? Waiting until the time that you're supposed to walk down the aisle to stop the wedding. I mean, honestly, there are so many other ways to stop your own wedding. Why wait until this last part? This seems like something Anna would do, not Brown.

I look over at Matt again and he still doesn't appear even remotely worried. In fact, he leans over to his best man, and from the chuckle that he gives, it would seem as if he just made a joke. Well, I suppose some people use humor to get through hard times. That's usually my go-to move, usually at a very inappropriate time, as well.

Just as I'm about to go out and find her, and the quartet begins to play the bridal march yet again, I see a flash of something white at the back of the door.

Brown's there with her dad, and they are walking. They are walking down the aisle. Good job, Brown! I let out a breath I didn't realize I was holding. I'm pretty sure everyone in the crowd did, as well. Not Matt, though. I peer over at him, and he's beaming at her as she walks down the aisle, and Brown is beaming back. Not a normal look for Brown, but I like it on her. She's radiant.

"Please be seated," the officiant says, and everyone does as directed. Well, everyone except the bridal party. We have to stand the entire time. I think at my wedding I will have chairs for the bridal party to sit in, since I plan on writing my own ridiculously long vows. Of course, I won't force the bridesmaids into horribly tall and somewhat frightening shoes, either.

I mean, if I ever *get* married.

As if Jared has read my mind, he smiles and winks at me. I blush, even though I know he's not a mind reader. Good thing Lia's not here to announce to the crowd that my aura is the color of la-la-land, whatever color that is.

The ceremony goes off without a hitch. Well, accept for the hitch of the bride not walking down the aisle right away. I'll have to pull Brown aside and ask her what the heck happened.

The officiant announces, "You may now kiss the bride," and Matt lays one on Brown that would have been a little over the top had we been in a church. Everyone claps and cheers. The bride and groom turn, the officiant introduces them as "Mr. & Mrs. Whitehead" (Brown only slightly cringes), everyone claps again, and then those Whiteheads (this new name for Brown is going to be so much fun) rush down the aisle with the rest of us following along. Thank goodness the recessional is so much faster than the processional.

There is no time to sit after the wedding. Much to my chagrin, we are immediately rushed off to take pictures around the grounds. I make a note to myself that if I ever get married (key word: if) I'll let everyone take a breather after the ceremony. And by breather, I mean a nap. I could totally use one right now.

The hotel is set on a beautiful golf course, and this

incredible May day will make for some stunning pictures, I'm sure. Although pretty much a guarantee, I try as hard as I can to not have any double chins or pirate eyes in the pictures. By trying, though, I may have introduced an entire new look to add to my non-photogenic ways: surprised constipation.

"So how does it feel to be Mrs. Whitehead?" I say to Brown while Matt and his groomsmen are posing for pictures.

She rolls her eyes. "You know what? It feels good." She beams happily.

"You had us all worried there for a second," I say, questioning her with raised eyebrows.

"Well, you know . . ." she trails off.

"Oh, so you freaked out again?"

"Only a little," she makes the sign for little with her thumb and pointer fingers.

"Oh, Brown, how far did you get?" I knew right away she tried to make a run for it. Just a little doesn't usually mean little in Brown-speak.

"The parking lot. But my dad found me and talked some sense into me." She glances down at her bouquet with a hint of shame.

"Really? What did he say?"

"Just that he almost made the same mistake and was forever grateful that he didn't." She looks up, the shame now replaced by admiration.

"Daddies are the best, aren't they?" I say and wink at her. I can't believe she will be gone for an entire month in Europe. An entire month! What will I do without her?

Matt calls Brown over to join the groomsmen for more pictures. I join the other bridesmaids and wait for our turn. I hope it's not much longer because I'm so ready to sit down.

~*~

Apparently, bridesmaids don't get to sit during weddings. I had no idea. My only other stint as a member of the bridal party was at Lennon and Jenny's wedding. At least at that one, Jenny had us all wearing ballet flats. We did have to carry pale blue parasols though. That was very laughable on me. I don't remember standing so much for theirs, but maybe I repressed it.

About the time that I'm pretty sure I'm going to start crying over my sure-to-never-recover feet, it's time to eat dinner, and we get to sit while we eat, which at this point is a bit surprising.

I won't get to sit next to Jared, which is a bummer. He's at a table across the room with Anna and Jonathon. My plus one doesn't even get to sit with me. Gosh, I love that: plus one. Brown was sure to seat him far from the Spectraltech bunch, although I doubt he would have cared if he sat next to them. For Jared, his time there was all business. That's just how he works. Not me. I'd feel guilty just looking at them. Even if they didn't know, I'd keep thinking somehow they did, and I'd end up all tongue-tied and would spill the beans myself. *Remember that time I was a consultant and laid off thirty percent of your company? Wasn't that so fun?*

"Julia, how are you?" Mr. Calhoun taps me on the shoulder, and I spin around to see him standing in front of me. I was just going to take my seat at the head table.

"I'm doing great. How are you, Mr. Calhoun?" I smile genuinely. I'm glad that I still see him every so often. Mr. Calhoun was one of the few people that I actually liked from my days at Spectraltech.

"Why all the proverbial formalities? You can call me

by my first name, you know." He winks at me and gives me a jovial grin. Ah yes, I see the misuse of the word "proverbial" is still in effect. I can't believe I'm going to say this, but I've sort of missed it.

"Yes, uh, sorry, Harold, it's good to see you." I've had a hard time with that. It just feels weird to call him by his first name after referring to him as Mr. Calhoun for ten years of my life.

"How did that cupcake battling thing go?" he asks, his hands intertwining and resting on his large belly.

"Well, I'm not contractually allowed to say. You'll have to watch to find out," I say happily.

He smiles, eyes squinting as his cheeks squeeze against them. "So, did you make the cake?" He gestures over to the cake that is displayed near the head table. I haven't even had a chance to see what Debbie and Patti did with it. From here, it looks fantastic. I won't be checking it out anytime soon. It's on the other side of the room from where I'll be sitting, and I'm fairly confident I won't make it there and back to the table in these shoes.

"Yes, I did," I say.

"Well, then I look forward to eating it," he says, the corners of his mouth turning up yet again.

"I'm sure you do," I say and then my eyelids shoot up. That just slipped right out. "I mean, er, yes. I hope it's good," I say, trying to recover, but instead just clumsily stumbling over my words.

Mr. Calhoun chuckles and then pats me on the shoulder and walks away, shooting a "talk to you later" at me as he saunters/waddles off back to his table, where Martha has been eying us from across the room. Don't worry, Martha, I'm not trying to steal your man.

"Hey, beautiful," I hear whispered in my ear from behind me, speaking of the main reason I'm not after

Martha's man.

I spin around and wrap my arms around Jared. I've been so busy doing bridesmaid's duties that this is the first time we've gotten to touch today. Only glances from across the room have been exchanged.

"You look amazing," he says as his hands rub up and down my waist. I pull back and stare down at my gown, and then, glancing back up at him, I grab one side of the dress with my hand and do a little curtsy.

Yes, I curtsied. Good hell.

"You don't look so bad yourself," I say, quickly letting go of my dress and wrapping my arms around him again. I reach up and kiss him lightly on the mouth. I'd love to attack him right here, but that's probably bad wedding etiquette.

Etiquette is so overrated.

"Sucks that I don't get to sit next to you for dinner," he says, giving me a smoldering expression that makes my knees wobbly. Of course, my knees were fairly wobbly to begin with. If he keeps this up, he might have to carry me.

"Oh, don't act like you aren't thrilled to converse with *Jooonathon*," I croon.

"Come on, he's not that bad." Jared gives me a little smirk.

"Yes, well you haven't spent enough time with him. Your opinion still needs to be decided."

"Okay, I promise to give him the chance to hate him." He chuckles slightly.

"That's really all I'm asking. Anyway, I don't hate him. I just don't enjoy him." I give Jared a tight squeeze with my arms, still wrapped tightly around his waist.

Jared looks at the head table and then back at me. "You're being beckoned." He tips his head in Brown's direction. I glance at her and she's squinting at me, probably scolding me for my public display of affection. She hates that stuff. I mean, I do too, but we've already established my exception to the rule. As long as it's me doing it, it's okay.

"Oh, fine," I let out a loud exhale and let my shoulders slump in defeat. "I guess I'll go sit in my designated seat before her highness blows a gasket. Go have fun with Anna and Jonathon."

Jared gives me a quick kiss and goes over to his assigned table while I go sit at my spot at the head table next to Paul.

Dinner tastes amazing. I don't know if I've eaten at all today. I was paying so much attention to my throbbing feet and tired legs, I guess I didn't realize that my stomach was suffering as well.

Although I'd rather be sitting with Jared, conversing with Paul isn't so bad. Actually, it's quite fun. He has kept me giggling while we people watch the wedding guests from our seats in the front.

"I really don't enjoy being in weddings," Paul says after he finishes eating, leaning back in his chair and throwing his cloth napkin on his empty plate. His long legs cross at the ankle and he puts his large manly hands in his lap. If I'm being totally straight up here, Paul is pretty darn good-looking. Maybe bordering on hot. Not Jared hot, of course. His dark, almost black hair is disheveled in a very handsome way. He's undone his tie and it dangles around his neck, his collar unbuttoned. So he might race right by the hot category, but I wouldn't know. I'm in love with Jared, after all.

"I'm not a fan of being in weddings, either. Especially with shoes that put your life at risk." I hike up the side of my dress just slightly to show off the deathtraps still strapped to my feet.

140

He whistles through his teeth. "Yes," he agrees. "I can see danger in wearing those. They should come with a warning label."

"They really should," I agree.

"So who was that guy you were practically making out with earlier?" he asks, giving me a small smirk.

"Oh." The heat crawls up my face, and I'm thankful for the dim lighting so he can't see my embarrassment. I now remember why I hate public displays of affection. People see you. "Um, he's my boyfriend?" I have no idea why that came out in the form of a question.

"Figured as much. I thought he might be a close relative or something." He gives me a mocking smile.

"Is that how you treat your relatives, then?" I say, my turn to smirk.

"Oh, yes. Didn't Brown tell you? We are very close in my family. *Very* close." His eyebrows shoot up just once.

"You're gross," I say, hitting him on the arm and giggling despite his grossness.

Silverware clinking against a glass sounds from somewhere down the head table. The maid of honor and best man stand up. It must be time for toasts.

The toasts are more like roasts. We all now know that Betsy was called "Wetsy Betsy" in middle school after an incident of water spillage that landed in an unfortunate area. No wonder she likes going by Brown. Too many embarrassing memories associated with the name Betsy. We also learned that Matt was a bit of a player in college, and there is a long list of hearts he's leaving behind now that he's settling down. Just the kind of info anyone would want to find out at a wedding. There will be none of that nonsense at my wedding — if/when that happens. When the long-winded best man finally sits down, the DJ takes over and the dancing commences.

"Well, that's my cue," Paul says, sitting up straight in his chair, getting ready to stand.

"You're a dancer, eh?" I move to the edge of my chair and place my palms on the table so I can lean my way up out of this chair and balance in my shoes.

"Totally. I was a ballroom dancer in college," he says, looking dead serious.

"Really?" I ask. I don't mean to sound so shocked, but he doesn't seem the type.

"No. Not really. I'm actually going to go have a cigar with the rest of the groomsmen." He jerks his head toward the door, and as if on cue, another groomsman gestures for him to join them.

"Well, have fun," I say as I start to get up. He jumps up before me and offers his hand, which I take because I honestly wasn't sure if I was going to be able to balance myself. The exhaustion has caught up and swooped right by. I feel like I'm barely functioning at this point.

I try to take my hand away, but he holds it in his, covering the top of it with his other hand. "I've enjoyed being your escort tonight, Julia." Something about the sound of his voice catches me. "If you ever get sick of that guy you're dating, give me a call."

With that, he gives me a wink, drops my hand, and walks away.

It takes me a moment to realize that my mouth is slightly open and I've forgotten to swallow. Well that was unexpected. But also quite flattering.

"Hey there." I hear Jared from behind me, and I jump slightly from the sound. I also feel suddenly guilty, for absolutely no reason. I mean, it was Paul who said that to me, not the other way around.

I turn around and Jared puts his arms around me. "Wanna dance?" He gives me a devilish grin, knowing fully well that I'm not going to step on that dance floor, especially when a fast-paced song by Beyoncé is playing. The song ends, quite suddenly, and then, as if Jared had paid the DJ off, a slow song starts.

"You will at least dance with me to this, right?" he asks.

"Okay, fine. I guess I can. But be forewarned, I have two left feet, and it's almost a guarantee at least one of your feet, if not both, will get stepped on," I say, pleading my case.

Taking my hand, he drags me to the dance floor. "I'll take my chances."

I'm not sure because my high school dance experience was pretty much non-existent, but if this were a school dance, I think Jared and I would be disciplined for how close we are dancing. There's not even enough space between us to slip in a ruler.

He's a good leader and I let him guide me around the dance floor. The only thing I'm paying attention to is keeping my feet to myself.

"How have you been keeping these dancing skills away from me?" I say as he swings me around with little effort.

"Bobby made me take lessons in high school. I hated it, but it's become very useful with the ladies." I lean my head back to see a mischievous smile playing on his face. If I didn't know better, I'd think otherwise, but Jared has never been a player. The last relationship before I came along was three years, and before that was another long relationship in college.

He leans down and kisses me lightly on the lips. Once again, my vow to never engage in PDA goes right out the door.

The music ends and something faster starts to play. Someone nearby us yells, "Oh, yeah, this is my jam!"

This is so *not* my jam. We walk off the dance floor and over to Jared's table, where Anna and Jonathon are still sitting. They appear to be celebrating something. Maybe it's the yearly anniversary or the day that . . . Wait, they haven't been dating long enough to have an anniversary.

"What are you two toasting about?" I ask as Anna and Jonathon clink their glasses together. "Or was it wedding plans? Oh, wait, I forgot, you don't like to do any of that, Jonathon." I couldn't help myself.

"Julia!" Anna says, appalled. Jonathon gives me a strange expression.

"No, we were just celebrating because Jonathon won another big case today," Anna says, giving me a smug look. Then she goes back to ogling Jonathon with sappy, in-love expressions.

Fantastic. Just what I wanted to hear right now.

Jonathon starts to open his mouth to talk and I quickly cut him off. "Just a second. We'll be right back." I take Jared by the hand and pull him a few feet away.

"So how about you tell me what's been going on with work," I say in his ear. This probably isn't the best time to bring it up, but it keeps me from having to hear Jonathon brag. Besides, I really want to know, and Jared has been in a much better mood these days. It seems like things have worked themselves out.

"Yeah, that . . ." he trails off, his mouth pulling into a frown. Okay, so things may not have worked themselves out, and I probably just opened up a deep wound for Jared. I have the best timing ever.

He takes my hand. "Let's go outside." He gestures toward the front of the ballroom.

"Okay," I say, suddenly feeling reluctant. He made it all too serious when he said we should go outside. Maybe we should just stay and listen to Jonathon talk about his favorite subject - himself.

Before I can protest, Jared is leading me away from the table and toward the exit. I give a little wave to Anna and Jonathon, but they don't even notice. They are too busy giving each other googly eyes.

The night air outside is cooler, and it feels so good to get some fresh air. We find a bench to sit on, not far from the doors to the ballroom where everyone else is still dancing and celebrating.

"So, what's been going on?" I say, not wanting to fuss around. The fact that he had me come outside is making me feel a little insecure. It's unfounded, but it's there nonetheless.

"Well," he reaches up and runs his fingers through his hair. "It's my job, my company."

"I thought as much," I say, feeling relived that it has nothing to do with me, even though he has already told me it has nothing to do with me. I'm such a dumb girl sometimes. "What's going on with your company?"

"Well," he reaches up, scratching the side of his jaw. His five o'clock shadow is pretty sexy. "It turns out, I've been outed."

"You've been what-ed?" I say, furrowing my brow.

"I pretty much pissed off the wrong person." He shakes his head slightly, as if he still can't believe it happened.

"Who?"

"Just another company I did some consulting for. One of the guys that made the list." He nods his head once. He knows that I know what "the list" is. No need for an explanation on that one. I was once on such a list.

"Okay, so what happened?"

"Well to make things short here, this guy basically used every avenue he possibly could to make it known

145

what kind of work I do."

"Oh, no, Jared," I say taking his hand. No wonder he's been so stressed. "So what does it all mean?"

"It means that my next three jobs have canceled." He stares at the ground, his shoulders slouching. He seems, I don't know, kind of defeated? This is a new look on Jared. I'm not sure I like it.

"Are you serious? Why?" I put his hand in my lap, holding it tightly.

"Because if everyone knows what I do, then I can't do . . . what I do. Not in that industry, at least." He looks up at me.

"Then change industries," I say simply. Seems like a perfectly good solution to me.

"It's not that simple." He runs his fingers through his hair once again. "That industry — backup software — is my expertise. It's a niche market, so it's easy for me to get word-of-mouth work, plus I know the business structure in and out. I can't just switch industries." He gives me a little shrug.

"So, what's going to happen now?" I ask, still not sure where this is all leading. Jared is a man who's always with a plan. He's not one to sit around and wait for things to come to him. That's something *I* do.

"Well, my company is officially out of business. I'm closing it down. As of," he glances down at his watch, "two days ago."

"Wow, that's . . . just . . . really . . . wow . . ." I trail off. I'm not sure what to say, but I'm also feeling a little upset that all of this was going on and he wouldn't tell me. "Why couldn't you tell me?" I ask.

"I didn't want to stress you out with everything going on. I talked to Bobby," he says, like that's supposed to reassure me that he was okay without me.

I realize I'm a relationship baby here, but when you're a couple, aren't you supposed to share things like this with each other? Rely on one another? I suddenly feel put-off. I try to tell myself that it's stupid of me, but really, it's not. I think I'm justified on this one.

"So what are you going to do?" I ask, instead of going into some relationship discussion that my inner-crazed-girlfriend wants to have right now.

"Well, that's the good news. I hope it's good, at least." He angles his body toward me, holding my hands in his. "I've been offered a job. A more permanent one, that's kind of my dream job, actually. I mean, if I can't own my own business, this is the next best thing." His countenance brightens at this piece of info.

"That's great news," I say, feeling my heart lighten a bit. My stomach is still slightly knotted. I'll have to talk to him about being more open with me, even if he thinks I can't handle it at the time. I don't want to go there right now, though.

"What's the job?"

"A large backup software company." He gives me a small smile. Of course, duh. I don't even know why I asked that since he already said he can't switch industries.

"It's a big title. His face lights up even more. "Great salary, stock options . . . a lot of money if I play my cards right. It could be life changing."

"Wow, that sounds amazing," I say.

"It is." He nods his head just once. "But here's the deal." He tightens his hands around mine and looks me in the eyes. I tilt my head, concern washing over me. There's a "deal?"

He swallows hard. "It's in New York. Manhattan, actually."

"What?" I pull my hands away from his. The job is in

New York? "What does that mean? You're moving to New York?"

"Well," he puts a hand through his hair, "yes. I accepted the job yesterday. I start a week from Monday."

I feel sick. My stomach actually feels sick. "You're leaving Denver? You're moving to New York? In a week?" I don't know why I need to ask him, when he just told me. I think I needed to hear it again for it to be real.

"Yes, but Jules, this means nothing for us." He points his finger back and forth between us.

"What do you mean? This means everything for us," I say, my voice escalating on its own. "You're moving across the country. How could that mean nothing?" I put my face in my hands, leaning my elbows on my knees.

Is this really happening? His traveling all the time was no fun for me, but now it's going to be a permanent thing?

"I've already thought this all through. I know I can't ask you to move to New York with me, with the bakery doing so well, but we'll make it work. I'll fly back on the weekends and you can fly out there to see me, too." He reaches over and puts a hand on my back, reassuringly.

But it's not reassuring at all. I find the gesture suddenly non-comforting. His touch makes me cringe back, my body reacting before my mind can tell it not to.

"Oh, well, I guess you've already thought it through, then," I say sarcastically, although I'm talking through my hands so the tone might have been lost.

"Jules, look at me," he demands, attempting to pull my forearm so he can see my face.

I look at him, my eyes glistening from unplanned tears that start to form.

"Jules," he says softly as he moves closer to me on the bench, putting his arms around me. "It's going to be fine. *We* are going to be fine. We can make this work."

This should feel convincing, him with his arms around me, telling me it will be okay. But it isn't.

"Why?" I stutter through a near sob that I manage to stifle.

"Why? I had no choice. The last consulting job I did wiped me out. Right now, they are refusing to pay and don't have a lot of liquidity. I need a job, Julia." His voice carries a hint of condescension.

"No." I wipe my now dripping nose with the back of my hand. "Why didn't you even think to talk to me about it first? Didn't you want my opinion?"

"Of course I wanted your opinion," he says, his tone more gentle. He wraps his arms around me, pulling me into him. "I just didn't want you to worry about any of this when you had everything going on with *Cupcake Battles*. And then there was no time to wait. They needed an answer. It all happened so fast." He rubs my back with his hand, soothingly.

But it's not soothing. Something is erupting inside of me that I'm having a hard time controlling.

"Oh, I see," I say, pulling back from him, pushing him away.

"What?" He looks confused.

"It's not that you didn't want my opinion, it's that my opinion didn't matter. You would have taken the job no matter what I'd have said." I keep my arm out, holding him away from me.

"Julia." He tries to pull me close to him, but I don't let him. Instead, I stand from the bench, not entirely sure where I'll go. But I don't want to be here.

"Don't," I say as he stands up next to me. "I just need to be alone for a bit. I need to think about things before I say something I'll regret."

"Okay," is all he says, which doesn't help my anger. It

only fuels it more. Why do men take things so literally? Women want to be fought for, for heaven's sake. But he doesn't fight. He just stands there.

Without making eye contact, I turn and walk toward the ballroom. This was certainly not how I envisioned this evening going. Not even close.

Chapter 15

"Mm-hmm," I say into the phone to a panicky Anna as she goes over everything that still has to be done before the wedding. The girl is freaking out.

I've never had a full-blown hangover before. You know, the ones that have all these weird food and drink concoctions that are supposed to fix it? I've never had to try that. But now I'm wondering if I should try something to help this crying hangover I have this morning. My head is pounding. Anna isn't helping.

"Anna, I know I've asked this before, but can't Jonathon do some of this? I mean, he's the groom after all." I don't know why I bring this up. It never ends well.

"Julia," she says in a weird, calm voice. "He's too busy. He's a lawyer, after all. An important one."

Oh, geez.

Not wanting to say something that will make this conversation go down a path I don't feel like going down, and because I need to find myself some aspirin for my throbbing noggin, I tell Anna to text me whatever she

151

needs me to help with, and I'll get right on that. And by right on that, I mean maybe sometime tomorrow. Maybe. I've got my own crap to deal with—like feeling sorry for myself and finding something sweet to drown my sorrows in.

I'd so love to talk to Anna about the Jared situation right now. I looked for her last night after I dramatically walked away from Jared, but she was already gone. It probably wouldn't have mattered anyway. If the topic is not about her wedding, then it pretty much goes in one ear and right out the other.

Jared must have gone after I left him sitting on the bench, because I didn't see him the rest of the night. I numbly went back to my wedding duties, trying in vain to appear happy and be there for Brown. Luckily for me, Brown was so busy with everything—talking to everyone, cutting the cake, throwing the bouquet (which in a horrible twist, I caught—that was a cruel move, karma), that she didn't have time to notice the heartbroken face I was probably carrying around. She would have been the only one there that would recognize it anyway.

With the people that I usually dump my problems on off doing their own thing, I'm on my own, I guess, although the devil and the angel are back on my shoulders, duking it out to try and persuade me to their side. The devil says I should just tell Jared where to go (hell, obviously), that apparently I'm not a priority in his life, not enough for him to even ask me my thoughts on the matter or seek out my opinion. The angel says I should let him speak and says something about forgiveness mumbo-jumbo. I think I'm siding with the devil on this one.

I honestly don't know how to feel about it all. I feel sad, but I also feel angry and slightly betrayed. That feeling came out of left field. I mean, it's not like Jared chose what happened to him and then did it all to spite me. But I feel minuscule in his eyes. Like he thinks I'm so desperate that I'll just hang around for him. Which, let's face it, I am. And maybe I hate myself a little for that as well.

I also just want to think that I'm important enough for him not to want to go, that our relationship means more than that, that he'd be willing to work as a janitor as long as he was near me. But that only happens in chick flicks, and I'm pretty sure that would bring up a whole other set of issues — resentment being the main one. I don't know if I'd want him to choose me and then resent me for it. Not that he's even offered that as an option.

A knock at my door makes me jump out of the blanket cocoon that I've been all wrapped up in on the couch. It's an eighty-degree May day (not normal for Colorado), so I cranked my air-conditioning down just so I could snuggle up with a soft blanket and feel sorry for myself.

"Just a second," I say to whoever is on the other side of the door. I take a quick glance at myself in the mirror by my door. Not pretty, but at least I took a shower this morning to wash off all of the makeup and hair products.

I open the door, not even thinking to peer out the peephole first, to find Jared standing there, holding a lunch-size plain, brown paper bag. I know immediately what that bag is, or rather what it has inside of it, without him even saying anything. It's a bag of buttermilk donuts from Amerigo Delicatus, an Italian bakery not far from my apartment. The line there is always too long for me to go as often as I'd like, and Saturday mornings are the absolute worst. That means he waited in that long line on a Saturday morning just for me, so I could have these ridiculously yummy donuts.

I know what this means. He's playing dirty.

"I brought a peace offering," he says, holding out the bag of fried deliciousness.

My mouth waters, but I try not to let on. I stand there with my arms folded, my game face on. If he wants to play dirty, then let's play dirty.

"And I'll accept the peace offering," I say, and completely abandoning my stance and game face, I reach out and grab the bag out of his hand.

Okay, so clearly, I don't know how to play dirty.

"Can I come in?" he says, still standing in the doorway.

This is an awkward question because pre-conversation last night, Jared would have waltzed right in and made himself at home. He has a key, for heaven's sake. But there is a different dynamic now. A stupid 1,800-mile one. I'm not even sure if New York City is 1,800 miles from Denver. Whatever it is, it's a new long-distance dynamic.

Without saying anything, I pull the door open wide and step aside. He walks into the apartment and I motion for him to take a seat on the couch.

I set the donuts down on the counter, but then decide I should at least have one since they are still warm, so I get napkins from the kitchen and then sit down on the couch, not too close to Jared, because I don't want him getting any ideas. I'm still mad, dirty-playing-donuts aside. We have things to talk about. And I don't want to share.

"Listen, Jules, I'm an idiot."

Well, that was a good start. I'd like to verbally agree, but my mouth is currently full of fried buttermilk awesomeness. So I just nod my head once.

"I should have talked to you first. It's just that it was bad timing with you doing *Cupcake Battles* and all. I was really thinking of you, I promise." He reaches over and puts his hand near me. Not on me, but close to me, as if he's testing the waters to see how close he can be.

I finish my donut and put the bag down on the side table by me. It's go time. Time for my speech. Okay, I don't actually have a speech. I'm just going to say what I'm thinking. From my heart.

"I guess you made me feel unimportant-"

"What? You're more than important to me, Jules," he says, his brow furrowed.

"Yes," I hold a hand up, "just let me finish."

"Okay," he says.

"This was a big decision in your life, and I know it's not my life, but by not even asking my opinion, you made me feel like you don't really care."

"I'm truly sorry, Jules," he says dolefully. "So then tell me, what do you want me to do?"

"Oh," I say, looking away. I didn't expect him to ask me that. But let's be honest here, he's just doing it to appease me. Too little, too late. He's moving. We both know this.

"It's too late to ask me, right? There isn't any other option at this point," I say. I glance at the donuts sitting next to me and want to shove another one in my mouth, but I'd totally be eating my feelings right now.

"I guess not. Not right now, anyway. But listen, Jules, I'm not selling my place here. I'm just going to rent it out. This job is just a pit stop in my plan. I want to end up here eventually." He gives me a half-smile.

"Yeah, but how long will that be?" I grab the bag of donuts. I don't care if it's emotional, I'm eating another one.

He shrugs. "I can't answer that."

We sit in silence for a minute, me chomping on a donut and Jared twiddling his hands in his lap.

"This sucks," I finally declare.

"Sorry, Jules."

He seriously needs another line. "Sorry" just isn't cutting it right now.

"So now what?" I ask, glancing at him.

"Now? I guess right now we just take it one day at a time. Me in New York and you here. I'll come home as often as I can, and you can come see me. It will be hard, but it's not like we haven't been basically doing the long-distance thing this whole time anyway, right?"

"That's true," I say as I look down in my lap and start to fold down the top of the donut bag, making the crease deep with my nails. I have no idea why I'm doing this. I'm about three seconds from chowing down another one. "But I also knew that most times you would come home for longer than a weekend, and that this — that Denver — was your home. Now your home will be in New York."

"No, my home is still here in Denver. New York is just temporary," he says, reiterating what he said before. The look on my face must be saying that I'm having a hard time accepting that it's just a "pit stop" in his plan. It doesn't feel like it will be.

"It won't be so bad," he says. "We can talk on the phone, video chat every day. You could text me sexy pictures . . ." He gives me a cheeky grin, reaching over and poking me in the shoulder.

"Oh, no. I've tried that. I won't be doing that again," I blurt out, without thinking.

"Huh?" he asks, confused.

That wasn't exactly a story I had planned on telling him, ever.

"Uh, nothing." I try to take on a tone of nonchalance, but I'm probably failing miserably since I start to feel panic instead. "Do you think it's going to work?" I say quickly, trying to steer the conversation away from where it was going.

"Will what work?"

"Us."

"Don't you want it to?" A flash of anger goes across his face.

"Yes, of course I do," I say, leaning back into the couch, turning my head toward him.

"Then that's all we need, right?" He reaches over and lightly brushes the top of my hand with his.

"I guess," I give him a tiny, closed-mouth smile. I don't know if that is all we need, but I have to at least try, right?

I feel myself conceding, but I still feel mad, as well. I can't seem to find any peace with it all. Not even a little. Maybe it will take time.

"You just . . ." he trails off.

"What?" I say, wanting him to finish what he was about to say.

"You have a little," he scoots closer to me on the couch. "You have some powdered sugar on your face."

"I do?" My hand immediately goes up to my face and I feel the heat wash over me as I blush.

"Yes." He moves in closer. "Just right . . ." — even closer — "here."

His lips move up to the side of my mouth, and he kisses me softly. "And here," his lips move to the other side. "And right here." He then kisses me behind my ear, just behind my lobe.

My favorite spot. I'm nearly positive I didn't get powdered sugar there. But, mmm, holy wow does it feel good.

Abort! Abort! Must use all of my resources to stop this!

"And here," he says, his hand moving up behind my head as he crashes his lips into mine.

Oh, screw it. I'll just be mad later.

Chapter 16

"There she is, Miss Winner of *Cupcake Battles*!" Debbie exclaims as I enter the kitchen Monday morning at a most ridiculous hour. As much as I try, I'll never be a morning person.

"Patti!" I say, giving her an irritated look—she knows we aren't supposed to tell anyone about winning. I mean, I did tell Jared, but that's the only person I told. Anna and Brown were both ticked that I wouldn't tell them, although they pretty much guessed it. Jared was right. I have a horrible poker face.

"Well, how'd you 'spect me to keep it from Debbie?" She puts her hand on her hip in full-on defensive mode.

"Well, obviously we had to tell Debbie, but you can't tell anyone else, okay?" I shoot her a you-should-know-better glance.

"Well, of course I told my husband," Patti says.

I give her a quick, evil stare. "Okay, fine. Nobody else, and definitely not any of our regulars. If they ask we'll just tell them that the show will be on in a month and they can watch to find out."

"Oh, this is so exciting," Debbie says, clapping her palms together.

Patti and I look at one another and smile, knowingly. Penis-gate is going to be more embarrassing rather than exciting. That, paired with having to watch myself on camera, is making it so I don't look forward to any part of watching it. But I will. My parents are planning a viewing party, and Jared said he will make sure he's in town.

And so it begins. My long-distance relationship with Jared. I've moved from the anger stage of my grieving process and am now into sadness.

"Patti? That guy you were talking about when we were at the battles — was it Randall?" I reluctantly ask Patti as she adds ingredients to the large KitchenAid bowl. I'm reluctant because I don't actually want to know what I'm about to ask, but I can't seem to stop myself, either.

"What about him?" she asks.

"What exactly made you break up?" I ask. Even though she's already told me the answer, I'm hoping it's different this time.

"Oh, it was a lot of things, but it probably had a lot to do with him being so far away. Kinda hard to have a life together when you have separate ones so far apart. Anyway, it's been my experience that distance does not make the heart grow fonder. I think it makes the heart wander," she says as she adds blueberries to the bowl.

Oh joy, a rhyme. A rhyme about the probable destruction of my relationship with Jared. His heart might wander? I didn't even think of that option. Not exactly what I needed to hear right now. There has to be someone with a different opinion of long-distance relationships.

"Debbie? Have you ever been in a long-distance relationship?" I ask, hoping she has some good news.

"Who me? I'm not in a relationship. Who said I was in a relationship? I'm not. Not me. Nope." A red hue starts from the base of her neck and works all the way up to her forehead, practically matching her red curly hair that is pulled up and away from her face.

"Whatcha gettin' all flustered over there for?" Patti points a measuring cup at her. "She was just askin' ya a question."

Debbie mutters something about the front of the store and leaves.

"Any clue what that was about?" Patti searches me, her eyes squinting, eyebrows creased.

"Not a clue."

"Well, whatcha asking all of these questions about long-distance relationships for anyway? Somethin' going on with Jared?" She furrows her brow even further.

"No, no. Jared and I are fine. I . . . I was just wondering," I say not very confidently and then busy myself with the croissants.

I don't really want to discuss this new wrench that has been thrown in Jared's and my relationship. I'm sure they'll say something like "You're the exception to the rule," but then behind my back they will talk about how we're doomed.

That's how I'm feeling about it. Doomed.

~*~

"Oh Julia, it's not a big deal," Lia says in her sappy-sweet voice, motioning for me to take a seat at the two person table where she always sits when she comes to the bakery. "Just let me give you a little card reading. Maybe it will make you feel better."

She's a tricky little witch. The Monday morning rush

was over and I came out to check on how disastrous the front of the bakery was. Lia was sitting at her normal table, ready to pounce, apparently. She beckoned me over to her, under the guise that she needed more coffee, only to bamboozle me with her witchy nonsense.

"I'm fine, Lia," I say, readying myself to about-face and walk away.

"No. You're not," she states. "Your aura says otherwise."

My dang aura. Always giving me away.

I have to admit, part of me is curious to see what she says. The other part of me thinks this is all a bunch of hokey crap and why waste my time? Plus, heaven knows I'll end up with a card that depicts the grim reaper, and that will mean I'm dying. I mean, if I bought into any of this.

"Don't worry. I won't be able to tell if you're going to die," she says as she mixes up the cards.

"How did you know—"

"That's the one thing everyone is afraid of when I do a reading." With her plump hands, she fans the cards out, face down on the table.

"Okay, fine," I say, plopping down in the seat across from her, my curiosity winning out as it usually does. "What do I do?"

"Just pick three cards," she says, motioning to the cards.

I stare at the cards all fanned out in front of me. Without thinking it over too much, I pick out three cards and give them to her.

"So we have the Two of Cups, The Judgment card, and the Three of Swords," she says as she lays them out in front of her in the order that I gave them to her.

She might as well have just read the ingredient label on

my shampoo bottle. I have no idea what any of those mean. But the pictures on the front are slightly daunting. One of them is a drawing of a heart with three swords piercing it. That can't possibly bode well.

"Interesting choices," she says as she studies them.

"What do they all mean?" I ask, my heart racing slightly. My, how quickly I've been sucked in.

"Well, the Two of Cups has to do with relationships. Often it's about a person that you have a special connection with, a soul mate perhaps. But it doesn't always have to do with soul mates. It could just be someone you love."

I perk up. A soul mate? Jared, maybe? Okay, this might be more interesting than I had envisioned it being.

"The next card is the Judgment card," she says just as I was going to ask her. "Judgment often says that a major change is headed your way."

"Oh, my gosh, someone is going to die! Is it me?" I blurt out, panic taking over in my chest. I know fully well that she said she couldn't predict death, but I also know that she could have said that to trick me into this.

She lets out a little, high-pitched laugh, a witchy one, actually. Does she practice that?

"No, Julia, Judgment is not destructive change, it's more like change that is under your control — one that you can even turn your back on if you wish."

I take a big gulp. "And the third one?" This is that card with the hearts pierced by three swords. I'm not sure I want to know what this one means.

"Ah, yes, the Three of Swords," is all she says.

"What does it mean?"

She adjusts herself in her seat, opening her mouth and starting to say something, and then shutting it as if she can't find the right words to say.

So clearly, this is a bad card.

I must remember that I don't buy into any of this, so why does the look she has right now make me want to cry and/or rip up these stupid cards?

"The Three of Swords," she finally says, "can often serve as a warning sign that something painful is possible."

"Painful?" My eyes widen as I picture myself being impaled by a knife or smashed in a head-on collision.

"Not painful as in actual pain. I mean heart pain. Things like heartbreak, separation, rejection," she says, looking down at the cards.

"Oh," is all I say.

"So putting these cards together, as I see it, there is a relationship in your life that will be going through a major change that could end in heartbreak."

"Oh," is all I say, again.

My heart sinks. Relationship. Major change. Heartbreak.

That's just too weird, right? I mean, if I'm not buying into this crap, then what do I think about this? Lucky guess?

"But listen, Julia," Lia says in soothing tones, possibly after seeing that I've gone completely pale, or perhaps my aura has changed to whatever color means "holy crap," "the Three of Swords can also be helpful."

"It can?" I brighten up with a little hope.

"Yes. By preparing for the possibly emotional blow, you can lessen it or even prevent it entirely."

I sit there for a bit, feeling a little cold, like my blood has run thin. Do I actually buy into this? I mean, yes, it's very . . . timely. But also, it's just a deck of cards, a deck of stupid, spot-on, I-want-to-put-them-in-the-blender-and-rip-them-to-shreds cards.

I should never have sat down in this chair. Even if this is a bunch of malarkey, it will now sit in the back of my mind, repeating itself, eating at me. This and so many other things that I had been trying to put out of my mind.

"Well, this has been fun," I say, standing up, wanting to go back into my office and shut the door so I can work on blocking out the past ten minutes of my life.

"Julia," Lia says as she starts putting the cards back into a pile. "All things happen for a reason. I do believe that." She gives me a small smile.

With that, I turn around and walk toward the back.

"What's the matter with you?" Patti says as I walk into the kitchen. "You look like ya've seen a ghost."

"Uh . . ." I shake my head and close my eyes, my mind feeling a little jumbled. "Lia was just reading my cards."

"Oh, whatcha letting her get into your mind for? That girl's as lost as last year's Easter egg. Don't you go believing anything she tells ya, got it?" She points her finger at me, one hand on her hip.

I give her an appeasing nod and hope she will drop it. Normally I'd say she was right, because I've never bought into that stuff, either. But she has no idea what Lia just said, nor does she know that Jared is leaving and moving far away.

Relationship. Major change. Heartbreak.

Crap.

Chapter 17

"Julia, darling, you look beautiful," my mom says rather loudly as I exit the dressing room wearing my maid of honor dress. It's the final fitting. Just over three weeks until the big day.

I'm so over weddings right now. And relationships. And cupcakes. And life. I'm just over it all.

I step on the large round stand, with mirrors at nearly every angle, and stare at myself. The dusty rose dress actually does look good and complements my skin well. I will not admit that to Anna, though. She will love it that she was right. Unlike the dress I wore in Brown's wedding, I might wear this dress again, if I had somewhere to wear it. A bakery owner does not need glamorous clothing.

"Oh, Anna," my mom says, her voice suddenly thick with emotion. I spin around to see Anna coming out of her dressing room wearing her dress and veil. It's the first time we've seen her in both. She really is stunning. Her dress is gorgeous, and her curly dark hair under the white of the netting on the veil makes a beautiful combination. I even start tearing up, which goes against my policy of crying in public. I've been doing that more than I like these days.

"Move it." Anna taps my side and jerks her thumb back, signaling for me to get off the stand so she can see herself. "Go try on the shoes you're wearing. Mom has them," she says as she steps onto the stand and adjusts her dress so the large train flows down the back and onto the floor.

My mom gives me a shoe box and I open it.

"Not deathtrap shoes again!" I say loudly when I see the shoes. What is the deal with all of these ridiculous shoes people are wearing these days? I pledge right now that if I ever get married, my bridesmaids can wear whatever the hell they want, even hiking sandals. And I *hate* hiking sandals.

"Julia, those are Tori Burch!" Anna exclaims as if I've said something sacrilegious against the style gods.

I take them out of the box and step into them. They are the most uncomfortable shoes I have ever worn, I don't care who Tori Burch is.

"Tori Burch, you bi—"

"Julia!" my mom cuts me off. We were never allowed to swear when we were growing up, which is why I still rarely do. Except for my attempt right now. I'll throw out the odd "hell" and "damn" just because I was so deprived of cussing when I was a kid. I don't know if my mom has ever uttered a swear word in her life. I think one time she said "Oh, crumb."

"Just suck it up, Julia. It's one day of your life. Then you can donate them to charity," Anna says, turning and checking herself out from different angles.

That would be an insult to charities.

I slip the shoes off and my feet thank me immediately. At least I'll have Jared to escort me around at Anna's wedding. She's not having a head table. Three of the tables in the front will be reserved for the bridal party and we get to sit next to our dates this time.

Just thinking Jared's name makes my stomach sink.

"Hey, so Anna, I have a question for you," I say as I put the shoes back in the box they came in. Anna is still primping. "What is your opinion on long-distance relationships?"

"They're dumb," is all she says, which is *super* helpful.

"Yes, but why are they dumb?" I ask.

"Because they never work, Julia. I mean, maybe a few months or so. But any more than that, the odds are against you. It's just a known fact. Why are you asking anyway?" She squints at me in the mirror.

"No reason. I was just talking about it with the girls at work." I slouch down in a seat across the room and start examining my nail beds, avoiding eye contact.

"Anyway, is this about Jared? Because it's not like you have a real long-distance relationship. I mean, this is still his home." She adjusts the comb of the veil so it sits more on top of her head. The new positioning must be satisfactory because she gives herself a little nod in the mirror.

Little does she know, this is no longer Jared's home. His home is now in New York.

I stand up and go to the dressing room because I can feel tears threatening to spill, and I don't want any questions from Anna and my mom. Besides, Anna is so caught up in her wedding, she wouldn't fully listen to me anyway.

With Brown on her honeymoon and Anna in bridezilla mode, I'm feeling totally on my own right now. I guess I'll just have to go with what my gut says. Only right now my gut is craving cheesy fries, so it's not very helpful either.

~*~

Later that night, I found myself doing what any girl would do if her most-trusted confidants are off being all wedding-y and lovey-dovey. I turned to another source. I Googled.

Let me just say that I found a lot of interesting information when I Googled "Do long-distance relationships work?" and by interesting, I mean horribly depressing and awful.

The very first listing on the page, *the very first listing*, was an article entitled "10 Reasons Why Long-Distance Relationships Don't Work," and they were a very valid ten reasons, all backed up with statistics and crap. It was like the article was written for me, especially the part where it said "one person in the relationship didn't have any say in the decision and feels powerless to affect how the relationship is evolving." Which, you know, is only exactly what happened.

I need some chocolate.

I believe it was while reading number nine, which was called "A Foggy Future" that I started to get super jealous of a completely fictional, made-up-in-my-head woman that I envisioned Jared becoming quite cozy with in a New York coffee shop. I hate that coffee-drinking tramp.

The worst one by far was the last reason, titled "Life Goes On." It said something about how couples in long-distance relationships might not even notice that they are being pulled apart emotionally since their interests and friends may cause them to drift apart slowly and subtly. Or, depending on how different the living environments are, it may occur quickly and noticeably.

Quickly and *noticeably*.

Anyway, the article was relatively unsettling, and so I did what any normal girl in my situation would do. I saved it to my favorites to read and obsess about repeatedly.

There were others, though — articles with terrible, doomsday information that made me want to throw things and eat my weight in baked goods. In fact, it was rare to find a positive one. There were a few scattered throughout, which I read. But even those said things like "If you're a couple lucky enough to make it through the long-distance thing, you are one of the few." You know, happy stuff like that.

I think what I need to do now is stop all of this — stop asking advice and Googling. I need to decide that I'm going to make this work, and Jared and I will be the exception to the rule. I've got my mind on board with that, I think. Now if I could just get my heart to believe. And also that damned little voice in the back of my mind that keeps telling me "this won't work." I've got to get her on board as well.

Chapter 18

On Friday nights, normal people in normal relationships go on dates. That's how things had been working for Jared and me, for the most part, at least.

Tonight, though, we are spending the evening packing up his apartment, with his mom, no less. I like packing about as much as I enjoy getting a root canal, and I especially hate it this time because of what it all means.

Jared. Moving. To New York City.

My dang heart still wrenches when I think about it. The odds are stacked against us, this I know. The universe made that perfectly clear. There is no end in sight for this long-distance thing. But what I do know is that I at least have to try my hardest. If I have to resort to sending Jared a sexy text every now and then to keep his heart from "wandering," then I will. I'll just quadruple check that this time it will go to Jared and not my father.

"Jared, honestly, all of your stuff isn't going to fit in one of those tiny New York apartments. What do you plan to do with all of this?" Bobby says as she comes out of Jared's bedroom, carrying a box.

"I'm putting some of it in storage," he says with a quick shrug. He takes the box from her and stacks it by the door.

She makes a tsk sound with her mouth, which she's been doing a lot. It dawned on me after several thousand tsks (only a slight exaggeration) that Bobby is probably having a hard time with Jared leaving as well. He's never lived this far away from her before. At least she and I can bond over him leaving, although that hasn't actually happened yet since I just recently realized that we had that in common. How very selfish of me.

Bobby has been packing up the bathroom while Jared and I work on the kitchen. She's come fully ready to pack up his apartment in jeans and, surprise, a white button-up shirt (my suspicions were correct—she wears the same outfit in the summer as well). I'm looking extra-specially lovely in an old torn up college sweatshirt and ratty worn out jeans. If I had some warning that Bobby was going to be here, then maybe I'd have tried a little harder. But I was not warned ahead of time. I'm only a little bitter about it.

"Where do you want me to put this?" I say, holding a box of cleaning items that I pulled from under the sink. I question why Jared had them in the first place since he had someone else clean his apartment, but then again, he has an entire kitchen full of cookware, and Jared doesn't cook.

"Over there," he points to a growing pile of boxes by the door.

The moving truck comes tomorrow and he flies out Sunday night. The first time he will come back to Denver is nearly three weeks after that for Anna's wedding, since he needs to get settled in his new apartment and job. It's not like we haven't been apart for that long before. With his last job, he had spurts where he couldn't come back every weekend. But for some reason this feels too long.

I guess I could go out there to see him, but with all of the wedding stuff for Anna and the fact that she freaked out that I was leaving to do *Cupcake Battles* a month before her wedding . . . well, she would probably lose her crap over me taking off anytime between now and then. So I'll stay put and go out there after everything has settled down here. A small part of me is looking forward to visiting Jared in Manhattan. I love many things about New York City, but I mainly love the food. So many bakeries to try.

"What's this?" I say to Jared, as I spy a shoe box sitting atop one of the moving boxes by the door.

"Just some old pictures. You can look at them, if you want," he says, as he starts to work cleaning out his desk.

I walk over to the couch as I open the box and take a seat. The first item I notice in the box is a picture of a young boy that is obviously Jared and his younger brother, Mark. I've only met Mark a couple of times. He lives in Boulder and works crazy hours doing something at a hospital. He doesn't seem to be as close to Bobby as Jared is. I think he's just very career-driven. But then again, so is Jared.

"Aw, look at you," I sing-song as I wave a picture of a baby Jared, naked in the bathtub.

"Give me that," Jared says, grabbing it from me, traces of embarrassment on his face. He doesn't get embarrassed all that often. I think I might enjoy it a little too much when he does.

"What are you looking at?" Bobby says as she carries another medium-sized box out of the bathroom.

"Old pictures," Jared says as he sits down next to me and starts perusing through the contents. Bobby comes and sits on the other side.

I watch and listen as Bobby and Jared reminisce over pictures. Every once in a while a picture of Jared's dad pops up and they tell the story behind the picture, which is usually followed by laughter or bouts of melancholy. Not as much sadness as I think I'd have if it were my dad, but I'm sure time does do some healing. Jared's dad seems like someone I would have liked.

Jared took me to his dad's graveside once a few months back. I remember the headstone was large and ornate and there were fresh flowers lying in front of it. I was pretty sure they were from Bobby, since she goes there regularly. James was his name. James Nathan Moody. He and Jared share the same middle name, which I think I'd like to do, if Jared and I ever have kids, that is. Kind of hard to get married and procreate when we'll live on pretty much opposite sides of the country.

In with the positive thoughts, out with the negative, my-life-sucks thoughts. I'm getting on my own nerves.

After the packing is pretty much done, Bobby heads home and Jared and I lay on the couch. His arms are wrapped around me and I'm resting my head on his chest, listening to his heartbeat. This is my favorite place to be, snuggled up in his arms.

I'm going to miss this.

~*~

"Julia, are you even listening to me?" Anna says somewhat loudly.

It's Sunday morning, the morning before Jared leaves. I wanted to spend all day with him, but he has some last minute things he needs to take care of this morning and Anna claimed she "desperately" needed my help.

"Huh?" I say, trying to bring my mind back from

wandering. It's been doing a lot of that lately. Currently, Anna and I are sitting in my parents' overly decorated formal dining room.

"Seriously? If you can't help me sort out this seating chart, then just say you can't." She squints her eyes at me.

"No, no, I can help. Sorry, I just have a lot on my mind," I say through a yawn.

"Yes, so do I. Like this stupid disaster," Anna glances down at the chart we've been working on. She's not being dramatic. It really is a mess.

"Now where were we?" I try to remember what we were talking about before my mind wandered. I think we were trying to decide if my dad's sisters Brenda and Melanie can sit at the same table as some distant cousin whom they've both had a falling out with at some point. Seriously, can't we all just get along?

"This seating chart is going to be the death of me," Anna says, sinking back into the high-back leather dining chair.

"I think you're getting a little too worried about it," I say in a kind (albeit forced) voice. If I said it sarcastically like I wanted to, I'd start another discussion about how I have "no idea" what she's going through right now. And I know I don't, but why does she feel the need to rub it in?

She sighs. Here we go.

"You're probably right," she says, leaning her head back against the dark leather.

Holy crap, did she just agree with me?

"Holy crap, did you just agree with me?" I say out loud, because I'm so shocked I couldn't help myself.

She opens her eyes and peers over at me, scowling. "Yes, I'm getting really tired of thinking about it." Her head goes back to lying against the chair and her eyes close.

"What's with you lately, anyway?" she asks, not turning her head in my direction.

"What do you mean?" I say, knowing exactly what she means.

"You're just distant and you seem, I don't know, not happy." She still doesn't turn toward me, her eyes still closed.

I'm honestly surprised she noticed. "It's just something with Jared," I say.

"What's going on?" she asks. She seems concerned, but in an overly tired way.

I pause to look over at her. She keeps her eyes closed, her head back. Butterflies of excitement suddenly fill my chest. Finally, someone to talk to! And it's even the one person I've wanted to talk to all along. Anna is who I trust the most when it comes to relationship talk. She can help me make sense of it all. She's been my sounding board when I feel insecure, which has been more than I care to admit.

"Well," I say, not sure where to start. "He's had some problems with his company and . . ."

Anna's head droops to the side, lazily. Her eyes are still closed.

She's asleep.

"Anna?" I say, touching her lightly.

She doesn't budge.

Well, I guess I'm on my own for this one, at least until this wedding is over and I get my sister back.

That can't come soon enough.

Chapter 19

"Whatcha wearing?" Jared asks, in soothing, seductive tones.

"Oh, just some old sweats and a ratty T-shirt." Yeah, I'm not playing along. I'm too tired. Plus, it's the truth.

We are on the phone — Jared in his new apartment in Manhattan, me in my condo in Denver. Day two of our new, long-distance relationship.

Putting him on the plane was difficult, even knowing that he would be coming back in just a few weeks. I'm not going to sugarcoat this—I blubbered, like, snot-nose, hiccuping, blubbered. In front of him, even. I tried to hold it in, at least until I got to the car. But something about hugging him in the airport with everything so permanent, well, it's a wonder I didn't hyperventilate (I do that sometimes when I cry too hard . . . quite embarrassing).

So far so good, though. We are totally kicking this long-distance thing's butt. We've talked both nights, FaceTimed one of them, sent multiple texts during the day. And one was even a sexy text from yours truly.

Successfully this time, I might add.

Okay, it wasn't sexy so much as a picture of my foot. But I had just gotten a pedicure and my feet looked gorgeous. Some guys get into that whole foot thing. Not Jared, but I figured I'd start small anyway. What's there to build up to if I start sending him pictures of my bra strap right away? It was a little awkward with a "thinking of you" text and a picture of my foot, because that doesn't make much sense now that I think about it. What does my foot have to do with missing him? Oh well, it was something different. He must, at least, appreciate that.

I'll do better next time.

"How are the bright lights of Broadway?" I ask as I lay on my couch, feeling exhausted. It's nearly my bedtime - 8 p.m. I truly live a glamorous life.

"I wouldn't know." Jared heartily yawns in my ear. "I haven't even had a chance to go anywhere near there, I've been so busy with work."

"Still liking it?" I asked him this yesterday, but I'm holding out for him to hate it and move back home.

"So far. Since it's only been two days, yes," he says, sarcasm swimming through his tone.

I hate his job, even after two days. Perhaps I can hate it enough for both of us. I thought I hated what he did for work before. Now I'd give anything for him to go back to it. Lesson learned — be careful what you complain about.

"Well, that's good I guess," I say in plain, unexcited tones.

"Jules, don't get all down on me," he says, fitting in a yawn after he said my name.

"I'm not," I blandly protest. "I just wish things were different, that's all."

"So do I," he says, and I believe him.

We're silent for a moment—me contemplating the

meaning of life, because I'm deep like that. Really, I'm just feeling sorry for myself. I need to lighten up.

"How are things at the bakery?" Jared asks after the bout of silence. I don't get nervous when we are silent. It's a comfortable silence with Jared.

"Good. Busy." I don't have much to offer. Not much has happened since he left. "Oh, wait," I say, remembering something that happened. "This morning when I went in I found a sock on the floor in the front of the bakery."

"A sock?" Jared says, confusion in his voice.

"Yes, a sock. It was totally random. I saw something peeking out from under one of the tables and so I went to grab it and it was a sock. A man's stretched-out, black sock, like my dad wears."

"That's weird," Jared says, even though I can tell he doesn't think it's weird at all but is just trying to appease me.

"I know you don't actually think it's weird, but think about it. Who would leave one black sock in a bakery? That's not a normal place people take their shoes off and relax."

"Very mysterious," he offers flatly.

"Could you at least try?" I ask, rolling my eyes at him even though he can't see me.

"Yes, yes. Black sock. Who left the black sock in the bakery? It's all very suspicious. Maybe you could get Sherlock on the case." He chuckles at himself.

"Well, maybe if I could get Benedict Cumberbatch to do it, I would," I say, in my best smarty-pants voice.

"Hey, now," he chides.

"Oh, and another sort of weird thing. I brought the sock into the kitchen and showed the gals and Debbie got all crazy and red-faced over it. I guess she thought I was saying it was hers? That's what Patti thought, at least."

That was very odd for Debbie. She's been acting so weird lately. Talking to herself when she thinks we aren't watching her, and then when we call her out on it, she turns red, mutters to herself, and walks away.

"Please make sure you keep me updated on the case of the mysterious sock," Jared says, unconvincingly.

"You know what? I will. Just because you clearly don't want to hear about it."

"Me?" He feigns innocence. "I was on the edge of my seat the entire time."

"Shut up!" I say, but I'm laughing when I say it.

He chuckles into the phone. He thinks he's so hilarious.

"Hey, so remember that time at Spectraltech when you practically attacked me in the conference room?" I say, deciding to change the subject since my sock story was going nowhere, except to give Jared the opportunity to tease me. Anyway, saying it out loud made me realize that it was, in fact, a completely pointless story. But it's still mysterious, even if pointless.

"Yes," he says. I can visualize him smiling. "Haven't we gone over this before?"

"Yes, but there is one thing I've never asked you that I've always wanted to know," I say, and then start chewing on my bottom lip.

"Shoot," he says.

"So that day, when you attacked me in the conference room—"

"I did not attack you. Would you stop saying it like that? You make me sound like some kind of pervert."

"Okay, fine, that day in the conference room when you romantically grabbed me and kissed me passionately—"

"Yes, much better," he says.

"Why?"

179

"Why what?"

"Why did you do it?"

He sighs. "Jules, you've asked me this question about a thousand times."

"I know. I just like the answer. Go ahead. I'm waiting."

"Fine. I kissed you because — even against my best judgment — I found you intriguing, irresistible, and cute."

"What? You said 'adorable' last time," I protest.

"Did I? Okay, fine. I found you intriguing, irresistible, and adorable. I couldn't help myself."

I sigh a heavy, dramatic sigh. "I just love that story."

"I know you do." He chuckles into the phone.

"I've got to go to bed," I say, sadly. I don't want to hang up the phone. Maybe we could just keep the call going while we sleep. How romantic is that? Although over the phone and not in his arms, my snoring — and possibly other bodily noises — would probably not come across as very appealing. So that might not be in my best interest.

"Me, too. I'm exhausted," he says. Like I hadn't gathered that from all the yawns.

"Talk to you tomorrow," I say, feeling another sad ping in my heart at the way things are now.

"Hey, Jules?"

"Yeah?"

"I love you," he says, simply.

"Me, too," I say, my heart warming up quickly. "I, er, mean, I love you, too."

I'm getting so much better at this saying I love you thing. Not really, but I'll keep telling myself that.

We hang up and I lay back on the couch, holding my phone against my chest. He loves me. I love him. Our love will get us through this.

Lia's stupid cards were so wrong. Google was wrong. We are going to be just fine.

Chapter 20

I'm just going to keep calm. Keep calm and not get annoyed that I haven't heard from Jared in nearly thirty hours. Yes, I've been keeping track like a stalker. I can't help myself.

It's no big deal that we haven't talked. This is not a sign of things to come. I will not believe Lia the Witch, or Google . . . or history. In with the *everything-is-fine* thoughts. Out with the *I-want-to-slap-my-boyfriend* thoughts.

After all, he's only been gone for nearly two weeks now. Everything was good in the beginning, great even. Things have been slightly strained as of late, though. Texts and calls were tapering off, but I wasn't freaking out (well, not totally) because I knew we had to find our groove, but then last weekend happened. Last weekend when I got super-duper-over-the-top mad that he was letting his ex-girlfriend, Kirsten (who happens to live in Manhattan), take him around to see the sites.

First of all, I had no idea that Kirsten lived in

Manhattan. That was never mentioned before, even though he actually knew that fact. He told me that he didn't say anything earlier because she's so unimportant to him that he didn't even think to tell me about her. I'd have given him the benefit of the doubt over that had he not just had lunch with her when he mentioned her living there. One would think that if you're having lunch with your ex-girlfriend, you should probably inform your *current* girlfriend prior to said lunch. But, apparently, that kind of information is not on Jared's radar. Especially when it "meant nothing to him."

Well, it meant something to me. We got in a pretty big fight about it, over the phone of course, since we are a bazillion miles away from each other. It's hard to fight over the phone—things sound harsher when facial expressions aren't involved. Things were said that would have come across less harsh (on his part) and less paranoid (on my part) if we had been speaking face to face. It was kind of worked out, or at least we came to an understanding of sorts, but it feels like things have been strained since. It's probably just me, because I'm a girl and I hold on to things, but it's strained nonetheless.

It was, once again, a reminder of how far away we are from each other and how easily things can slip away and then off into someone else's arms. Or something like that. It's not that I don't trust Jared. I do. I just don't trust that tramp, Kirsten. I've never met Kirsten, so I'm only assuming she's a tramp. But I'm probably right.

So it's pretty obvious why it would bother me so much that we haven't talked in so long, because when I don't hear from him, my horrible, girlish mind likes to punish me by envisioning him and Kirsten the Tramp running off into the sunset together. And then that little, annoying voice in my head gets louder and louder saying, "This isn't going to work."

Currently, I'm trying to stop myself from going there, because I'm stronger and better than that. Nope, I will not go there.

"WHAT THE HELL!" I scream from my office and slam my smart phone down on my desk.

Then I quickly pick it up to make sure I didn't do anything to it.

"Who peed in your Cheerios?" Patti yells from the kitchen where she's working on cookies for the lunch rush.

"Jared did. Jared peed in my Cheerios," I say as I walk out of my office. I start pulling out supplies to make lemon bars, slamming each one on the counter as I grab them.

Note to self: slamming a bag of flour down on the counter (or any surface for that matter), is a bad idea. Now I have a mess to clean up. I blame Jared for that, too.

"What did Jared do?" Patti asks, her forehead creased with concern.

"It's not what he did. It's what he *didn't* do," I say as I poorly try to sweep up the spilled flour. I abandon it quickly though, and decide to start cracking eggs for the batter. Breaking things just feels right all of a sudden.

"Okay, so what didn't he do?" She puts her hand on her hip. Patti does not like to beat around the bush.

"I've only talked to him one time since yesterday morning. One time! How are we supposed to carry on a relationship if we are already not talking on a regular basis, not even a couple of weeks into it?" I say, yelling at Patti. Even though I don't mean to direct my frustration at her, I can't help myself.

He did warn me yesterday that he had a client dinner that night and might not be able to call me, but promised to send a text at the very least. But he didn't send the text, and here we are, late afternoon the next day, and still nothing. Not a peep.

"I'm sure he's just super busy—"

"Don't give him excuses. You know, I believed you and Debbie when you said we would be fine, that this whole long-distance thing would work out. But now I think you were just saying that." I stare down into the mixing bowl. I've just cracked about a dozen eggs into it without even knowing. I only needed six. Great. Now Jared is making me waste supplies.

I wasn't going to say anything to Patti and Debbie just yet. But I needed to talk to somebody or I was going to explode. Their words and even their expressions didn't give away the fact that they might have thought Jared and I were doomed when I explained what was going on. Either they have really good poker faces, or they truly do believe it. But even if they do believe it, what do they know? They are both ridiculous, hopeless romantics. I never told them about the whole Kirsten wrench— probably because it's not actually a wrench and I most likely overreacted. I don't want to hear them tell me that.

"There's gonna be some adjustment time," Patti says, using tones that she's obviously trying to force. Soothing and coddling do not come easy to Patti.

"Yes, adjusting to being away from each other and getting used it, and then getting comfortable with it," I say, tearing up. Dang you Google. If I hadn't read those articles, the thought wouldn't be in my head. I also blame Lia, that stupid witch. She totally hexed me. I think I'm going to have to ban her from coming into the bakery with her bad juju.

My phone beeps to alert me that I have a text. I run to my office. It must be Jared. My heart lightens slightly. I'm not that high maintenance, I swear. I just need a little communication here. That's all I'm asking for.

I grab my phone, already thinking of replies. Most of them consisting of "Where the H have you been?" But when I look at the screen, it's not a text from Jared. My heart sinks. It's a text from Anna.

Help! Wedding disaster! Need ur help!

Yes, perfect. My boyfriend who's far away is frustratingly unreachable, so to help pass the time until I reach him, karma has sent my whiny, bride-to-be sister. Well played, karma, well played.

I start to write her a text to tell her I can't meet up until after the bakery closes, but then I decide that getting out of here early might be just what I need. I'll stay through the lunch rush and then ask Debbie and Patti if they mind closing up shop.

Whatever this disaster is, I hope it's going to help me change my focus. I'd be willing to wager money that it's not, though.

~*~

It turns out the emergency is that Anna, in her wedding planning craze, forgot to find a going away outfit for after the reception.

So not even remotely a disaster.

I have to say, some retail therapy has actually helped ease the fact that I *still* have not heard from Jared. That little annoying voice in the back of my mind is gnawing at my brain, repeating "this is not going to work" over and over again. I try to shake it off, but it's hard.

It's just that, Patti and Debbie aside, it feels like the universe is trying to tell me something. I've never been a huge sign-seeker before . . . Oh, who am I kidding? Of course I have. I search for signs everywhere. I need to stop.

"What do you think?" Anna says as she comes out of the dressing room, modeling probably the fiftieth dress (only a slight exaggeration).

"Great," I say flatly. I've liked pretty much all of the dresses she's picked out. This shouldn't be that hard.

"What's your deal?" she asks, giving me snooty-faced duck-lips.

"Nothing. I just haven't heard from Jared." I slump back in my chair, grumpily.

"Where is Jared these days?" she asks, surprising me that she even heard what I said.

"He's in New York," I say.

"How long will he be there?" Her eyebrows pull together and down.

"Um, who knows?" I don't want to talk about it right now because it needs to be a longer discussion, and Anna does not have the capacity to talk for longer than thirty seconds about anything that is non-wedding-related. Plus, she could fall asleep on me again. There's just no point.

I cannot wait until this wedding is over so I can have her back. Well, except that she'll have Jonathon in tow then. But I'll learn to deal with him. I hope.

"Well, he better be back for my wedding. If he's not there, then it will mess up the whole seating arrangement," she says as she slumps down in the open chair next to me.

"He'll be here," I say in monotone. I have no idea why one person would mess up her entire seating chart, but I don't feel like asking.

"Hey, have you worked on your toast yet? You know the maid of honor has to give a toast," she says, a worried look on her face, probably because she thinks I've forgotten.

I had forgotten, but I won't be telling her that.

"Of course," I fib, trying quickly to think up something in case she asks me for a sample of what I plan to say.

I'm totally drawing a blank at this point. Luckily, she doesn't press further.

Anna rests her head on the back of the seat. "I'll be so glad when my wedding day is here."

You and me both, kid, you and me both.

"It seems like so far away, and it's next week," she says, closing her eyes. "And there's still so much to do."

Yes, like your maid of honor needs to write her toast.

"Can't Jonathon help out more now that he has those two big cases behind him?" I ask, using my best I'm-not-attacking voice.

She stares me down, annoyed. "Julia, he has other cases that he's working on. You, of all people, should know how that works, since both our dad and our brother are lawyers."

"Yes, but Dad's his boss. Can't he cut him a little slack?" I give her an annoyed look back.

"No way! Jonathon wouldn't want to look like a weakness to the firm," she says, putting her head against the backrest and closing her eyes once more. "Besides, I can handle this."

Of course dear, sweet, pompous little *Jooonathon* wouldn't want to seem weak. Heaven forbid he act like a real human being and not just a robot lawyer.

"I'm starving," I say, changing the subject. "Let's go get something to eat." Maybe, just maybe, if I get her to go out to eat with me, Anna might have time to listen to the whole Jared moving debacle and give me some sound advice.

"No can do," she says, placing her hands on the tops of

her knees as she goes to stand. "I'm on a juice fast until the wedding."

"Anna, you can't do that. It's still an entire week until the wedding. You need to eat," I say, a sudden protective, big sister feeling rattles through me. Plus, I want her to go out with me.

"Oh, Julia." She bats a hand at me. "I'm eating one real meal a day. It's just that I had that meal when I had lunch with Jonathon, so I have to have juice for dinner." She rolls her eyes. "I need to make sure I fit into my wedding dress."

I give a non-approving "hmph." I'm pretty sure her dress will fit just fine. I've been with her for nearly all of the fittings, and it fit every time. I'm also perturbed that she wasted her one meal with Jonathon. It might not have felt wasted to her, but still.

So much for having a little time with Anna. I guess I'll just have to keep waiting . . . impatiently, apparently. Maybe this is a sign. Maybe it's time I stood on my own two feet and went with my own gut and didn't rely so heavily on Anna and Brown. Honestly, I'm old enough to make my own decisions, or rather too old to let other people help me make my decisions for me.

My phone rings. Finally, Jared. I tell Anna I'll be right back and walk out of the dressing room.

Okay, Julia, time to put on your big-girl pants.

"Where have you been?" I ask, not even saying hello. I seek out the closest exit to the department store we are in and go outside.

"Is everything okay?" he asks, sounding a little panicked.

"Yes. Well, no. I mean, I'm annoyed that I haven't heard or spoken to you since early yesterday," I say boldly, which is not something I normally do.

"Are you serious?" he says, frustration ringing through his tone. "Julia, my phone wasn't working, and then suddenly I got a bunch of texts and voicemails from you. I thought something horrible happened."

"Well, sorry to disappoint. It was just me, freaking out over this whole thing," I say, not meaning to say it, or at least not like that. But it's out there now.

"What do you mean, this whole thing?" he asks, sounding even more put off.

"This whole thing—you, me, this long-distance thing," I say, somewhat loudly.

"Julia, it's been a long day at work. Are you seriously going to be mad at me because I haven't been able to call you for a day?" Now he's the one talking loudly. "Is this about Kirsten? I told you not to worry—"

"No," I cut him off, stopping him there. I'm not worried about Kirsten. There are bigger things I'm worried about. "It's not about her, and it's been more than a day since you called."

"Julia—"

"It's not just that. Don't you think it's a sign of things to come?" I say, trying to keep my voice steady and calm. "If we can't even communicate on a regular basis in the first two weeks, if things are already tapering off now, what happens next?" Water starts to gather in the corners of my eyes.

"I think you're being totally irrational right now," he says.

That actually quiets me for a few seconds, as I count the days to make sure I'm not PMSing and that this isn't just a hormonal rage. When I realize it's not, my heart sinks. This is coming from me and only me. No hormones involved. This is how I really feel.

"I'm not being irrational. I just feel like—"

189

"Like what?" he cuts me off.

"Like this isn't going to work." I say flatly. I don't want to say it, but now it's out there. All of the stories and the Googling and the ex-girlfriend and the hexing have brought me to this point. Now it's his turn to tell me why I'm wrong.

Instead, it's just quiet.

"Well," he finally says, "if you're already thinking that way and it hasn't even been two weeks, then maybe you're right."

Okay, so that was a pretty crappy way of telling me I'm wrong.

"Julia," he says in a quieter tone, "I've had a rough day. It sounds like you have had one, too. Let's not do this over the phone."

I don't say anything. Mostly because the tears that were gathering are now sprouting from my eyes. I'm basically a sprinkler at this point.

"I'll be there in a week for Anna's wedding. We can talk about it then, okay?"

"Okay," is all I can say.

"Let's just take some time to cool off and think about things. We'll talk when I get there."

"Okay," is still all I can say.

"I'll be in touch," he says and then hangs up.

Well, that . . . was not good. Actually, it was horrible. I don't know what I was expecting from this conversation, but it certainly wasn't that.

Chapter 21

Currently, I'm having fake discussions in my mind with Anna and Brown over what to do about my crumbling relationship with Jared. I don't actually know if it's crumbling. We haven't spoken in four days. Four days, two hours, and twenty-two minutes, to be precise.

I honestly didn't think we would really take time to "cool off." I figured one of us would give in and call the other, only I thought Jared would figure it should me, and I don't want to be the first one to call back. I think it should be him. After all, this is all his fault. He took the job in New York. He moved far away. He claimed we would be fine. He forgot to tell me about Kirsten. He got caught up in his new life and lessened the lines of communication. It was all him.

Okay, and it was some of me — my mind, my Googling, my witchy clients. Mostly my mind. What can I say? I'm naive when it comes to relationship stuff. That's why my fake conversations with Brown and Anna have started happening.

The verdict so far? They are both telling me to jump ship before my heart breaks even more, to rip the Band-Aid off fast rather than a slow-form-of-torture rip. Long-distance relationships don't work, especially ones with no end in sight. That is what my fake conversations with my two most-trusted confidants are amounting to.

So I'm taking their fake advice into account, as well as my own feelings, which are confusion mixed with doubt mixed with heartbreak mixed with the desire to eat something chocolate. I seriously wish chocolate would magically fix things. I always think it will, but the only thing it does is temporarily relieve me of my stress. Very temporarily.

I don't want things to end with Jared. That is the truth. I also know I have to protect myself, and if the signs are there, that might just be what I do. Protect me. But I'm not making any rash decisions. I'm going to wait until he gets here tomorrow. We will have a conversation—one in which he tells me he can't live without me and is moving back. (That's the chick-flick version of what I've come up with.) Yes, I've been having fake conversations with Jared, as well.

For now, I have to focus on Anna's cake. Tomorrow is the rehearsal dinner and with all of the wedding-y things I have to do tomorrow, I need to be ahead of the game. Tonight I'm making the cakes. Then I'll cool them and put them in the walk-in. Tomorrow I'll fill and frost them while Patti works on décor, which is going to be a mix of fresh flowers (roses) and gum paste flowers (that's where Patti comes in). On Saturday, Patti and Debbie will deliver and assemble the cakes. I could not have done this without them.

The bakery is totally my sanctuary, especially at night when I'm the only one here. Although there have been moments when I've heard things. One night in particular, I practically ran out screaming (and by practically, I mean I actually did), because I swear a psycho killer was hiding behind the front counter. I may or may not have watched a scary movie the night before.

I'm listening to the radio while I make the fillings and the frosting. I've got it on that cheesy Delilah station. Although I find her normally soothing voice rather grating right now, the music tends to be on the side of sappy and that's all I feel like listening to. It reminds me of high school when I found out my crush was dating another girl. I think I listened to "My Heart Will Go On" by Celine Dion about one hundred times.

Oh, joy of joys. And now on Delilah, because karma truly has a sense of humor, some guy named Tony is sending out a dedication to his girlfriend who's far away, and he knows "they will be together soon." Really, Tony? Will you? And even if you are, will it all work out? Don't be so frickin' naive, Tony.

There's a leftover chocolate chip cookie in the walk-in, calling my name.

~*~

I get up early Friday morning to go to the bakery. Today Jared arrives. I'm sort of freaking out, honestly. Every time I think about it, my heart races a little. Has he cooled off? Have I cooled off? I don't feel very cooled off, myself.

I can hear arguing as I make my way back to the kitchen from the front. Patti and Debbie are already at it this morning. I wonder what the argument is today. Yesterday they were arguing over whether okra was a fruit or a vegetable. We had to look it up. Well, Debbie and I did. Patti "knew all along." Apparently, it's a fruit, which is what Patti said it was. How dumb of us to question a Southern lady's knowledge of okra.

As I walk to the back, something sparkly under one of the tables toward the front of the store catches my eye. I squat down to get a closer look. It's a hair clip, a silvery, butterfly hair clip. I pick it up and take it into the kitchen with me.

"Debbie, I think you dropped this," I say as I walk into the back and hand the clip over to Debbie. I knew exactly who it belonged to. What surprises me is that no one found it the night before when we were cleaning up. Maybe we need a checklist to make sure we are getting everything clean before we close up.

I glance over at Debbie. A bright red flush starts from her neck and travels quickly up to the top of her forehead.

"I, uh, I must . . . I think it came out when I was cleaning," she says, stumbling over her words.

I scrunch my face at her, squinting. "I'm not accusing you of anything. I just thought you would want it back."

"Yes. I mean, no. I didn't think you were accusing me. Sorry," she mumbles. She puts the clip in the pocket of her apron and goes back to making dough for what will probably be cinnamon rolls.

"There ya go again, getting all flustered over somethin'," Patti says, her big blonde hair bouncing as she shakes her head at Debbie. "What is with you these days?"

I look over at Debbie because I've been wondering the same thing about the blushing all of the time, the weird mumbling, and the talking to herself. The other day I caught her dancing some sort of one-sided waltz in the walk-in cooler. There is definitely something strange going on.

"Nothing is with me," Debbie says defensively.

"Well then stop acting like there is," Patti says, pointing a long, bony finger in her direction.

Debbie makes some sort of hmph sound and mutters a couple of things under her breath. She starts the large KitchenAid mixer. The noise covers up anything else Patti might have to say.

I get to work on the croissants. The goal today is to keep myself busy until Jared gets here, which I don't even know when that is. Normally I'd know this information. I should text him and find out.

No, I must be strong. I'm not entirely sure what I'm being strong for. Oh, I'm so confused by everything. Wearing big-girl panties sucks. My own brain is pushing and pulling me from one thought to another. I can't even bring myself to have a full and complete thought on the matter. Not one that makes me feel better, at least.

Nothing is making me feel better. Not even chocolate.

~*~

The bell chimes and I look up, which I've done at least a hundred times today, hoping that the person walking through the door is Jared. But it hasn't been him so far. He's being such a weenie about this whole thing. That's right, I said weenie. He's supposed to walk through the door and over to me, pick me up in his arms, and carry me out while the song "Love Lift Us Up Where We Belong" plays in the background.

Clearly, I'm still envisioning a chick flick ending to all of this.

He said he would be my date at the rehearsal dinner, so I guess I'll see him then. At least I hope I'll see him. So far, Jared has always shown up when he said he would.

But I'm not sure about this Jared — the one who needed to "cool off" and is taking his own stupid time doing it. I feel like kicking something.

I decide to abandon all hope that he will come to the bakery, so I head to the back and start working on the filling and the frosting for Anna's cake. Patti is in the back working on gum paste flowers for the décor.

"Ya think you've got enough fillin' there, darlin'?" Patti says, gesturing toward the middle tier of Anna's cake that I just mindlessly piled filling on. It's slopping over the sides.

"Crap!" I yell as I start scooping off as much as I can. I grab a spatula and clean up the sides. If this cake turns out, it will be a miracle. I've been absentmindedly making it. Neither my brain nor my heart, has been in it.

Anna is most certainly going to notice. She'll notice a hair out of place for this wedding. She's paid way too much attention to detail. I envision her saying something like "You've ruined my cake and my entire wedding! How could you?" I'm not sure how a cake can ruin the entire wedding, but Jared not showing up was going to ruin the seating chart, so I'm betting a botched cake would be way worse.

Of course, everything is so up in the air right now with Jared, I might actually be ruining the cake and the seating chart after all.

I hear the door chime, but I'm in the kitchen so I'm unable to look, as I've obsessively been doing all day. There's no point anyway. I've given up hope.

"Julia, someone is here to see you," Debbie says, raising her eyebrows. I know immediately who's here, because she gives me the same eyebrow raise every time.

It's Jared. He's here. Why do I feel like I'm going to throw up all of a sudden? It's just that I've spent the last five days completely building up this moment, and most of the time in a fairy-tale kind of way. Who could possibly live up to that?

I wipe my hands on a towel and take a couple of deep breaths.

I walk out of the back of the kitchen and into the bright sunlit front of the bakery. The lunch rush is over and a few stragglers are still sitting in the dining area.

"Hi, Julia," says someone who's *not* Jared.

"Paul?" I ask, totally confused. What is Brown's new brother-in-law doing here?

"Yeah, Paul," he says, pointing awkwardly at himself.

"What are you doing here?" I say a little crasser than I mean to. "I mean, how are you?" I try to recover, albeit poorly.

"I'm doing good," he says, apparently oblivious to my crassness. "I was just down the street and thought I'd pop in."

"Well," I shake my head to try to get myself out of the disappointment that he's not Jared, "I'm glad you did." I give him a smile and hope that it doesn't look too forced.

"Can I get you something?" I ask, motioning toward the nearly empty display case behind me. "Sorry, the lunch rush wiped us out."

"What about one of those?" Paul says, pointing to a massive chocolate cookie, the only one still left by the register. It's wrapped in cellophane, with a Julia's Bakery sticker slapped on the middle. I love those stickers. It makes my heart ache slightly when I see them wadded up in the trashcan. Surprisingly, all anyone ever cares about is what is inside the wrapper, not my beautiful label with my bakery logo on it.

"Of course." I smile. This time it's genuine and not forced. It's good to see Paul—in an awkward, I-don't-know-why-you're-here way, but good nonetheless.

I walk over to the counter near the register, grab the cookie, and hand it to him.

"What do I owe you?" he asks, reaching for his wallet.

"No," I hold my hand out toward the wallet as he pulls it out of his back pocket. "Don't worry about it. It's on the house."

"Really?" he says holding up the cookie that's practically the size of his face.

"I insist."

"Well, then okay," he gives me a big, dazzling, smile. If my ever-growing annoyance with Jared wasn't causing me to hate all men at this moment, I'd probably appreciate it more than I do. Right now, it's just an obviously dazzling smile and that is all.

"Care to share it with me?" he asks, tilting his head at an empty, two-person table that he's standing next to.

"Um," I say, not really sure. I have things I should be doing, but maybe sitting down with Paul for a few minutes would get my mind off of everything, even for a small while. "Okay," I say and take a seat.

"So what are you baking?" he asks, gesturing toward my chest.

"Huh?" I say, and then peer down at my flour-covered apron, most of the flour in my chest region. There's a smudge of frosting, or possibly filling, on there as well. Lovely. "Oh, I'm making my sister's wedding cake, and apparently it's all over me."

He grins. "Your sister?"

"Yep. My baby sister is getting married. I get the pleasure of making the cake." I make sure the word pleasure oozes with sarcasm.

"Ah. I see," he says, as he starts ripping open the plastic wrap on the cookie. He's careful not to rip the label on the front, which I find odd but also appreciate at the same time. "When is the wedding?"

"Tomorrow. I'll be glad when it's over." I sit back in my chair, attempting to relax a little.

"Oh, right, you're the one who hates being in weddings." He winks at me as he breaks off a small piece of cookie and puts it in his mouth. He breaks off another piece and hands it to me but I decline. I've had quite a bit of sweets today, I think. Eating my feelings has only proven to give me a stomachache.

"As I recall, you hate being in weddings as well," I say, cocking my head to the side, accusingly.

"Yes, you would be correct in that recollection," he says after he swallows the bite of cookie. "I don't envy you in the slightest."

"I don't envy myself," I say and half smile.

"So how does the whole cake making process go?" he asks, breaking off another piece of cookie.

"You really want to know?" I scrunch my face, confused.

"Sure. I've always been interested in the inner workings of a bakery," he says, looking around the bakery.

"Well, I have to go and finish it. You can come watch while you finish that cookie." I gesture toward the cookie that looks barely touched, even though he's eaten quite a bit.

"It could take me a decade to get through this." He holds it up so that it covers his face.

I laugh. A *real* laugh. Not the fake kind I've been doing for the majority of the week. It feels good.

"Okay, come on back," I say, getting up from my chair.

He follows me to the back and I show him around the kitchen, introducing him to Patti and Debbie. I get started on the cake and he leans up against the counter not far from me, watching me as I work. Out of the corner of my eye, I catch glances from Debbie and Patti, who both look none-to-pleased by the handsome stranger that has invaded the kitchen, as if his very presence means I'm cheating on Jared.

I'm not cheating on Jared. What I'm doing is biding my time until I see him, whenever that is. It's helpful that Paul just happened to be around to help me through this rough day that I'm having. It's a welcome distraction, even though I was initially disappointed that it was him that came through my bakery door and not Jared.

The conversation stays light and easy-going with Paul. We discuss the bakery and business, and he tells me what he does for a living (graphic design, which explains the way he handled the label on the cookie with such regard — graphic designers appreciate graphic design).

Debbie and Patti pipe in every now and then with questioning that sounds more like detective work ("And how do *you* know *our* Julia?") rather than polite conversation. Luckily, Paul doesn't notice.

I show him my technique for frosting. There is actual real buttercream frosting on this cake. None of that fondant nastiness. I can do fondant, but I don't like it.

"So, why buttercream frosting?" Paul asks as he tries to scoop a finger-full off the side of the mixing bowl. I'm able to snatch the bowl away before he's successful. He's got a lot of nerve trying to stick his finger into my mixing bowl. We barely know each other.

"Because it's amazeballs," I say, not meaning to say it. It just comes out.

"Um, who says 'amazeballs' in their thirties?" he asks, still trying to reach for the bowl to sample some of the frosting.

"I believe you don't have to worry about it until you're in your forties," I say, grabbing a clean spoon from the adjacent counter. I spoon out a good amount and give it to him.

"Thank you." He takes the spoon out of my hand. "You must have gotten that article from Brown as well."

"Yes, I did," I say, picking up a spatula. I spoon out a large amount of the buttercream and dollop it on top of the cake. "I should have figured she would send it to everyone."

"I think she's single-handedly trying to eradicate the word," he says between licks of the frosting.

"Well, amazeballs wasn't actually a part of my vocabulary until she sent me the article, so the joke is on her."

He snickers at that and then tries to swipe another spoon full of frosting, but I'm able to ward him off.

Before I know it, Patti and Debbie have left for the day and it's time to go home and get ready for the rehearsal dinner. Time flies when you have someone to distract you from your real life, I guess.

"Well, thanks for the cake-making lesson," Paul says as we walk out the front door of the bakery. "I don't know if I'll ever look at a cake in the same way again."

"How did you look at a cake before?" I ask with a smirk.

"With awe and admiration, of course. Now I know it's just a baked slab of pastry stuck together with filling and frosting slopped all over it." He smirks.

"That is not how I just made that cake," I deadpan.

He nudges me with his shoulder to demonstrate that he's joking around as I lock the deadbolt that keeps my bakery somewhat safe. As if that really keeps it safe. I mean anyone could throw a brick through the glass and break right in, but for some reason that deadbolt makes me feel like the bakery is protected. I've even gone all OCD and had to check it five times before I knew it was locked for certain. Luckily that doesn't happen all that often to me. It's super annoying when it does.

"So are you still with that guy?" he asks as I turn toward him.

"Huh?" I ask, taken aback by the question.

"That guy, at the wedding. The PDA one?"

"Oh yes, that guy. Um, yeah, I'm still seeing him. I think," I say, staring down at the concrete sidewalk, trying to keep my face from blushing after the PDA comment. It doesn't work.

"You think?" he asks, obviously hearing me even though I thought I had said it under my breath.

I shake my head. "It's complicated."

Ugh, did I really just say that? I hate it when people say that. I feel like I've just publicly changed my Facebook relationship status.

"Complicated," he states. "What's so complicated?"

"Well, it's just that," I look down at the sidewalk again, feeling awkward. "You know what? I don't feel like talking about it," I say and then give him a closed-mouth smile.

"Gotcha." He nods once. "Well let me know if your status ever changes to no longer being in that complicated relationship." He smiles. Not smirks. Just a nice, genuine, teeth-filled grin, and nice teeth, to boot.

"Um," I say, not sure what to say to that. This is the second time that Paul has pseudo-hit on me. Since Jared is my one and only boyfriend and has been for the past ten months, I'm not sure how to respond.

"See you around, Julia," Paul says without giving me a chance to even retort.

With a small wave, he walks away. I stand there, slack-jawed, with what I'm sure is a shocked expression on my face. I've had two encounters with Paul and both times it's ended with me caught completely off guard and speechless.

It's been a while since I felt off my guard and speechless. In fact, it was about a year ago, in an office building not far from here.

Spectraltech. Jared. That feels like ages ago.

Chapter 22

I've never been able to figure out why we have to have a rehearsal dinner. I'm totally okay with rehearsing the wedding, and then just going home and going to bed. But no, tonight there will be a rehearsal for the actual wedding, then a dinner, and then instead of going home to my bed, I have to go to a hotel suite with Anna, my mom, and the rest of the bridesmaids, so we can braid each other's hair and have pillow fights. I've never had to spend the night with the bride and a bunch of giddy bridesmaids before, so I have no idea what will happen. I truly hope it's just sleep because that is what I need.

"Julia!" Anna yells from behind me. "You're going way too fast. Cut the music!" she yells to my mom, who's playing a classical piece from a portable stereo. "Julia." I turn to see her walking toward me. "You're not staying with the rhythm of the music. Let me show you one more time."

She's in full controlling mode. I can see the madness behind her eyes. She's stressed and tired. She should be happy and enjoying this moment in her life, but instead she seems on the verge of a nervous breakdown. I kind of know how she feels.

I can hear the tired frustration in her voice. This is the second time she's stopped everything to show me how to walk down the aisle. I can't help it. She picked the hardest song to walk to. Or perhaps I was not meant for matrimony. I probably would care more if I actually cared, but I don't, not today, at least. Jared is supposed to come to the rehearsal dinner, and I have no idea if he will be there. All I know is that the longer I go without hearing from him, the angrier I get at the whole situation. The fact that he can just shut me out, and easily do so since he's a zillion miles away, is just one more reason why I see that long-distance relationships have no hope. My stomach is tied in knots, so obviously I have much more important things to think about than whether I can walk down the aisle in a perfect march.

It also doesn't help that I'm walking toward *Jooonathon* with his perfectly coiffed hair and tailored business suit. He looks smug standing up at the front next to his groomsmen, waiting for all of us to walk down the aisle. He's done nothing for this wedding, and now he gets to stand up at the front while the rest of us have to do the walking. How fitting.

I try my very best the next time, only because I don't want to do it again, and because tomorrow I'll be doing this in front of bunches of people. And if I go too fast or fall flat on my face (which is highly likely in the shoes I'm wearing — Tori Burch, my butt), that will only add to the shame of my being the eldest of the Ray Dorning family and still not married.

Marriage. Love. I spit on all of it.

I make it down the aisle, this time without being

stopped by Anna. Either I did it correctly, or it was not terrible enough to be stopped. I'm okay with either reason.

I stand up at the front and watch as the other bridesmaids come down the aisle, one by one. Jonathon's parents are seated in the front row, both carrying smug looks. What is with this family? It's as if they all think they are the best family ever. Does Anna really want to marry into a family like this?

Finally, it's Anna's turn to rehearse walking down the aisle. My dad escorts her to the back of the chapel and they start walking perfectly to the music.

I hope this doesn't take too long. It's not a full rehearsal, of course. No vows. Those will be saved until tomorrow.

Now that I've got a perfect view of Anna's face as she walks down the aisle, she looks pretty pale. Is she having second thoughts? Will I have to do a pep talk like I did with Brown? I'm not sure I could be so peppy with Anna. I think I'd end up convincing her to run away.

"Stop!" Anna yells from halfway down the aisle. Her voice is loud, but wobbly. "Just stop," she says more quietly as she unhooks her arm from my dad's and sits down in the pew that they were just about to pass. My mother cuts the music.

"Anna?" Jonathon says as he walks quickly over to her, with me following him. "Anna, are you okay?"

"Yes," she says quietly. "Yes, I'm just light-headed all of a sudden."

"Everyone stand back," my dad says because a bunch of us are surrounding her at this point. "I think she needs some air."

"I'm fine," Anna says, her voice a little less wobbly. "Just give me a second, okay?"

Everyone gives her space except for Jonathon, who's sitting next to her, holding her hand and whispering something in her ear. His other hand is caressing the back of her hair. I'm standing in the aisle, just next to the pew, but far enough away as not to crowd her.

I knew it. She took on too much. How can he just sit there and try to calm her down when he's the cause of all of it? I have half a mind to say something. But just as I go to open my mouth, my mother comes in with a glass of water and some crackers and gives them to Anna. She eats and drinks, and almost immediately some color starts to come back to her face.

"This is ridiculous," I whisper to my mother, who looks wrought with concern. "She's been spread too thin."

"I know. But it's not our place to say anything," she whispers back to me.

I roll my eyes. That's how we Dornings handle most things, just roll over and take it. I'm sick of being that way. I'm taking this whole long-distance thing from Jared; I'm watching Anna take this whole wedding on by herself without saying anything. It's not right.

Anna stands up and declares that she's ready and we all go to our places. Luckily, she does not make the bridesmaids walk down the aisle again, we just start from the part when she comes in. I don't know if I have it in me to do it right one more time, and if I do, I need to save it for tomorrow.

Except for the concerned glances everyone keeps giving to Anna, the rehearsal goes on without any more drama. Anna appears less pale as they go through the steps with the wedding officiant.

Once we've finished with the wedding rehearsal, we all load up in cars and head over to the restaurant for the dinner part of this rehearsal. This is the part where Jared is supposed to join me, only I have no idea if he will. And if he does, what will we say? I'm at the point of lashing out at him or something. I can feel myself riling up by the second. My anger with Jonathon and worry for Anna definitely pushed me further with the riling. My stomach is so full of pukey butterflies and my mind is such a jumbled mess of thoughts that I'm unable to talk during the car ride. I just sit in the backseat of my dad's car and listen to the talk radio that is blasting through the speakers. Oh, Rush Limbaugh, I haven't missed you at all.

A chill runs down my spine as we get out at the valet and file into the restaurant. It's not a particularly chilly night; in fact, more the opposite, but it feels chilly all of a sudden to me.

Walking into the restaurant lobby, I look around, frantically hoping that Jared is here. I probably seem a little freakish to anyone who might be watching me. I'm past the point of caring. I've moved to full-blown crazy person in my mind. No one is paying attention to me anyway. Everyone is crowding around Anna, still concerned for her as she reassures them that she's fine. Jonathon has had her in close proximity since the episode at the church.

In my peripheral vision, I see some movement in the corner of the lobby and I sweep my head around. Sitting in the corner, in a large, tall-back leather chair is Jared. He's here. Jared's here. I had thought that seeing him would put a halt to all the thoughts that have been racing through my brain, but instead, the sight of him breaks my heart into a million stupid pieces.

He stands up from the chair he's sitting in and starts walking toward me.

"Hello, Jared." My dad stops him before he can make his way to me. He shakes Jared's hand with a firm grasp and pats him on the back with his free one. "Good to see you. Where have you been these days?"

Jared gives me a strange look. "I've been in New York. Didn't Julia tell you?" My dad shakes his head because I haven't told him. I haven't told anyone yet, except Debbie and Patti. "I've taken a permanent job there."

"Oh," my dad angles slightly toward me, "no, she hasn't told me." He keeps shaking Jared's hand, taking turns looking at him and then at me. It gets awkward, actually. "Well, we'll catch up later. Glad you could make it," he finally says, relinquishing Jared from his grip.

Jared gives him a quick nod and then walks over to me.

"Hello," I say in a stubborn sounding voice.

"Hey," he says back.

So now is the part where he takes me in his arms and says he can't live without me, and that he was miserable not talking to me this past week, and thereby squelching the angry fire that is burning inside of me.

I swallow hard. He doesn't do any of that. We just stand there, staring at each other.

Someone announces that we can all go back to the dining room, but my legs are rooted to the ground where I am, and food does not sound even remotely appetizing.

"Let's talk," he finally says, taking me by the hand and leading me outside.

I follow along, but not before I make eye contact with Anna and she gives me a questioning look. I just shrug my shoulders and mouth to her that I'll be right back.

Jared leads me to a bench outside the restaurant. Letting go of my hand, he motions for me to have a seat. But I don't want to sit down. I need to stand. It just feels like I should be standing. So he follows suit and stays standing. He turns and faces me.

"Julia, I've had some time to think and—"

"I'm so glad you've had time to think while you've left me completely hanging over here," I interrupt him.

"Well, what did you expect me to do?" His voice gets a little stern, but not louder. "You practically freaked out when I hadn't talked to you for one day. I thought we were doing just fine."

I shake my head. "It wasn't just the one day, Jared. It was the slow progression over the time since you left. I've tried to think positively, that this could work. But how can it?"

"Where is all of this coming from?" he asks, frustration in his tone.

"From many places, starting with the fact that you didn't even care what I thought and just took that job in New York." I glance down at the sidewalk, tears stinging my eyes.

"Julia, I thought we worked that out? I told you I didn't have much choice. I really wish there was another option."

"Do you?" I ask, not convinced that he believes that. "Did you even try to look in Denver?" A single tear escapes and leaks down to my chin.

He doesn't say anything, answering with his silence. "It's not that simple," is all he says.

"I don't know if I can do this, Jared," my mouth says, not consulting my brain first. And there it is, the plain truth. I really *don't* know if I can do this.

"What can't you do? Be in a relationship with me?" His face flashes red.

"It's not that. I just don't think this long-distance thing will work." I look down at the floor. I'm not holding back, I'm saying what I feel. This is not how I usually deal with things. It feels weird, but also sort of validating.

"Jules, I love you. We can make this work. I know we

can." He reaches out to take my hand, but I shake him off.

"I wish I felt like it could work, but there's just no end in sight. I don't know if I can invest all this time trying, only to realize it won't work because you'll be living your life in New York and I'll be living my life here."

"New York won't be forever, Jules," he says, his eyes searching my face, pleading with me.

"Okay, so how long then? Give me some sort of ballpark guess," I say, hoping that he might have an answer, even though I already know he doesn't.

"I can't do that," he says, which is exactly what I was expecting.

"I don't think that's enough for me," I say quietly, looking down at the floor. Am I really saying what I think I'm saying? Is this what I truly want?

"What are you saying then?" His face red with anger. I don't know if I've ever seen him this mad.

I pause, swallowing deeply, taking in everything that has just been said by both of us. I've told him my thoughts, and he has not said anything to make me think otherwise.

"I guess I'm saying that I think maybe we should break things off now, before it gets messy and even worse later on."

He just stands there staring at me. "Don't do this," he says, finally.

"I'm sorry," I say through the tears now pouring down. "I don't see any other way."

He looks me up and down and then, without saying a word, he turns and walks toward the parking lot. I just watch him. Part of me wants to chase after him and tell him never mind and that I'm an idiot. But the other part of me knows that this is a lost cause, and that if Brown and Anna were here, they would tell me just that. It's better to end it now. Pull the Band-Aid off now.

I hear a car door slam and then seconds later, tires peel out of the parking lot.

Did I really just break up with Jared? I should feel the slightest bit of closure, like I did the right thing. But I don't feel like that at all. I feel like my heart is literally broken, and all I want to do right now is curl up in a ball and cry. Forever.

Chapter 23

The cold water I just splashed on my face does nothing to tone down the large, red blotches that dot my complexion. I look like a clown. Actually, I take that back. A clown looks better than I do right now.

I've been in the bathroom for the past fifteen minutes, trying to talk myself into bucking up and going into the rehearsal dinner without buckling at the knees and falling to the floor in a ridiculous, overly dramatic fashion. I really want to do that. But I must fight my drama instincts and be strong for Anna. I can do this for her. I can't take away anything from this wedding that she has worked so hard for. I will not make this about me.

I sniff hard. I open the little hand bag I brought with me and pull out the pressed powder I'd normally have left at home, but since I was running late tonight, I had put makeup on in my dad's car on the way. That certainly worked out to my benefit. I put powder all over my face. I look a little better, but there is nothing I can do about my red, bloodshot eyes. The restaurant has dim lighting. I'll just have to hope no one can tell.

In order to make it through tonight, I'm going to have to avoid thinking about what just transpired outside fifteen minutes ago. I'm going to have to push it out of my mind and make it through this night for Anna. I will not even think the name Jared.

Crap, I just thought it. And double-crap, there're the waterworks again. I blot the tears away quickly with a tissue. I can do this. Well, I probably can't, but I'm going to try my hardest.

The room that is reserved for Anna's rehearsal dinner is in the back of the dining room. After taking many deep breaths, I work my way back there, taking the longest way possible to give me even more time to pull it together. It's definitely dim in the restaurant, but I can see that the lights are brighter in the back room where everyone is gathered, celebrating my sister and her betrothed.

The room is a nice size with tables put together to make a big square. Everyone is sitting around it enjoying appetizers and drinks. I see a spot by Jenny and Lennon and work my way over to it, trying not to make eye contact with anyone.

"Where's Jared?" Anna asks as I take my seat next to Lennon. Just his name makes my eyes immediately well up. I blink back the tears as fast as I can.

"He had to go home," I say, trying desperately not to look her in the eyes. "He wasn't feeling well." Good cover-up, Julia. Now I can use that same excuse tomorrow when he doesn't show up and ruins the whole seating chart. I'm still not sure how that all works.

"Oh, no! I hope he feels better for tomorrow," she says, of course making Jared's fake sickness all about her big day. I welcome it, though. I need Anna to be so caught up in the glow of wedding bliss that she won't notice my

Debbie-downer facial expressions, blotchy red face, and the tears threatening to spill at any time. I never thought her spoiled ways would become useful to me.

The server comes by and against my better judgment (a.k.a., the angel on my shoulder), I have him pour me a glass of the champagne everyone else is drinking. Not a great idea. Alcohol is a depressant after all, and I'm pretty sure I don't need any more of that. But I need to feel numb if I'm going to make it through this night without completely breaking down. Even with warning signs in my mind flashing "BAD IDEA! BAD IDEA!" I gulp down my first glass without taking a breath and then signal for the server, who hadn't gotten far away, to give me a refill.

After the second glass, I'm already starting to feel a little light in the head. I think I can count how many times I've drank on one hand. Actually, I can count it on two fingers, so twice. I had a bad experience both times that I'd rather not repeat. But how I'm feeling right now, this numbingly giddy feeling, is just what the doctor ordered. The server comes by again with an open bottle, ready to pour, and I cover my glass signaling for him to not refill mine. I may be starting to feel tipsy, but I'm not going to push it.

Jonathon stands up from where he's sitting at the head of the table and raises his glass. Oh yes, words from Jonathon, just what I need.

"I'd just like to thank everyone for coming tonight," he says, looking ever-so-smug as his eyes move around the room. "Anna and I wouldn't want to spend this night with anyone else."

"Here, here!" one of the groomsmen cheers and everyone joins in.

"I'd also like to thank Anna," Jonathon says after everyone calms down. "She put this all together with very little help from anyone."

I snort. Everyone looks at me. I didn't mean to do it, it just came out. Dang alcohol.

"I'm sorry, Julia," Jonathon says. "Did you have something you wanted to say?"

"Um, no. No, I don't," I say, grabbing a shrimp appetizer and shoving it in my mouth. Everyone's focus goes back to Jonathon.

"Anyway," Jonathon goes back to his smug gaze. "I just want to give kudos to Anna for all of her hard work."

I snort again. I swear it was unintentional, mostly. All eyes are back on me.

"I'm sorry, Julia," Jonathon says once again, "do you have a problem?"

"No, I don't," I say. But inside me something is rumbling like I've never felt before, and it's not indigestion. It's anger . . . mixed with champagne. So, anger champagne. "Actually, yes. I do have something to say."

"Julia," my mother says from the other side of the large table.

"It's fine, Katherine. Let her talk." Jonathon waves a hand at my mom, keeping his eyes on me the entire time. Meanwhile, Anna isn't saying anything. She's just sitting there looking dumbfounded. That seems to be the general look around the table.

"Okay, fine. I guess we're doing this," I say half under my breath. "I was just thinking that here we are, celebrating this wedding for you and Anna, and you get to be all calm and just show up while Anna has been running around doing everything." I spit out the word "everything" as harshly as I can. "She almost fainted tonight. She needed help."

"Enough, Julia." Anna finally pipes in in squeaky

tones. She gets squeaky when she's angry.

"No, Anna. This needs to be said," I say, standing up from my chair.

Whoa, apparently heartbreak plus champagne equals an angry Julia. But I feel something different than just anger, more like kick-butt. I could totally kick somebody's rear right now.

"You think you can just waltz in here and marry my sister when she has been doing all of the work and you have done nothing? Not one person in your family has lifted a finger for this wedding. Wait," I pause dramatically. "I take that back. Your mother," I point at his mom who's sitting to the left of Jonathon, looking quite shell-shocked. "She wrote a check for this dinner. Oh, and the flowers. So I guess a finger was barely lifted."

"That's enough, Julia," my mom says, angrily. "This isn't the place or time."

She's right. I do realize that. Even in my champagne/heartbroken stupor, I know this is neither the time nor the place. But even knowing that, I can't help myself.

"You have no idea what you're talking about," Jonathon says, glancing back and forth between Anna and me.

"I don't? Well then what's your rebuttal, Mr. Big-time Lawyer?"

"JULIA!" a bunch of people yell at once. I'm not even sure who all yelled my name.

"Anna didn't need my help," Jonathon begins his rebuttal. "I offered, believe me. I offered so many times. But she would just tell me she had it all handled." He furrows his brow, confused. "Anna?" He looks to his bride-to-be.

"I . . . I didn't want to bother you." She shrugs, trying

to feign innocence. "I knew you were busy with work."

"But you turned my mom down when she repeatedly offered to help." He gestures toward his mom. "She doesn't even work. She would have loved to help." Jonathon's face starts to turn a crimson shade.

The tension in the room is palpable. I don't know if anyone is even breathing at this point.

"You said you had it handled," Jonathon says almost timidly.

"Jonathon," Anna stands up. "I did have it handled." She motions with her hands around the room that she set up, that she ordered all of the food and drinks for. "I got everything done in time."

"But," he says, a confused expression on his face, as if he's going over previous conversations they had had in his mind, "you did it all by yourself, even when I offered to help. Even when I said I wanted to . . ." He trails off, searching the room with his eyes. Then Jonathon's eyes widen, as if a light bulb has gone on in his head, like he's come to some huge realization. "Excuse me," he says as he hurriedly walks out the door.

The silence in the room is deafening. What have I done?

"You." Anna points at me, speaking in mostly psycho tones. "You, with your big mouth. What the hell is wrong with you, Julia?" She throws the napkin that she had been holding onto the table and storms out of the room after Jonathon.

We all sit in silence, each of us taking in what just happened. After what feels like the fiftieth glance in my direction, I gaze down at my hands in my lap, the fire in my face burning to the tips of my ears. What have I done? I'm such an idiot.

"Julia," my mom finally says, and I look up. "Go fix

this. Now."

I know that tone. It's the tone we would get as children when my mom had gotten to her breaking point and wanted something done without further question. Further questioning only led to bad things.

I stand up from my chair and do a whole new walk of shame that I've never done, out the door of the rehearsal dinner that I pretty much ruined, and off to try and fix something I have no idea how I can fix.

I've really messed things up this time.

Chapter 24

I walk out of the dining room and into the lobby, keeping my eyes peeled for Anna and Jonathon, but they are nowhere to be found.

I walk outside into the night air and spy them standing at the exact same spot where I just ended things with Jared. Seriously, karma? There's like a hundred other places they could have gone.

"Anna, I don't know if I can trust you now," I hear Jonathon say as I get closer to them.

"Jonathon, please. Please, just listen to me," Anna pleads, which is a tone from Anna I'm pretty sure I've never heard.

"Um, hey guys," I say weirdly. This is one of those situations where no intro is really appropriate. Variations like "What are you two up to?" or "What's going on over here?" just seem inappropriate. "Hey guys" ranked up there too, but I was going off the cuff. There wasn't a lot of time to think of an intro.

"What are you doing here, Julia?" Anna practically

spits my name, total hatred filling her voice. "Get out of here. You've done enough."

"I'm really sorry, I had no idea—"

"You had no idea that you would ruin my wedding?" she says, walking toward me.

I crouch back. I'm pretty sure she wants to slap me. I don't blame her. I'd probably want to slap me.

"The wedding's not ruined," I say, trying to calm her down.

"It's not?" She's sounding shrill at this point. "Well, then tell Jonathon that. He's just called off the whole thing."

With that, she makes a rather loud wailing sound. She buries her face into her hands and quickly walks away.

Jonathon folds his arms and looks out into the parking lot in a very leave-me-alone stance.

I ignore it, of course. "Why did you call it off?" I walk closer to him. He braces himself as if I'm about to slap him. I wasn't going to, but the thought sounds a bit appealing now that I've had it.

"Because. I can't trust her," Jonathon says simply.

"She planned the wedding without your help. Why can't you trust her?" What a strange thing to lose trust over. Jonathon just gets weirder by the second.

"Because this isn't about her planning the wedding by herself. She didn't want the help. I didn't see it, probably because I didn't want to. She clearly has control issues, and I don't want someone who has to control everything." His arms unfold and drop to his sides. He looks defeated and sad . . . and human. I feel a ping of sadness for him, which feels weird for me to have. I've spent too much time feeling annoyed by him.

"Jonathon." I stand a little closer to him, putting a hand on his upper arm, which also feels weird. I'll do what it takes to fix this. I must. "You love her, don't you?"

"Why do you care?" he asks me, shaking me off with a jerk of his arm.

"What do you mean? She's my sister," I say, scrunching my face at him. What a stupid question.

"I mean, you don't even like me, so why do you care whether I love your sister or not?"

"I li . . . li . . . like you," I stutter out. That was hard.

"No, you don't," he says flatly.

I'm having a hard time controlling the liquid courage that is racing through my veins because it's making me want to say things I'd never say. "I think I just need to spend more time with you," I say, which is a much tamer version of what I was thinking of saying.

He just stares at me. So I feel the need to defend myself. "It's just that you're always bragging about the cases you've won."

"I've never been a bragger," he says, appearing completely appalled at the notion.

"But you're always talking about your cases."

"That was Anna. She's always talking about my cases, not me."

That gives me pause. This entire time, did I think Jonathon was the one bragging when it was actually Anna? Anna doing the bragging does make much more sense.

Thoughts and memories of my time with Jonathon suddenly start filing into my brain. "Oh, my gosh . . ." I trail off, so many things coming to light. It was Anna the whole time. Anna did the bragging. Anna wanted to do the wedding without any help. It was Anna. Not Jonathon.

This makes me suddenly realize that I have no idea who Jonathon is. I was only seeing Anna's version of him.

Maybe he doesn't even go by *Jooonathon* and that was Anna too.

"Hi," I reach out my hand to shake his. "I'm Julia, and you are?"

"Are you drunk?" Jonathon asks, staring at me as if I've lost my mind.

"Slightly. But that's not the point. I've just realized that I don't know you at all. So, hi," I say again, holding out my hand. He reluctantly reaches out and shakes it. "I'm Julia, and you are?"

"Jonathon," he says, barely playing along.

"It's nice to meet you, Jonathon. Can I call you Jon?"

"No," he says firmly. Okay, so that part wasn't just Anna.

"Okay, well Jonathon, I look forward to getting to know you better after you're part of the family." I smile sincerely.

He looks at me and I feel like I'm seeing him in a whole new light. I had so many things wrong. I mean, he still has a smug face, but then again, so did his whole family. Maybe it's not actual smugness, but just a family trait? So much to learn.

"Didn't you hear your sister? I've called off the wedding," he says, his eyes shiny. I pray silently that he won't break down. I'd have no idea what to do.

I put a hand on his arm again. I must be one of those touchy drinkers. I hate that. I seriously should never, ever drink again. I leave my hand there anyway, and this time he doesn't shake it off. "Jonathon, do you love my sister?" I ask him once more.

"I don't know any more," he sniffs. Oh, please don't cry.

"Really? You can just all of a sudden fall out of love with her?" I squint, unbelieving.

"Of course I love her," he says after a slight pause. The tearing up appears to have stopped, although his eyes are still fairly shiny.

"Then you have to love everything about her. Yes, Anna can be a little controlling, but that's what makes Anna, well, Anna. Honestly, her heart is in the right place. As controlling as it all seemed with the wedding, she does like to be in charge, but I know she was also trying to be helpful to you. She loves you. I've never seen her so in love before. If you truly do love her, then you have to take her with the good and the bad. And she has many good qualities."

"Like?" he asks, raising his shoulders.

"Like . . . like . . ." I trail off. Oh, gosh, why am I having a hard time answering this? "Well for one thing, she gives great advice." Hey! That was true. "And . . . and she has an incredible sense of style and loves to go shopping." Okay, so that was probably not a quality I should be using to convince him. This isn't working. I love her as my sister, anyway. It's different. "Why don't you tell me what qualities attracted you to her in the first place?"

"Well," he peers up at the sky as he thinks. "She has a great sense of humor and a beautiful face. And when she gets really excited about something she has an almost childlike excitement that is so . . . so infectious." His expression lightens up as he talks about her.

"Go on, this is good," I say.

"You're right about the good advice. She's smart. Smarter than she gives herself credit for." He lifts his chin up, a look of pride suddenly washing over him.

"So now," I say, putting my hand on his arm once again, "now what you need to do is figure out if life is better with or without her."

"That's a very good way to look at it," he says, his eyes

brightening even more.

"Yes, a very smart person—smarter than she gives herself credit for, asked me that same question once." A smile spreads across Jonathon's face. I grin back, but then I think about how that advice was about Jared and my happiness fades. And now . . . now I wish I could go back to that time when Anna gave me that advice, to when things were new. The beginning of it all. Life was better with Jared, but it was the separation part that really messed things up.

"Thank you, Julia," Jonathon says. This time it's him that touches my arm.

"You're welcome," I say. "Now go back in there," I jerk my head toward the restaurant, "and save my butt because if this wedding doesn't happen I'm pretty sure it will be on my head."

"The wedding is back on, if Anna will have me," he says. I notice this time when he smiles, it's not as smug as it used to be.

Sheesh, you think you know someone and then you get tipsy, ruin things, and then find out they aren't what you thought they were. How very strange.

The alcohol, and then subsequent drama with Anna and Jonathon that I single-handedly caused, had one positive note. Well, two actually. The first is that I no longer dislike Jonathon, which is a good thing, I think. The second is it helped me to not think about Jared. But now that it's all over, the sadness rushes through me quickly. So quickly that tears instantly sting my eyes.

Maybe some more champagne will help me get through the rest of this night? On second thought, I think I'd best not. Who knows what I'd do next?

Chapter 25

There's a hole . . . in my sock.

But also, there's a hole in my heart. I feel a bit like crawling under a rock and coming out only when I feel better. Which, I'm pretty positive, will be never.

Have I made a huge mistake? Even when I think of calling Jared and telling him that I was just kidding or had a moment of complete insanity, I just know it was best for things to end the way they did. It would have been worse if it happened later.

My heart aches every time I think of how angrily he looked at me last night, which is why I'm trying desperately hard not to think of it. And even though I swore it off the last time, I Googled. I searched "How to stop thinking about someone" and read the first article that popped up. There was some very good advice that I won't be using. It's just too much work. Besides, I don't want him to be out of my head. I just want the pain to go away. Something tells me it will be a while until that happens, if it ever does.

The rest of the dinner was drama free and when I walked back into the dining room, Anna came over and gave me a big (albeit undeserved) hug, for talking some sense into Jonathon. Check me out, I've saved two weddings, first Brown's, now Anna's. I'm like the wedding whisperer. Sure, it was me who ruined Anna's in the first place, but I think we should just focus on the fact that I fixed it.

I made it through the rest of the night without a huge breakdown, which I think was a miracle. I just focused on Anna and tried to be the best maid of honor I could be, after being the absolute worst one. I even participated in the slumber party, although my bed, a box of cookies, and Charlie sounded so much more appealing.

It's been a long time since I was part of a slumber party with a bunch of women, but apparently, it's still the norm to talk about boys and relationships. So that pretty much sucked. I avoided talking about me and luckily no one asked me anything about my love life. They probably just figured I was Anna's sad older sister who has no future.

I couldn't sleep after everyone had snoozed off, so I got up and sneaked out. For some reason home seemed sad and lonely, so I went to my favorite place in the world, my sanctuary, the bakery. I figured I could work more on Anna's cake, saving Patti and Debbie from having to do too much. Really, it was just something to get my mind off of Jared. I've realized, though, that weddings are not exactly the best way to get your mind off of love.

Even though it's a struggle, I make all of my thoughts about the cake. It's turning out beautifully, I must say. I've even made a few gum paste flowers, though Patti has already made all of the ones we need. I just wanted to try it. I thought I was horrible, but either I'm not that bad, or the gods of gum paste were watching out for me because if the flowers had turned out horribly it might have been the straw that broke the camel's back and I'd have completely lost it.

A noise makes me jump, and I nearly knock an entire mixing bowl of icing off the counter. It was the bells jingling from the front door. In my depression coma, could I've forgotten to lock the front door? I've never forgotten before, but there have been a lot of firsts in my life recently.

I must have forgotten because there are now sounds coming from the front of the bakery. Oh, gosh, this is not good. With so many freaky people downtown, this could be seriously bad. I hear more noises coming from the front. I can't make out anything, but I can hear two muffled voices. A man and a woman, it sounds like. I pick up my phone as quietly as possible and get ready to dial 911. I slowly walk to the opposite side of the kitchen, trying carefully to not make a sound, and grab a large butcher knife. Thank goodness I'm in a bakery. There are a lot of items at my disposal to use as weapons.

I carefully walk over to the door that separates the kitchen from the dining room and press my ear to the door. Whatever the intruders are searching for, I don't think they are going to find it here. We have very little cash on hand, especially on Saturdays when the bakery is closed. Plus, any leftovers are donated to a local soup kitchen, so there are only ingredients to steal and, I suppose, expensive equipment. Maybe that's what they're after. Yes, perfect. I've lost my boyfriend and now I'll lose my large KitchenAid. Could this weekend get any worse?

It's quiet. Maybe they've realized there was nothing for them and gone? I can hope.

"Oh, George," a woman says, or rather moans. Okay, so they didn't leave. Crap.

Wait, the woman's voice sounded familiar.

I push the door open ever-so-slightly and peek out. "Oh, Debbie," I hear as the sight unfolds before me.

George. Debbie. Slightly compromising position in my dining room. *My* dining room, where people eat.

So many levels of gross.

I quickly go back into the kitchen. They don't know I'm here, which means if I don't let them know that I'm here the situation could escalate to something that will probably scar my brain for life. I suppose I could go out the back door, but that is an emergency door that opens up into an alleyway that gives me the creeps. Plus, the door will sound a ridiculously loud alarm, giving me away completely. I think I need to signal them that I'm here. But how?

Realizing, rather quickly, that I'm surrounded by things that make loud noises, I start banging kitchen items on the stainless steel table I'm working at. It's too noisy for me to know if it scared them off. I'm not sure I'm willing to try listening for them again because I'm scared of what I might hear.

I don't think this is their first tryst in my bakery, by the looks of things. What if they made it to the back? To the kitchen? I glance around my kitchen. A horrific picture fills my mind. Oh, my poor stainless steel counters. I'll never look at you the same.

"Julia?" From the doorway, a very red-faced Debbie speaks loudly over the noise of the mixing bowl that I'm currently banging on the possibly despoiled stainless steel counter. "What are you doing here?"

"Um, I'm uh, just working on Anna's cake," I say, not wanting to admit that I just saw what I saw. Maybe if I just don't bring it up, neither will she.

George. Debbie. Wait. George and Debbie. Oh, my

229

gosh, George and Debbie! Even though they may possibly have defiled my bakery, I'm suddenly feeling so happy for my friend. She deserves happiness. I just hope George is the man for the job.

"Oh, well that's what I came in for, too," she says easily. Too easily. Although, that might be the real reason she came in, she just decided to let George come with her so they could take advantage of the dining area with no one around. And even though I'm so happy for her, that is still super gross.

"Great," I say a little too brightly, sounding fake. "I guess I will leave you to it, then," I say as I take off my apron and quickly grab my purse. The longer I stay here, the more chance there will be for me to accidentally say something. Something needs to be said, but not right now. Not today.

Oh, my gosh, the sock! And the hair clip! Now I know why she was acting so weird when I asked her about it. I can't wait to tell Jared the reason behind the mysterious sock. Oh, wait. I can't tell him. Maybe I can give him a little time and we can be friends? Maybe the sock story will give me a reason to talk to him?

Gosh, I hope so.

~*~

"You look so pretty, Anna," I say and sniffle. I told her I wouldn't tear up, but I didn't get any sleep last night and so it's going to happen. She's just going to have to deal with it.

"No crying, Julia," she says as she checks herself out in the mirror. "I'll end up crying with you and completely ruin my makeup." She makes an "O" with her mouth and wipes the corners clean of any seeping lip-gloss.

She looks more than pretty, stunning is more like it. But I can't tell her that because it would tread too far into that after-school-special feeling we so try to avoid. My family is not the best at admitting our feelings about each other. We get embarrassed by it. Which might be why the words "I love you" could never just spill out of my mouth when I said it to Jared. That actually makes a lot of sense. I can't believe that's the first time I've thought of that.

I've always coveted Anna's brown, bouncy-curly hair, but today her hair goes way beyond coveting. More like full-blown hair envy. It's been straightened and then curled, the loose ringlets cascading down her back. I hadn't realized how long her hair really was.

And then there is the dress. I'm not sure how she did it, but she obviously crawled into my mind and stole my dream dress. It's exactly what I'd have wanted, simple, yet elegant. I want to hate her, but I'm just so darn proud of her, even if she's marrying a guy she only dated for six months. I'm not going to think about that right now.

I'm also not going to think about Jared, which is pretty much an impossibility. Of course I'm going to think about him. But I'm going to try to push the thoughts out because if I'm going to make it through this day, and I have to make it through this day, I can't think about anything having to do with Jared.

"Is Jared coming?" Anna asks as she primps more in the mirror.

Well, that really doesn't help my vow of not thinking about Jared. I guess it was coincidence that she stole my dream dress. Anna obviously cannot get into my mind. If she could, then she would know that just saying his name is like driving a hot, searing knife into my heart.

"Um . . ." Deep breaths, Julia. Deep breaths. "No, sorry. He's still sick," I continue with the lie I started yesterday.

"Oh. Too bad," is all she says. What? No freaking out over the seating chart?

"Sorry about your seating chart," I say, and then mentally slap myself. Why would I even say that out loud? Am I trying to send her into a rage right before she's to walk down the aisle?

She waves it off with her hand. "Oh, Julia, it's no big deal." She gives me an eye roll, like I shouldn't even be mentioning it.

"Did you take a Valium?" I ask, actually concerned.

"What? No!" She stares at me like I'm ridiculous.

"Well, it's just that you don't seem to be reacting to things you would have normally reacted to."

"Julia, this is my wedding day. All of the other stuff, the planning and everything else? That suddenly becomes unimportant when the day is finally here. I just want to marry Jonathon. That's all I care about. You'll see when it's your turn." She pats me on the cheek in a patronizing way. It would have been patronizing, if it weren't a joke we sometimes do—making fun of my mom's sister, Aunt Louise, who always pats our cheeks as if we are still babies. She's going to be here today. Lovely.

"Oh, no," I say, just realizing something.

"What?" Anna says looking frantically at her dress as if I just spotted a stain on it.

"I just realized that all of the relatives are going to be giving me the 'your day will come' lines all night. I don't have a buffer!" I say, panic in my voice.

"Oh, Julia." She purses her lips briefly. "Who cares what they say. You have Jared now."

"Yeah," I say sadly. But she doesn't notice. And she shouldn't notice. This day is about her, and I will not make it about me. When she gets back from her honeymoon, I can tell her everything and then when she tells me I did the right thing, I'll feel so much better about it all. I can hold on until then. If only Brown were around, I could at least talk to her. But she's still off honeymooning in Europe.

There's a knock on the door. "Are you ready?" my dad asks.

Wedding number two, here we go.

Chapter 26

I made it down the aisle. I did it. I didn't trip, I didn't face-plant. I even kept with the rhythm of the music. With my mind so terribly full of things, it's quite the incredible feat. Jonathon winked at me as I passed, and I beamed at him. I'm going to enjoy having him in the family, I think.

Even though I knew he wouldn't show up today, I had a little hope that when I got up to the front and turned around, I'd see Jared sitting there in the pews. It was a dumb, chick-flick girl-fantasy. I should probably stop watching chick flicks or reading romance or chick lit for a while. I need to be in the real world, I think.

Anna is practically glowing as she walks down the aisle with my dad escorting her. No pale face, no stressful looks, just beautiful and happy. Even in my sad state, I can feel the joy radiating off of her. I feel something like pride well up in me, and it's hard to keep my eyes from tearing. Then, of course, I make the mistake of glancing at my mother who has tears streaming down her face. That does not help matters at all.

The look Jonathon has as he watches Anna walk down the aisle is, I dare say, quite adorable. He is sharp in his black tuxedo, with black tie and vest. He even looks handsome, I'll admit. Now that I know he's not actually as smug and pompous as I painted him to be, he seems that much more attractive. Still not even remotely my type, which is a good thing, after all, since he will be my brother-in-law in a matter of minutes.

I listen as the officiant welcomes everyone and then gives a little talk about how Jonathon and Anna are each other's happily ever afters. A wave of sadness rushes over me. I thought Jared would be my happily ever after, but now . . . now I'm not even sure I'll have a happily ever after in my life. Nor am I sure I'd want it with anyone else but Jared. There is the incredibly small hope that he will move back and we might find each other again, but I doubt Jared will stay lonely long. Someone will dig her claws into him as soon as she can, probably that trampy Kirsten. I, on the other hand, may live a long life of solitude with cats. My life has come full circle.

Anna and Jonathon say their vows and they are beautiful and heartfelt. Jonathon's are not long and drawn-out like I had originally thought they'd be. In fact, most of his vows are clever, and he gets the congregation to giggle a couple of times, like when he vows to keep Anna's wallet full of shopping money. He knows her well.

With vows completed and rings exchanged, the officiant pronounces them husband and wife and tells Jonathon he "may now kiss the bride." The kiss is sweet and not quite as PG-13 as Brown's and Matt's was. After the kiss, everyone cheers and they turn and walk down the aisle and out into the church lobby.

I can't believe it. My baby sister is married. It's the end of an era. But I guess the beginning of a new one. New beginnings. I need to find one of those.

~*~

"Oh, Julia dear," Aunt Louise pats my cheek, patronizingly. "You're so pretty. Why haven't you been snatched up yet?"

"Oh, well . . ." I trail off, not knowing what to say. I've thought of lying and saying my boyfriend isn't here because he's sick, but then I'd probably start rumors of a fake boyfriend I've made up in my mind. Which would be true, since my real boyfriend is no longer my boyfriend and isn't actually sick. It's very complicated.

I manage to get away from Aunt Louise before she's able to give me advice on how to land a man. She'd started to, but then my dad cut in and saved the day. I don't need her advice right now. I don't want to talk about my love life, even though everyone else wants to talk about it. I need to remember not to do this to anyone else, if the situation ever arises. It's a crappy place to put someone in.

I go to the table where I'm assigned to sit and plop down at the seat where my place card is. To my left there is "Jared Moody" on the little white card at the head of the place setting next to mine. I want to take the place card and rip it into tiny pieces, but instead I turn it around so his name won't be staring at me, taunting me. It's bad enough that I have to sit next to an empty seat all night.

I look over to see Anna and Jonathon laughing and smiling as they talk to their guests. The reception hall is gorgeous. Large billowy clouds of fabric hang from the ceiling, the colors Anna chose are all over the room in complementary ways. It's elegant and romantic, like something out of a bridal magazine. It's hard to believe that Anna pretty much arranged this all by herself. Maybe wedding planning is her calling in life.

During dinner, I only had a few questions about where Jared was and why there was an empty seat next to me, so it was only a few times that my heart was basically gutted from my chest. It felt worse than that, if I'm being honest.

I keep to myself, trying desperately to avoid relatives and long-time family friends that will ask me questions I don't want to answer. Luckily the dancing starts and there's been just enough alcohol to get a large crowd to the dance floor. With the focus on dancing and the loud music, I'm able to sit at my table without any interruptions.

The music switches to a slow song and the dance floor fills with couples, holding each other and swaying together to the music. Perfect.

"May I?" A hand reaches out in front of me. I look up to see my dad.

"Sure," I say, standing up and following him to the dance floor.

"You don't seem like yourself lately, Julia," my dad says once we are moving in slow circles on the dance floor. My dad knows about my two left feet and is keeping it simple.

I give him what I'm sure is a very vacant smile. "I'm just tired, that's all."

"Is it anything to do with Jared not being here?" he asks.

I look down quickly, not wanting to make eye contact, which is pretty much a non-verbal way of telling him that I'm about to lie. Hopefully he's not that astute and doesn't pick up on it.

"No, everything is fine, I'm just tired," I say and look up at him again after I get the lie out. It's not entirely a lie.

I'm really tired.

He gives me a closed-mouth smile. I think he knows I'm lying, but he doesn't press further, which I'm grateful for.

The rest of the night, I'm able to stay in the shadows, avoiding as much as I can. Jonathon asks me to dance with him and we only make it through half of a song before Anna cuts in. I'm left out on the dance floor without a partner only momentarily before Lennon steps in.

"So I guess we are now related to Jonathon," I say to Lennon as we make our way around the dance floor to the slow song that is playing.

"I guess so," he raises his eyebrows high on his head.

"And how do you feel about that?" I say, knowing that Lennon wasn't a fan either and wondering if like me, he's changed his mind.

"I think he'll fit in just fine," he says, smiling slightly. "He just needs to remember to stay away from you when you've had champagne."

"Hey!" I protest and then slap him on the shoulder with my hand. "Yeah, you're probably right," I concede quickly. It's the truth after all.

Soon after dancing with Lennon, the DJ announces that it's toast time, so I make my way over to the microphone to give my speech — the speech I so lovingly prepared for my baby sister, for her wedding day.

The speech I forgot about until just now.

I would totally freak out, only there is no time to freak out, so I'll have to do what my speech professor in college told me *never* to do (not the class, just me). I'll have to wing it.

Heaven help me.

"Um, hello, everyone," I say nervously, after the DJ hands me a cordless mic. The entire room's attention is turned to me.

I can totally do this. Not really, but I'll delude myself into believing it, and maybe it will actually happen.

"So, Anna, Jonathon," I say, motioning toward them. "Here we are. Your wedding day."

Crickets. Chirping. Seriously, no one is even talking. Everyone is paying attention to me, waiting for beautiful, melodious words to come from my mouth, and not only do I have nothing prepared, but I have nothing coming to me.

Think, Julia, think.

"Anna," I start, "you look so beautiful today, and you too Jonathon. I mean, you don't look beautiful, you look handsome . . ." I trail off with a nervous laugh. Someone in the crowd of people surrounding me stifles a giggle.

MAYDAY! MAYDAY! Abort! Abort!

But I can't abort. Everyone is holding their flutes of champagne, waiting for me to say something poignant, so they can say "Here, here!" and drink.

Anna gestures at me with her facial expression that I need to say something - anything better than what I've said.

I take a deep, obvious, breath. Here goes nothing.

"When Anna came to my apartment just three months ago and announced that she was going to marry Jonathon, she definitely caught me off guard. They had only been dating for just over three months at that point. I was a little in shock and because of that, I don't think I gave her the proper congratulations that a big sister should give to her baby sister when she finds out she's getting married. So I'm going to make up for that now." I take a deep breath and pause for dramatic effect, and also to buy me some time to get my words straight.

"Anna, I'm so incredibly happy for you. You have truly

found your soul mate in Jonathon, and I know that he will make you happier than you have ever been because I see how you look at each other. I don't need to tell you to cherish one another or to be there for each other because I know you will be. You have found in six months what some people search a lifetime for." I pause to swallow the large lump that is forming in the bottom of my throat and my eyes well up as I see Anna's doing the same. "I love you both," I finally choke out.

"So here's to Anna and Jonathon!" I say as I raise my glass, and everyone in the room joins me.

I walk over to my sister and her new husband after my toast and give them each a big hug, to which an audible "ah" runs through the crowd.

I hug Anna just a little longer than Jonathon because it's a rare moment when we allow this kind of thing to happen, and I want to cherish it and remember it forever.

"That was perfect," she whispers in my ear before we let go.

In your face, college speech professor! I can so totally wing it. In fact, that was probably the most perfect off-the-cuff toast ever given. Well, it was for me, at least.

At the end of the night, we light sparklers and line up, holding them out as Jonathon and Anna run through them to their car and then drive off. It was a fairytale ending to a fairytale wedding, I'd say. The rehearsal may have been full of drama, but the wedding itself went off without a hitch.

I made it. I made it through this day without taking anything away from Anna or burdening anyone with my drama. Now I just have to make it home so I can curl up with Charlie and have a good cry. I think I've earned it.

Chapter 27

"This is so exciting," my mom says as she sits down on the couch in my parents' living room.

My parents decided that it would be fun to throw a big party for the premier of my stint on *Cupcake Battles*. I tried to warn them that they could end up mortified, but they didn't believe me, and my contract forbade me from giving them details. At least they can't say I didn't warn them when the phallic display I created shows up on their very large-screen television.

They've invited neighbors, and Lennon is here with Jenny and Liam, of course. Anna is still on her honeymoon and won't be back for another few days. Brown was going to come but couldn't make it. I was hoping she would so I could get her alone and tell her about everything that has happened with Jared. As it stands, I haven't even seen her since she got home a couple of days ago. She's been so busy catching up with work and newlywed life that she hasn't had a second to spare. I guess I'll just have to wait for Anna. Thank goodness, because of Jonathon's loyalty to the firm, they were only able to get away for a little more than a week. No month-long European vacation for them.

I desperately need to talk to Anna. I feel like I might explode at any moment. I haven't even told Patti and Debbie, for fear that they would lecture me on my stupidity. They would never see that this was the right thing to do. I'm not sure I even see it. The last thing I need to do is follow their crazy romantic advice, only to have it blow up in my face.

Speaking of Patti and Debbie, I wanted them to come to my parents' party tonight, but Patti decided to have a party of her own and Debbie wouldn't say where she would be. I'm willing to bet all of my worldly possessions that she's with George. She has still not admitted to seeing him romantically and I haven't had the nerve to ask her about it because she will know how I found out. She seems very content these days, which does make me happy for her, even though in my heart of hearts I hate everything about love and relationships right now. But that's probably just my problem.

"It's starting!" My dad says loudly, and everyone comes in and takes a seat. The couches are filled, and they have brought in chairs from the kitchen and dining room for extra seating. I look around the room as everyone sits down. I guess I didn't realize how many people were here. It's pretty crowded.

"Welcome to *Cupcake Battles*," Franky Jackson croons with his sexy made-for-television voice.

Well, ready or not, here we go.

~*~

My mother is in tears. She can't stop crying. "Oh, Julia,

you won! How did you keep that a secret from us?" she says as she's hugging me. Everyone is cheering and gathering around to congratulate me. My mom stands back and everyone starts taking turns shaking my hands and giving me hugs.

I feel like a superstar. And for one night, I sort of am. Seeing myself on the screen was both exhilarating and horrifying. Parts of it, I was actually proud of myself for how I looked on screen and how I handled the tasks given to me. But during some parts, I wanted to crawl in a hole and die. Like the part where I lost my Rock Star drink in the trash can - that was a super bad part. Well, at least for me, it was. Everyone else was delighted and laughed hysterically at my expense. But that's what the producers wanted people to do. So I gave them a good show, I suppose.

The other parts that were not so pretty were the portions of my audition tape that they chose to use for the show. I cringed until I couldn't cringe any more. It was, in a word, excruciating. Somehow though, everyone in the room found it to be delightful and well done. I guess hopped-up-on-Percocet makes for a more interesting Julia? I thought I was annoying and I was totally slurring my words. Regardless, I won't be trying that again to find out. Not any time soon, anyway.

The phallic cupcake display wasn't half as bad as it was in the studio. They edited so that only parts of it were shown and rarely the full display. Although a sidebar interview from Josef had him in hysterics as he said it looked like a cupcake-filled penis to him. Nice.

As suspected, Patti was the star of our duo. At least I thought she was. She was clever and down-right-Southern adorable. Every time she was on the screen, giggles would start even before she said anything. They just knew it was coming.

It was very interesting (and enlightening) to see what the other competitors were saying about me behind my back during their interviews. Of course, Cool Cakes had nothing good to say, and at the end, they were so devastated by the loss that they both kept crying during the final interview. I don't think this was good advertising for them. Or maybe it was the best advertising ever. People love a good train wreck, and they were definitely a train wreck. They might be evil geniuses, actually.

"Good job, Julie-Bear," my dad says as he hugs me. Since he's invested in the bakery, this is a win for both of us. I'm really interested to see the kind of business it brings in. I hope it was all worth it.

My phone vibrates in my pocket. I pull it out and see that I have text from Jared. My stomach drops immediately and my heart starts pounding. This is the first I've heard from him since the rehearsal dinner nearly a week ago.

With shaky hands, I click on the text to open it up.

Saw the show. You did a great job.

I quickly text back.

Thanks. It wasn't half as embarrassing as I expected. :)

My phone quickly sounds again. Another text from Jared.

I miss you.

Oh, gosh, my heart seriously aches when I read those words. I don't know if I've ever missed someone so much in my life. To say it back to him is an understatement for how I've been feeling. Why did this long-distance thing have to happen?

I miss you too.

I text it to him anyway.

I stare at my phone hoping for it, or rather willing it, to beep again, but it's silent. Maybe, just maybe, this could be the start of something. We could be friends. I seriously hate that word, especially if it has to do with Jared, but if it keeps me in touch with him, then I'll take it.

~*~

The next morning, I finally get to post the sign in my window that says I'm a *Cupcake Battles* winner. A winner! That's not something I've been able to say much about myself. That sounds pathetic and sad, but honestly, it just makes me appreciate this win all the more. If I won at everything, then this would be just another win and not as huge as it is.

I walk back into the kitchen and tell Debbie and Patti that I've just put up the sign. They both clap and cheer, and Patti proclaims something Southern that I'm pretty sure meant happy.

"Since we are declaring such happy things, I guess I should admit something to you," Debbie says. The red immediately starts creeping up her face. "I've been seeing George."

"So? We see him every day," Patti says, sounding confused.

"I mean George and I are dating," she rephrases and then smiles sheepishly.

"Well, it's about darn time!" Patti says, walking over and throwing her arms around her, careful to keep her flour-covered hands away from her hair. She stands back. "See? I'm always right." She puts a hand on her hip and pops it out, a very know-it-all stance.

"Congratulations, Debbie," I say and mean it. I'm glad she's happy. She deserves it. "Now, if you could just find a different meeting place to get together, other than my bakery," I say and cock my head slightly to the side, pursing my lips together as I out her for doing naughty things in my store.

"Oh," she declares, putting a hand over her mouth.

"What?" Patti asks, not understanding.

"The sock? The hair-clip? I found them in the bakery because Debbie and George have been meeting up here after hours." I raise my eyebrows as I tilt my head briefly, gesturing toward a now beet-red Debbie. Mortification would be an understatement. She looks positively sick. I suddenly feel horrible that I've embarrassed her so.

"Debbie!" Patti yells her name, but then admiration washes over her face. "Well, well. I didn't know ya had it in ya, ya old bag." She laughs lightheartedly.

"Oh, you . . ." Debbie trails off, batting a hand at her.

I put an arm around her. It's the least I can do after causing her so much trauma. "I'm happy for you," I say and grin at her.

"So how did it happen?" Patti asks Debbi.

We all get back to work as Debbi tells us how she and George came to be. After Patti had told her to go for him, she started thinking about it, and then it was like the universe had heard and brought them together because the very next day, George asked her out for coffee. They hit it off from there. Apparently, both of them have adult children living at their homes (I knew this was the case for

246

Debbie, but obviously not about George), and so the bakery was the best place for them to meet up where they could hide out and be alone, much to my grossed-outed-ness.

"I'm sorry, Julia," she said, her eyes lowering to the floor sheepishly.

"Don't worry," I said, putting her mind at ease. I'm not that upset by it, just slightly uncomfortable. "I'm just glad you're happy. Anyway, now that you've outed yourself, can't you finally tell your kids?"

"I guess we probably should. I just don't know how mine will take it, since this is the first time I've dated someone since Roger died," she says, somberly.

"Oh, they be happy for ya," Patti says. "You'll see."

The morning goes quickly as we work. Patti and I throw out a few jabs about Debbie and George, and Debbie acts insulted even though I know she's loving it. New relationships are so fun. But once the honeymoon phase is over and reality starts settling in, then one person moves across the country and everything is ruined. Okay, well that may only be my experience. But still, the honeymoon part doesn't last forever.

The front of the shop is much busier today. I think we are already seeing the effects of *Cupcake Battles*, which is exciting and slightly overwhelming. If the pace keeps up, I'll have to hire someone else for sure. It will take a strong person to make us want to turn our trio into a quartet. The thought of adding someone to our group makes me kind of sad. We have a good thing going, Debbie, Patti and I.

"Hello, Julia," a sappy-sweet voice says.

"Oh, hello, Lia," I say, willing my aura to appear bright and happy. I'm not sure that's even possible, but I don't need her reading my aura or bringing any more of her bad juju into my life. Just because she's usually right doesn't mean I have to like it.

"I had a dream about you," she says, slightly raising her eyebrows.

"You did?" I question. I don't really want to know the details of her dream. I'm sure it will be off-putting no matter what.

"Yes. You were with a tall, dark, and handsome stranger." She gives me an insinuating stare. It's unsettling, actually.

"Oh," I say, not quite as put-off as I thought I'd be. "What was I doing with this tall, dark, and um, handsome stranger?"

"I'm not sure, exactly. I think you were on a date or something," she says matter-of-factly. Obviously, she thinks this dream is going to come to pass. I highly doubt it. I do not see any tall, dark, and handsome strangers in my future.

"Well, thank you for telling me," I say, wanting to be done with this so she doesn't tell me anymore of the dream. I'm worried that the rest of the dream consisted of this tall, dark, and handsome stranger killing me in some way.

"What can I get for you today?" I ask, signaling to the line of people that has been growing behind her.

She places her order with no more words about her dream or my aura or anything thing else that's hocus-pocus-y, thank goodness. I don't even have the time or the desire to dwell on the tall, dark, and handsome stranger dream.

Later in the afternoon, Patti, Debbie, and I all sit down in the front the bakery and I let out a loud sigh. What a day. It was one of our busiest ever, and people actually wanted to take pictures with me! Pictures! I felt like a star.

I didn't even care that there are probably lazy-eyed pirate pictures of me now floating out on the Internet.

"Well, ladies, I guess we should get used to this," Patti says, sitting tiredly in the chair.

"You think?" I ask.

"I think this is just the beginning," she says with a wink.

Just the beginning. Maybe even a new beginning? I guess time will tell.

Chapter 28

Anna is finally home. Finally! In fact, she's coming over right now so we can hang out. To my utter delight and benefit, Jonathon will be working late hours at the firm to make up for all the billable hours he missed while they were on their honeymoon. That means Anna has nothing to do but have sister time with me. Well, I'm sure she thinks she has other things to do, but I have a pan of hot, just-out-of-the-oven brownies that will convince her otherwise.

It will be so great to have her back. I have so much to tell her, so much to talk about. And I'm sure she will have so much to tell me as well.

I have to tell her about Jared, and also Paul. It turns out Lia's tall, dark, and handsome stranger dream was not far off. She just didn't realize that he was not a stranger to me.

Just before I locked up the bakery last Friday, Paul stopped by to see if I was free to have lunch with him the next day. I agreed, but on the condition that it wasn't a date. He didn't know that I had broken up with Jared, and

I didn't want him to know.

The lunch was nice. Paul is charming and funny and very handsome (okay, very, very handsome). But he has one big fault. He sniffs his nose *way* too much. Okay, he does do that, but that wasn't his big fault. The biggest fault is he's not Jared. And I'm just not ready to be with anyone else. Not now. And if I keep feeling the way I do, not ever. I hope Anna can talk some sense into me.

There's a knock at my door and I run to open it. Anna is standing there looking happy and tan. The cruise they took for their honeymoon must have been a good one. I can't wait to hear all the details. Well, not *all* the details.

"You made brownies," she says, her eyes widening with delight as the chocolate aroma spills out into the hallway.

"Yes, I did. Want some?"

"Yes, I do," she says as she walks into the apartment.

We grab brownies and milk and sit down on the couch. It's just like old times, and I've needed these old times so very badly.

"So how was the honeymoon?" I ask and then take a big bite of brownie.

"So amazing," she says and then goes on to tell me about the cruise and the food and the ports they stopped in. It sounds like the perfect honeymoon. I find myself feeling envious that I couldn't be there. But it was her honeymoon, so that would have been awkward.

"So how about you?" she asks when she's done telling me about her trip. "I saw that you won *Cupcake Battles*." She smiles brightly.

"You saw it already?"

"Yep, Jonathon and I watched it on the DVR as soon as we got home." She gets up and walks to the kitchen to get herself another brownie. "Want one?" she asks before coming back.

"No, thanks," I say. The one brownie was pushing it. My stomach is in knots. I nibble my bottom lip like I usually do when I get nervous. I just want to talk about Jared. I'm about to pop.

"What are you going to do with the ten grand you won?" she asks as she plops herself down on the couch, brownie in hand.

"Probably just funnel it back into the bakery," I say.

"That's boring," she declares.

"Well, that's what you do when you own a business." I give her a little smirk.

"How's Jared?" Anna asks.

Impeccable timing, I was just going to bring him up, only because I couldn't hold it in any longer.

"Actually, we broke up," I say, searching her face for a response.

"WHAT?" She exclaims loudly. "You broke up?" She sets the brownie down on the coffee table. Apparently, this bit of information is more important than food. "How? When?"

So I tell her. I tell her about how he took the job in New York, and how he didn't telling me until after the fact. Then I tell her about how things went downhill after he left, and about Kirsten, and then how I cut things off at her rehearsal dinner.

"You broke up with Jared at the rehearsal dinner?" she asks, looking confused, as if she's trying to remember everything about that night and putting the pieces together.

"Yes, that is why I stupidly drank and then, you know . . . " I say, motioning with my hand that she knows very well what happened that night.

"Right," she shakes her head, recalling.

"Julia," she angles her body toward me, taking both of my hands in hers. Here it comes, the part where she tells me I did the right thing. "I say this with the most love I can give you as a sister, but, are you a complete idiot?"

"Huh?" That was not what I was expecting her to say. I pull my hands out of hers. "What do you mean?"

"I mean, are you a complete and total idiot?" Her voice gets a little louder. "Julia, has Jared ever been mean to you or treated you badly?"

"No. Why are you asking me that?" I scrunch my face, not sure where she's going with this.

"I mean, besides moving away from you and not being totally forthcoming about it, which, come on—he had a point. He would have totally killed any chance of you winning *Cupcake Battles* if he had dropped that bomb on you then." She tilts her head to the side, giving me a knowing glance.

"Yeah, I guess." I really don't guess. I know. It would have killed what little game I had.

"So then why would you throw away something so great with Jared, just because he moved away?" She looks like she wants to shake me.

I look at her and my breath gets heavy. Suddenly my face goes into my hands and the tears come quickly. In an instant, I'm literally sobbing, like, hysterically.

"Julia?" She reaches over and touches my trembling back. "You're not an idiot. I mean, well, you sort of are. But I guess I didn't mean to be so harsh."

Wow. Anna should quit her day job and go into counseling. She would be amazing.

"No," I say as I try to calm the tears, try to get my breathing back. "I'm just so, so glad you said that."

"What? I'm confused," she says. I pull my face out of my hands to see her looking at me oddly.

I shake my head. "I was so afraid you were going to tell me I did the right thing, and I really never felt like I did. I tried to convince myself, but I just couldn't do it."

"Then how did you get to the point that you even broke up with him in the first place?" She furrows her brow.

"Well, you said yourself that long-distance relationships are stupid and don't work," I say, recalling our conversation in the dressing room when she was trying on her wedding dress.

"Yeah, I didn't mean it for you," she says.

"But it wasn't just you! Everyone was telling me the same thing. Patti, Google, Lia's stupid cards . . ." I trail off, thinking of all the reasons I got to the breaking point.

"Lia?" she asks, no clue who I'm talking about.

"She's a witch," I say, as if she should know that.

"Huh?" She gives me a confused look.

I bat my hand around, dismissing the subject. "I'll explain later."

"Okay, so besides Google, when you were asking everyone about long-distance relationships, did you tell them you were talking about you and Jared? Or were you asking hypothetically like you did when you asked me?" I can tell by her know-it-all mug that she already knows the answer to this.

I don't say anything. I've been such a fool.

"So what are you going to do?" she asks.

"I don't know. I can't just call him or send him an e-mail, can I?" I raise my eyebrows looking for her approval.

"Of course you can call him," she says.

"Really? Shouldn't it be a bigger gesture than that?"

"Oh, Julia, you watch too many chick flicks," she whacks me lightly on the arm. "Just call him. Do it right now."

With shaky hands, I pick up my phone. I'm not sure what I'll say when he answers, but I pray that it will come to me.

But he doesn't answer. In fact, the phone never rings. It just goes straight to voicemail. I try again, but it goes directly to voicemail once more.

"Should I leave a message?" I ask Anna.

"No, don't leave a message," she says and I hang up quickly. "I've changed my mind. I think it needs to be big."

"Really?" I ask. Anna is so confusing sometimes. "Okay, fine. What should I do?"

"I don't know. I think we need reinforcements." She pulls her phone out of her purse and starts texting.

Fifteen minutes later, there is a knock at my door.

"Julia, what have you done?" Brown says as she walks into the room. "Do I smell brownies?" Her eyes widen at the scent.

"Yes, do you want one?" I ask in vain, knowing fully well she will decline, like she always does.

"No. I ate way too much on my honeymoon. I'm just going to stand here and smell it for a second, though." She inhales deeply.

"Julia needs help salvaging her relationship with Jared," Anna says from the couch, once Brown has sniffed sufficiently. I'm surprised she wasn't concerned that she would inhale the calories.

Brown and I join Anna on the couch and I let Anna explain everything that happened. Hearing her say it in her smart-alecky voice—annoying as it is—makes me realize all the more what an idiot I've been.

"Jules, how could you think that you would know if long distance would work after three weeks?" Brown asks, looking appalled.

"I know! I know! Geez you guys! I want to fix this. Help me fix this," I plead to them with my hands.

"Just call him," Brown says, picking up my phone from the coffee table and handing it to me.

"I've tried already. It went straight to voicemail," I say. "Besides, Anna and I decided it needs to be bigger. I want him to know that I'm serious."

"So what, then?" Brown asks, her eyes moving back and forth from Anna to me.

We sit there in silence, contemplating my choices, which are fairly limited at this point. Calling isn't working and now feels too trivial. E-mailing would be a cop-out. What am I supposed to do? Send him a message that says, "Do you still love me?" with a box that says "Check yes or no." I could send him flowers, but that just seems cheesy.

"I've got it," I say, realizing what I should do and mentally slapping myself for not thinking of it sooner. I get up from the couch and go into my room to get my laptop computer. I come back and sit between Brown and Anna, who are both looking very skeptically at me. I don't blame them. Left to my own devices, I do tend to make some stupid choices.

"Don't leave us hanging here, Jules," Brown says as I open the laptop and pull up the internet.

"You aren't going to send him a singing telegram or something tacky like that," Anna says, eyeing me with disapproval.

"No. I'm not doing anything like that," I say as I type in the web address at the top.

"Then what are you going to do?" Anna asks, impatience in her tone.

"I'm going to fly there tonight and tell him myself," I

say, clicking on the travel site I had been looking for.

"Well," Anna says, "Julia Dorning, I had no idea you had something like this in you." I look over to see her smile admiringly.

"Nice one, Jules," Brown says, agreeing with Anna.

We sit on the couch and search for flights. As it turns out, all of the flights are booked until tomorrow afternoon, so my crazy out-of-character trip will have to wait until then. But I don't care. I'm doing this no matter what.

"What are you going to do when you get there?" Brown asks as I click the last button, finalizing my trip to New York.

"Oh," I say, sitting back against the couch. I look back and forth between the two of them. "I hadn't thought of that." My eyes start to dart around as new and scary thoughts dawn on me.

Crap. I didn't think this through. I just had this romantic notion and ran with it, not even thinking what I'd do once I got there. I have no idea where Jared lives or whether he'll even answer the phone. I don't even know what he's been up to. Who knows? He might already be dating someone since we broke up. That Kirsten tramp probably hopped right on into his life.

Oh, gosh.

"Julia," Anna puts a hand on my arm in an attempt to steady the panic that is rising in my body. "Don't get caught up in all of the details."

"Yeah, that's how you got yourself into this mess in the first place," Brown adds.

Nice.

"Everything will work out how it's supposed to. But you have to try, right?" Anna says, looking me in the eyes.

"Yes, I know I have to try," I say, feeling a little less

apprehensive.
    And try I will.

Chapter 29

"You are dumber than a billy goat," Patti declares after I finally tell her and Debbie what actually transpired between Jared and me.

Debbie nods her head, agreeing with Patti.

"I know, that's why I have to fly out there and fix it," I say for like the fiftieth time.

"You betcha do," Patti says and then clicks her tongue curtly.

Can't anyone give me a little credit here? I mean, yes, I did screw it up. I did get carried away with my own brain. But I've realized the error of my ways, and now I'm going to fix it. Well, hopefully.

Oh, gosh.

No, I'm going to push the negativity out and focus on the positive. I will not picture myself wandering around Manhattan, bawling my eyes out when I find out I'm too late. I will not go there. I want a chick flick ending here, not a drama flick.

It worked out well that I couldn't fly out until this

afternoon because I'd have left Patti and Debbie in a real bind had I just up and left last night. The bakery has been busy — probably too busy — for just the two of them. I'll be here to help today, and then I've called Beth to come and help out tomorrow. My bakery will be in good hands. At least I won't have to worry about that part.

The morning rush takes off with a bang, with many more customers than our normal Thursday rush. *Cupcake Battles* has definitely been beneficial. I'm grateful for the busy day, as it has been a welcome distraction from all the thoughts filtering through my mind.

"Julia," Lia greets me in her sweet and sickly voice, as she comes up to the counter. Great, just what I needed right now. "Your aura," she says, pointing above my head. I look up instinctively, but realize that I can't see my own aura. Actually, I can't see anyone's aura.

"What about it?" I ask and then silently pray that she won't tell me some prophetic thing about how my aura says I'm taking a journey and it will be a waste of time and/or I will die.

"You look hopeful," she says, sounding as if she can't believe that's possible. "It's not the muddied blue one you have been carrying around for weeks."

"Oh," I say, not expecting that. "I guess you're right. I'm hopeful." I give her a smile and then quickly ask for her order. I don't want to hear any more of what she might be seeing. I prefer to be surprised.

Like breakfast, the lunch rush is super busy. Again, another welcome distraction. As the clock ticks closer to the time I need to head to the airport, the butterflies start multiplying. I'm not sure I can do this, but I know I must.

Around two, the bakery starts to empty of customers and it's time for me to get my bags and go to meet my fate with Jared. My flight doesn't leave for a few hours yet, but

I need to take a shuttle and I don't want to risk missing the flight. I need to be in New York tonight. I need to see Jared, and I need to make things right.

I grab my carry-on from my office and tell Patti that I'll see her on Monday.

"Good luck, darlin'," she says with a wink. Apparently, she has forgiven me for my billy-goat-like stupidity.

"Thanks," I say as I open the kitchen door, walking out to the front of the bakery.

Except for a few stragglers, it's fairly empty of people. At least I can feel good that Patti and Debbie won't have much to do for the rest of the day except clean and lock up.

I realize before I leave that I should double check that I have my license. As I'm searching through my purse, the bells on the door sound as someone comes in.

I look up. It's Jared. Jared is in my bakery.

"Hi," he says as he sees me.

"Hi," I say back. I'm so confused right now. "What are you doing here?" I ask, not in an accusatory way, more like a non-believing way. What *is* he doing here?

"Well," he says, taking two steps toward me to lessen the gap between us. "I flew here to talk some sense into you."

"Jared, I—"

"Before you say anything, just hear me out," he says, holding up a hand as he cuts me off.

"Okay," I concede, swallowing hard.

"Listen, I know you think that we can't make this work, but you're wrong—"

"Jared, I—"

"Please, just let me finish," he cuts me off again. "Julia, I love you. I've been miserable without you. I'm not going

261

to lose you over some distance between us, and so I'll move back if that's what I have to do."

"Jared," I shake my head, "you can't move back for me. I—"

"Yes, I can," he cuts me off again. "I need you in my life." My mind flashes back to the last time Jared said those exact words to me. It seems like so long ago, but it's been less than a year.

He looks me up and down, searching me. Then his eyes catch on something, and his brow furrows. "What's the suitcase for?" He dips his chin, gesturing to the carry-on that is slightly hidden behind me.

"Oh, that." I look behind me at the teal suitcase. "I was just leaving for the airport."

"Where are you going?" he asks, confused.

I smile. "To see you and beg you to take me back," I say, looking up at him. He breaks into a large grin and takes another step toward me, removing nearly the entire gap that's between us.

"You were coming to see me?" His smile gets even bigger.

"Yes, I was. But you're here now," I say, dropping my purse on the floor and wrapping my arms around his neck.

He leans down and kisses me hard on the mouth. Not soft and tender, but hard and passionate, as if he's making up for lost time. After a minute, he breaks the kiss, leaning his forehead against mine, both of us trying to catch our breaths.

I forgot about the stragglers that were still in the bakery. They are getting quite the show of PDA. I know I swore that off, but now I can't remember why, nor do I care.

"I'm sorry," I say. There's so much more I want to say,

to apologize for, but that's all that comes out.

"Me, too," he says, and leans down and kisses me again, this time softly and tenderly. My knees feel wobbly.

In my head, I envision a movie camera zooming out from Jared and me to the front of the bakery and then into the sky. Just like the ending to a good chick flick. Only this beats any ending to a chick flick I've ever seen.

My own happy ending. Or rather, happy new beginning.

I like the sound of that.

Two Months Later . . .

"Julia, would you just trust me?" Anna says as she drives me in the new Audi that Jonathon just bought her. She's ridiculously spoiled and loving it. Marriage has been good to her.

I'm blindfolded in her car driving to who knows where. She's got some "epic" surprise that she's been working on for me. She made me get all dressed up. I'm scared to find out what it is. Whatever it is, I hope it's not something grand. I truly hate being the center of attention. My intuition is telling me it probably is, so I try working up my courage as we drive.

Whatever it is, nothing can top the surprise I got last week. Jared called me to say he's moving back to Denver. He's starting his consulting business back up, but this time he will have other people doing the work for him so no one will catch on. It's a brilliant idea, and the consulting work flooded in as soon as word got around. The best news? He doesn't have to travel even a quarter as much as he did when he was doing the work himself.

He moves back home next week, so I don't think anything can top that. Even something "epic."

I start to feel the car slow down and then it comes to a complete stop. I hear the car door open and the clicking of Anna's heels on the ground beneath her as she gets out. She shuts the door and the car shakes just slightly from the force of it closing. It's silent for merely seconds before I hear the clicking of the door handle next to me and feel the breeze whip in as it opens.

"Time to get out," Anna says. "We're here." She grabs me by the arm and helps guide me out of the car.

"Can I take off the blindfold now?" I ask, impatient. Blindfolds make me feel claustrophobic. I'm not sure how much longer I can stand it.

"Not yet," she says as she guides me to wherever we are going.

We stop and I'm pretty sure she opens a door, as I can feel a blast of air-conditioning hit me in the face. I also hear bells chime, similar to the ones that I have on the door at the bakery. Actually, they sound exactly like the ones at the bakery. After hearing them so many times, I think I'd recognize them anywhere. But I don't smell the normal bakery smell that usually wafts through the door when it's opened. What I smell is burning wax. Maybe these aren't the bakery bells after all?

"Come on," Anna grasps my arm tighter as I try to pull back, not sure I want to go inside wherever she's dragging me.

Once inside she lets go of my arm and I hear the bells chime as the door shuts behind me. It's completely silent and the smell of melting wax is even stronger now.

"Anna?" I reach out, trying to find her.

There's no answer and I can't feel her.

"Anna," I say again and then wait. There is still no

265

answer.

"Anna," I grab the top of my blindfold. I don't care if she didn't tell me to take it off yet. "Anna, this isn't fun—"

I stop and stare, my mouth falling open as I pull the blindfold off my head and take in the scene around me. I'm in the bakery. The reason I couldn't smell the normal bakery scent is because all of the lights are off and candles are everywhere, Standing in the middle of the room is Jared.

"You're back? Already?" I say, a smile spreading across my face. Okay, this really is an epic surprise.

I walk over to him. He's smiling at me in a way I've never seen him smile before, almost as if he's nervous.

"Hi," he says simply.

"Hi," I say back.

"What's going on?" I gesture around the room with outstretched arms.

He licks his lips quickly, another thing I've never seen him do. It makes me think again that he's nervous. What would he have to be nervous for? I'm here. I'm his. Nothing he can say to me will make me change my mind, not ever again.

He holds my hand in his and looks me in the eyes. "Julia," he starts and then stops as if he wants to change direction from what he was about to say. He doesn't speak, though. Instead, he starts to move downward, getting on one knee.

Oh. My. Gosh.

"Julia," he begins again and my heart starts beating rapidly and loudly. "Being apart from you these last few months, I don't think I can stand to do it ever again. I want to spend the rest of my life with you and know that you legally have to spend it with me."

I snort-laugh, which is par for the course with me. Even at possibly one of the most important moments of my life, I can still be a total circus freak.

"So," Jared says, oblivious to my freakish antics. "Julia Dorning, will you marry me?" He looks into my eyes.

"Oh, my gosh," I say. Is this really happening?

"Was that your answer?" he says, giving me a small smirk — a smarty-pants smirk on the face that I love so much.

"Yes," I say. "I mean, no, that's not my answer." I shake my head. "My answer is yes. Yes, I will marry you." I obviously can't see myself, but I'm willing to bet that I have a ridiculous giddy look on my face.

Jared stands up, letting go of my hand. He reaches in his pocket and pulls out a little, black, velvet-covered box. He opens it slowly to reveal the prettiest ring I think I've ever seen. Princess cut, sparkling brightly even in the candlelight, it's perfect. He takes the ring out and slides it gently on my ring finger. Okay, really he gets it half-way and then I have to finish. Why do they always make it seem as if the guy can just slide the ring on in the movies? It never works that way.

I gaze at the ring, now twinkling on my finger. Then I look up at him smiling at me. He puts his arms around my waist and I put my arms around his neck. Kissing me, he lifts me off the floor and spins me around.

Best. Surprise. Ever.

I can hear a knock on the window behind me as he sets me down, and I turn my head to see everyone I love standing outside the bakery windows. My parents, my siblings, my coworkers, my friends, they're all here. Jared and I walk over to the door and let them in. A celebration springs into action as they join us inside the bakery.

Twinkling lights suddenly shine above me, and as the

room lights up, I see a table of food to my right and a large cake that says "Congratulations Jared and Julia" sits front and center on the table. How did I not see any of this when I first came in?

I'm not sure because it isn't over yet, but so far, I don't know if this night could be any more perfect.

Surrounded by the people I love and the man I love, I take back what I said about not wanting to be the center of attention. I think I'm going to enjoy this.

The End

Visit Becky's website and sign up for fun giveaways and
e-newletters

www.beckymonson.com

Join Becky on Facebook
www.facebook.com/AuthorBeckyMonson

Twitter: @bmonsonauthor

Acknowledgments

This book would not have been possible without help from so many people.

Many thanks to Robin Huling and Lori Schleiffarth for being inspirational and talking me down from the "proverbial" ledge that I find myself so often on.

Thanks to Kathryn Biel, my fellow author and friend, who understands what I'm going through on this book-writing journey, and also allows me to vent when needed.

I cannot thank Karey White and Chrissy Wolfe enough, for editing and making sense out of some of the nonsensical things I write

Thank you, thank you, thank you to the incredibly talented Mark Hamer who did my cover art. You saved the day!

I must also give shout-outs to my amazing parents and siblings who are always supportive of my crazy ideas.

Last, but not least, my husband and my kiddos who inspire me and love me even when I'm certifiable (which happens more than I care to admit). I love you more each day.

77746633R00151

Made in the USA
Columbia, SC
26 September 2017